The tremors woke both Darcy and Alex from sleep. They met in the hallway, he wearing boxer shorts, she wrapped in a robe.

"Explosion?" they both said at once.

Darcy added, "It felt like an earthquake."

"We have them from time to time but not often and not very strong. That must have rattled the whole town."

Darcy bit her lip. "How can we find out?"

She'd barely spoken when sirens began to howl in town. Fire truck. Police. She looked at Alex, spared a wish they had time for her to enjoy the sight of him so scantily clad, then without a word she turned back into her bedroom. "Let's go."

She dressed swiftly in her overalls and work boots, and grabbed her gloves. Back out in the hall she met Alex once again.

Neither of them said another word. Darcy felt her heart beating nervously, and all she could think was that if she were better at her job, this might not have occurred. What if someone had died? What if she still couldn't find the perp?

* * *

Be sure to check out the rest of the Conard County: The Next Generation miniseries!

* * *

If you're on Twitter, tell us what you think of Harlequin Romantic Suspense! #harlequinromsuspense

Dear Reader,

Sometimes life deals us hard blows that are difficult to live with. Not everyone can cope with what has happened to them by continuing in their old paths. In this story a Vietnam vet has never recovered from his injuries in the war, and he's become embittered because he feels like he was part of a cover-up. We also have a former FBI profiler who quit his job to escape the nightmares. And then we have a young man who gets himself entangled in the wrong side of the investigation because he wants to join the ATF but doesn't think he ever will. Bad things happen to him, too.

But bad things are a part of life, some worse than others. Like it or not, we have to carry on. In the center of this storm we have an ATF agent who is on her first solo assignment, wanting to do well to prove herself but needing some help anyway.

It's all about helping each other. When those bad things happen, we need our friends and family. Going it alone is a dangerous road.

Enjoy!

Rachel Lee

CONARD COUNTY REVENGE

Rachel Lee

HARLEQUIN®ROMANTIC SUSPENSE

Recycling programs
for this product may
not exist in your area.

ISBN-13: 978-1-335-45631-1

Conard County Revenge

Copyright © 2018 by Susan Civil Brown

Printed in U.S.A.

www.Harlequin.com

Rachel Lee was hooked on writing by the age of twelve and practiced her craft as she moved from place to place all over the United States. This *New York Times* bestselling author now resides in Florida and has the joy of writing full-time.

Books by Rachel Lee

Harlequin Romantic Suspense

Conard County: The Next Generation

Harlequin Intrigue

Conard County: The Next Generation

Visit the Author Profile page at Harlequin.com for more titles.

Chapter 1

ATF Agent Darcy Eccles wondered what the hell she was doing driving into a small one-horse town that might as well have been named Nowhere, Wyoming, instead of Conard City. *City?* The name was ironic, if not a downright joke. Someone had once cherished grandiose dreams for this place.

Aw, heck. She wasn't the snob her thoughts made her sound like. Small towns were wonderful places. The fact that her adult life had largely been lived in bigger cities didn't change the fact that a bomber had struck here, and like it or not, her job required her to investigate.

She only wondered where to stop first. The sheriff's office had called for ATF's help, but the fire department might have more information on the bombing. All of which would have been shared with the sheriff, of course. Or should have been.

Unfortunately, she'd run into territorial political bailiwicks before. She wondered if she'd find them here. There didn't appear to be a lot of anything to fight over, but people were the same everywhere. Too many wanted to be the biggest frog in even the smallest pond.

Sheriff's office, she decided as her GPS guided her along a relatively straight route.

No, her whole problem in being here was that she'd been pulled off a large case of suspected terror bombing. The work had been challenging, finding all the bits even more so, and supporting the conclusion… Well, they'd been getting closer.

Now here she was, a solo flight to find out why an explosion had happened in one corner of a high school shop. And the main reason she was here was the sheriff's request had included the acronym ANFO.

Before she even started asking questions, she suspected she'd find out the whole thing had been accidental, some high schooler's experiment gone awry. Kids were wont to try things out to see if they worked.

But she had to admit, building an ANFO bomb wasn't easy. More of them failed than succeeded unless you had pure anhydrous ammonia and the best measuring equipment. Lots of terrorists and soldiers tried to make them on the fly. Many never exploded.

But someone in this out-of-the-way place had succeeded. Not good for anyone, least of all the perp if they found him. Mercifully, from her understanding, no one had been killed.

Picking up her cell phone, she found she had a signal again. She pulled over on the shoulder and checked the GPS. Her satellite phone was in the trunk, but she hadn't exactly needed it until she found herself in a cell dead zone. Then she didn't need it because she rode the state highway all the way to town.

She punched in the number of the sheriff's office and spoke to the dispatcher. "Special Agent Eccles, ATF," she announced. "Please let the sheriff know that I'm twenty minutes out. He should be expecting me."

"He is," a croaky voice answered. "We'll get the fire chief over here, too."

"Thank you."

She sat for a moment while her engine idled, trying to shift mental gears. Part of her was still very absorbed in the investigation she had left behind. Now she needed all her attention on the school bombing, like it or not. It would be easy to write it off, but that was not her ethic, nor the ethic of the ATF. There was a job to be done, and she'd give it her best.

The sides of the state highway began to sprout houses, and as the next miles passed, the density grew until there was no longer any question that she was reaching Conard City.

There was a loop that could take her around town, but she drove straight in, toward the city center. The trees grew leafy with the light green of spring, the houses gracious despite their ages. *A lot of history here*, she imagined. Families with deep roots. *Deceptively calm*, she supposed. Although she doubted they had many bombs exploding around here.

At the first, and only, traffic light she encountered, she found the sheriff's office on the southwest corner of Main and Front. Several angled parking spaces remained open, none of them labeled, so she pulled into one.

Pretty courthouse square, she thought, looking around as she climbed out and stretched her legs from the long drive. It looked as if it had been transplanted from New England, the courthouse an edifice of red brick and tall white columns with an imposing staircase. It even had a dome atop it.

The square itself contained the obligatory statue honoring war heroes, but she wasn't interested in that. Stone tables and benches were scattered along flower-lined walkways, and at some of them older men sat playing chess or checkers. Bucolic.

Then she turned and faced the sheriff's office. A storefront, it boasted institutional green paint on the wood framing the windows, looking as if it needed a touch-up. Gold lettering in large windows. The door right on the corner.

She stepped through the door and was greeted by rows of desks, mostly unoccupied, and a dispatcher sitting at a console that looked as if it had been around for a while.

"Hi. I'm Agent Eccles."

The wizened woman at the dispatcher's desk nodded. She sat beneath a no-smoking sign, convicted by an overflowing ashtray to one side. Darcy felt a moment of amusement.

"Just head straight on back," the woman said, pointing to a hallway. Her voice rasped, probably from all those cigarettes. "First door on the left. They're waiting for you."

Despite the fact that it was late spring, even the air

in the office seemed chilly and Darcy was glad she'd decided to wear pants.

The office couldn't be missed. The door was wide-open, but she could see the black lettering on frosted glass: Sheriff Gage Dalton.

Two men were inside and rose to their feet as she entered. Immediately she found both men striking, but for different reasons. The tall man behind the desk wore a khaki sheriff's uniform and seven-pointed badge. He had burn scars on one side of his face, and experience screamed at her that he'd been the victim of a bomb. The other man was attractive and big, wearing the blue daily uniform of a firefighter with a captain's insignia embroidered on the shoulders and the familiar fire department four-leafed badge embroidered on his chest. He could have posed for one of those fund-raising calendars. A whisper of a smile ghosted across her mouth.

"Gage Dalton," the scarred man said, extending his hand and wincing as he did so. So, more than burns affected him. "This is our fire chief, Wayne Camden."

She shook Camden's hand as well and pulled out her credential wallet to show them. "Darcy Eccles. You have an ANFO bomb?"

"Had," said Dalton drily as he eased back into his seat and waved her to the remaining chair. "Wayne's chemical sniffers detected the ammonium… Wayne?"

"Ammonia. Gasoline. Not a clean burn."

She nodded. That meant inexperience, which was good. "Anything else?"

"You need to come out and see it," Wayne said. "Judge for yourself. It might have been an accident."

She nodded, then caught something in his tone. "You don't think so?"

Wayne shook his head. "Plenty of space out here if you want to play with bombs. You don't need to do it at the school. If someone had been using lab equipment…" He shrugged. "We should have found a body. But it happened at 2:00 a.m. on a Sunday morning. Nobody was in that school."

"Theoretically," she said.

"Theoretically," he agreed.

Gage Dalton leaned forward, placing his elbows on his desk. "We're questioning everyone with any association with the school, but that's damn near everyone in the county. Agent…"

"Darcy, please."

"Darcy." He nodded. "I realize you ATF people have bigger things on your plate. I get it. I used to be DEA. But the thing is, what if there are more? What if it happens again in a building that isn't empty? We don't have your expertise in learning things from the bomb that might help us locate the perp. And the mere fact that Wayne here sniffed ANFO chemicals doesn't mean that was just an ANFO bomb. Something else could be involved."

"I agree, especially given how difficult it is to make a successful ANFO bomb. Far easier to set off a few sticks of dynamite. The purpose of ANFO is to build a bomb without leaving the kind of trail a dynamite purchase would leave. But it needs to be in an enclosed space, unlike dynamite."

Gage nodded slowly. "So you're saying it had to be inside the building."

"Or in a pipe. Some enclosure." She looked at Camden. "Anything?"

"Not yet. We're still scouring the site."

She nodded. "Okay, then. I've been driving since the wee hours. If I can grab a bite and some coffee, I'd appreciate it. Then we can go look over the site. Have you checked if anyone around here has received a tank of anhydrous ammonia for fertilizer?"

"Running it now," Gage said, "but I haven't heard of any, at least not in a while. We're not intensive farming country for the most part. We rely mostly on ranching, sheep and cattle, and I hear there's plenty of manure compost."

"Bags of dry fertilizer can be used, too," she remarked. "It's just harder. Thank you, gentlemen." She rose. "Point me to someplace where I can eat and I'll be back here in a half hour or so."

"I'll show you," Wayne said, rising. "Maude takes a little getting used to."

Darcy wondered what in the world he meant by that. They hadn't exited the front office, however, before a tall, well-built man with blond hair and blue eyes arrived. A beardless Viking. He looked at Wayne. "This is her?"

Darcy halted, surprised.

"Yeah," said Wayne. "Darcy Eccles, ATF, meet Alex Jansen, our shop teacher. Also former FBI."

Oh, boy, Darcy thought as she shook his hand. Former FBI? Helpful maybe. Trouble maybe. Hunk, definitely.

"Yeah, the explosion was in my part of the building," Alex said. "I'm naturally…involved."

Yep. Great. She forced a smile. "I was on my way to lunch."

"I'll join you," Alex said without hesitation.

Double great.

"It's just a half block from here," Wayne said as they stepped out onto the quiet street. "Afterward, we'll meet my wife out at the school. She's our arson investigator."

How interesting, Darcy thought. In her world, such a relationship would have resulted in reassignment. Out here, it probably never made any difference. The chief and his wife most likely shared the same goals and interests.

But in a criminal investigation? Well, that depended, didn't it? She almost sighed.

Alex spoke. "Maude, the diner's owner, is a law unto herself, Agent. So are her daughters. Just ignore the rudeness. The food and coffee more than make up for it."

Well, there didn't seem to be any other place to eat along the street. She was sure she could handle a little rudeness. Must be a little beyond average, though, if both of these guys thought she had needed a warning.

The diner showed its age. Colored duct tape had sealed cracks on some of the red benches and chairs, but aged or not, the interior appeared spotless. Alex guided them to a table as far from other patrons as they could get, which wasn't far. The restaurant wasn't huge, and a number of people were scattered around in booths, all of them engaged in conversations that stopped the minute they saw Darcy.

Hers was a new face, something interesting around here. She smothered another sigh and joined Wayne and Alex at the table. Almost instantly menus were emphatically slapped down in front of them. Conversation resumed around them.

Darcy looked up into the face of the gorgon, sour and unfriendly. "Coffee?" the woman demanded.

Alex spoke. "You want a latte, Darcy? Or just regular leaded?"

A latte? Why should that surprise her, but it did. It certainly wasn't on the menu. "Latte, please."

The men chose black coffee, then turned their attention to the menus. Darcy scanned hers with a vague surprise that it didn't feel sticky. Cleanliness around here evidently went past the floor and tables. It wasn't a long menu, but all the offerings, except the salads, appeared to be rib-sticking food. No one with a cholesterol problem ought to eat here, she decided, allowing herself another moment of amusement.

Why not be amused? She was in the middle of nowhere on an assignment she didn't want, and she felt like Alice slipping down the rabbit hole. This was so far from her usual environment she had to be careful she didn't offend needlessly with an absent-minded comment.

She hadn't eaten since last night, so she passed on the salads and asked about the steak sandwich.

"It's the reason most people love to eat here," Wayne told her. "But it's huge. You might need a doggie bag."

"That's fine. I need to eat tonight, too."

After the woman, whose name tag identified her as Maude, took their orders, Darcy looked at her two companions. "So your wife is the arson investigator?" she asked Wayne.

He nodded. "She was an investigator for insurance companies until we married a couple of years ago. Now she's with the department as both an investigator and a firefighter."

"Cool," Darcy answered, though was wasn't sure she thought so. Then Alex. "You used to be FBI?"

"Behavioral Science Unit."

Well, that could *be useful*, she decided. Her latte arrived in a tall foam cup and she wrapped her hands around it. Her fingers felt chilled and she hoped enough heat would escape to warm them.

"And you?" Alex asked bluntly.

"Ten years with ATF as an investigator. Right across the spectrum."

All right, then, with creds established among them they fell silent as their sandwiches were slammed in front of them. No one seemed surprised by the loud clatter.

Darcy hadn't expected to be working alone—that would have been ridiculous—but she wasn't sure how Alex fitted in unless someone thought he could profile a perp. She knew better than that. The idea that anyone could pull a suspect out of their hats was for the movies. A so-called profiler could use evidence to piece together a behavioral picture of a perp, but there was no magic to it. Just skill and a lot of ugliness, from what she understood.

She finished her first bite of sandwich and forgave Maude for all current and future rudeness. When their eating began to slow, she focused on Alex. "What brought you to be a shop teacher?"

"I enjoy working with my hands." He paused. "And frankly, I'd had enough of the underbelly of humanity.

It's peaceful here, and I enjoy my students. Creating something is a great source of healing."

His forthrightness surprised her. She sat looking at him—well, admiring his appearance if she was to be honest—but astonished by how much he had just revealed with a few brief words. So the BSU had left him emotionally scarred in some way. She understood the job could be really dreadful, but she hadn't ever pondered how it might personally affect those who did it. No reason to. Her own job could get horrible enough at times.

She looked from Alex to Wayne. "This bombing must be…shocking to the town." And to them, though she didn't say it.

"It's not something that happens here," Wayne said. "Although most everything else has at one time or another. It's not like evil never touches us. But this is a new one."

She looked down at her sandwich. "I hope it was an accident. But…"

Wayne nodded. "I did some research on ANFO bombs. They don't happen by accident. Usually."

"Not unless we're talking about a fertilizer plant. So nobody uses anhydrous ammonia around here?"

"Not that I know of," Wayne replied. "Alex?"

"Me neither. But I don't need to tell you how hard it would be to know for sure. Once those tanks are delivered, all identifying information is removed so no one should know it's there. Basic safety precaution. Heck, even when it gets to construction sites where it's in heavy use, they take all identifiers off it. It should be recorded somewhere safe but…" He paused and shook his head, smiling faintly. "I'm preaching to the choir. I'm sure you know better than I do. You guys write a lot of the rules."

"Interstate Commerce does mostly. Hazardous cargo. But I read you." Liquid anhydrous ammonia made it much easier to build a bomb, so its presence was concealed as much as possible. All labeling was reserved for when it was being transported. On farms all over this country, tanks full of it resided without even a single marking to identify it as hazardous. "Where would it be recorded if someone had it?" She knew what the answer should be, but she wanted to know the procedure here.

"With the fire department," Wayne answered promptly. "We'd be the first responders in case of a breach. I have my assistant looking back through logs for the last ten years. Lots of stuff comes into this county that we track in case, but so far no anhydrous ammonia."

Very professional, keeping the record of hazardous materials with the first responders. She felt a prickle of annoyance with herself that somewhere inside she must have expected something different. What did she anticipate? Moth-eaten records in some damp, moldy basement? "Well, the storage tanks can be distinctive," she remarked. "They have to endure such high pressures, you can sometimes pick them out if you know what you're looking for. But say this guy didn't have access to the liquefied stuff."

Two men exchanged looks. "Then we're in trouble," Alex said. "Hundreds and hundreds of square miles out there where fertilizer could be stashed. But, Darcy, you know it's close to impossible to use ammonium nitrate fertilizer for an explosive."

"Close to, but not impossible. Oklahoma City."

The words fell into a dead silence among them. After a few moments, Darcy spoke again. "Nothing's impossible, gentlemen, when it comes to explosives. Some of it is just more difficult. Using bags of ammonium nitrate fertilizer has worked, as we all saw. As a result, these days we keep a record of large purchases, but you don't need enough to blow up a big building to make a bomb. Or you can acquire smaller quantities over time that wouldn't draw any attention."

Alex watched Darcy eat with a healthy appetite. Clearly she wasn't a rabbit-food-only woman. He liked that. Judging by her nice build, at least as much of it as he could see through her gray suit, she kept in great shape. So naturally, she had to eat decently.

She was also pretty, but he wasn't exactly prepared to notice that, not her bright green eyes or dark auburn hair caught in a businesslike knot on the back of her head. She was a Fed. He'd been a Fed. He wanted nothing to do with that world ever again.

Although the bombing early Sunday morning at the school had kind of dragged him back in. He was sure the first suspects would be his students, especially given the location of the blast, but he was equally certain none of them would have put a bomb in the school. Some were adventurous enough to try it out in the barren areas around here, he supposed, but none of them were the kind of stupid that would put it in the school in an area that would draw attention their way.

There was going to be some push and pull here, he thought, bending his gaze once again to his sandwich. Skills he had tried to bury were already springing to life. He wanted to protect the students in his shop classes. He wanted to get the real bomber. And he was quite sure he didn't want to fight with this Darcy Eccles all the way.

"The timing creates a problem," he said a while later. "Two in the morning on a Sunday? Nobody in the building, not even a janitor? Property damage only? No point to it unless you hate band saws."

He was pleased to see a smile tug at the corner of Darcy's mouth. Okay, then, she wasn't that uptight.

She answered, "It does seem like an extreme way to drop a class."

While he and Wayne both smiled, Alex felt his innards coiling. She could joke about it, but he was quite sure every single one of his students was going to be put on trial in this woman's mind.

Fairly, he acknowledged that was part of her job, to regard everyone who might be involved as a potential suspect. But he'd left that world behind and he had come to understand since the bombing just how protective he felt of his students. They were the bright and shiny future he'd once sought only to lose it in the bowels of criminal minds. Especially that last case. He closed his eyes momentarily and shoved the memories aside.

Anyway, because of those students he had a bright and shiny present, and he wanted to keep it that way, mostly for them. The microscope of suspicion could cause a lot of damage, and by the nature of her job, Darcy brought suspicion. Much as he didn't want to get involved with the work again, it appeared he would have to. Who else could ride herd on her? Or even guide her to a reasonable list of suspects? Therein lay a great deal of his training.

It wasn't as if he would start rustling up his training now that she arrived, though. Hell, no. He'd begun gathering evidence from the moment he learned what had happened. Some things never turned off.

But that didn't mean he wanted to dive in full strength.

Wayne's elbow brushed his. "About ready?"

Alex looked down at his plate. Two mouthfuls remaining. "When are we meeting Charity?"

"Twenty minutes."

"Then give me a minute to finish. I can't bear to waste any of this sandwich."

Wayne laughed. "Have at it." Across the table, Darcy had stopped eating. Slightly more than half her sandwich was gone. "Need a container?"

"Please."

Wayne waved and moments later Maude stomped over with a foam container. "More coffee?" she asked as she put the container down on the table.

"The latte was great," Darcy said pleasantly. "I'll be back for another later."

Alex took the last bite of sandwich because it was a great way to stifle his grin as Darcy watched Maude stomp away without the merest acknowledgment of the compliment. Darcy shook her head a little and put her sandwich in the container. "My truck's just outside the sheriff's office. I can follow you."

"It's not that far," Alex said. "Down the street out there toward the north of town. No turns. You can't miss it."

She nodded and rose, lifting her box. "I'll meet you at the school then."

Alex watched her walk over to the register and pay for her lunch. Per diem, he thought. She'd come with cash to cover her expenses, maybe a credit card for the motel, and she wouldn't allow anyone to pick up her tab. He was familiar with the protocol.

Wayne stood a moment later. "You coming?"

"Of course." His gaze followed Darcy through the door.

Wayne laughed, drawing his attention. "Watch it, man. I was a fool to fall for Charity when I thought she'd be leaving in a week or two. But I was lucky."

Alex gave him a crooked grin. "I'm that obvious?"

"I'd be looking, too, if I weren't happily married. She's a stunner, all right."

"As long as she doesn't catch me drooling, we'll be fine."

Wayne laughed again as they went over to the register. "I thought you were done with the Feebs."

"I sure thought so."

"Funny how circumstances can change things."

Chapter 2

As promised, Darcy had no difficulty finding the high school. It kind of hit her in the face at the north end of the street. It also looked sadly deserted except for some people working inside a police-taped area toward the rear corner, under a large canopy. Yellow evidence markers covered the ground, looking like a field of out-of-control dandelions.

She sat studying the destruction from the parking lot, taking it in, estimating the explosive force involved. Pure guesswork at this point, but the damage to that corner of the school was extensive. A fertilizer bomb. She'd encountered them before during her years with ATF, but quite a few of them had been duds. Seriously, it wasn't easy. Timothy McVeigh had had a lot of time to experiment beforehand. Yeah, he'd thrown the final bomb together at the last minute in the back of a rental truck, but he'd had plenty of experience and experimentation to back up that effort. Plus, a great detonation system.

Detonators weren't exactly easy to come by, either. They had to be signed for. Permits were required. Plenty of people had legitimate reasons to get them, but they left a paper trail. Possible, of course, to make a detonator if you knew what you were doing. She was looking forward to finding out if they'd recovered any remains of the ignition device. Given the hour of the night when the bomb had exploded, a timer had to be involved. A timer or a cell phone. Curiosity began whetting her appetite for this job.

Athletic fields spread out from the school building, large and spacious because this county had the room. Some trees lined the north and west ends of the fields, most likely as a windbreak. In the winter it was probably very stark, but now, in the late spring, it was simply relaxing and beautiful.

Until she trained her gaze again on the scarred building. Annoyed as she had been to be pulled off the other case, that was forgotten as she looked at the new challenge. Build a case. Find a perp. Ascertain every part of the bomb that had been used here and try to trace it to someone. Excitement began to rise in her. A whole new case, entirely her own, unless she needed to send for assistance. A lot of trust from her superiors. For the first time it struck her that she'd had a kind of promotion by being sent out here to do the job herself. She'd never headed up a task force, but she was doing that now, even without the accompanying manpower here.

Resources would be at her disposal back at the field

office. Other agents would be assisting *her*. A new level of responsibility. She was determined not to fail.

Both Wayne and Alex had parked nearby, and she realized they were waiting for her to exit her vehicle. Time to start earning her spurs.

She climbed out, carrying her notebook computer and a legal pad on which to scrawl notes to herself. The computer would make taking photos easy, but she'd never mastered the art of holding the tablet in one hand and typing with the other. A few key identifiers, yes, but actual notes? She preferred to write them on paper and organize them later on the tablet.

She also retrieved some evidence bags and some rubber gloves, stuffing her pockets with them. Best to be prepared, although right now it appeared that the local authorities had matters well in hand.

She switched the computer on as she approached the two men, and was glad to see she was getting a wireless signal. She'd discovered quite a few dead zones on her way to Conard City. Apparently that wasn't a problem in town.

Summoning a smile, she reached the two men.

"That's my wife, Charity," Wayne said, pointing.

Darcy picked out a blonde woman who was probably stunning when she wasn't wearing suspendered fireman's pants and boots and heavy gloves. Good clothing choice for the job. Darcy's fresh-from-the-office outfit was going to hinder her until she could change. At least she'd worn sensible black flats.

Charity waved at them and strode toward them. "Hi," she said, accepting a quick kiss from Wayne. "You must be Darcy Eccles." She waved her glove, stained with soot. "I'll shake your hand later."

Darcy liked her immediately. "That can wait. How's your investigation going?"

"Like most investigations. The cause is obvious. Finding all the pieces is a bit more difficult. We did find some slivers of PVC pipe, but at this point we can't be sure it didn't come from the building and not the bomb. As you can see, it was a decent blast, but not huge."

"Any sign of the ignition source?"

Charity shook her head. "Agent, I'm going to let you go through all the pieces. I've never dealt with a bomb and I couldn't recognize a lot of items that might be significant. We're mapping our finds on a grid, taking photos, bagging stuff we don't want to leave out in the elements. Mainly, we're trying not to disturb anything. Is that good?"

Darcy was surprised that she was being asked, then wondered why. Bombs were her area of expertise, not the arson investigator's.

"That's great. I'm going to need someplace where I can lay things out and look at them. And if you don't mind, I'd like to take a few pictures right now if I won't get in your way."

Charity lifted the yellow tape. "Have at it. I've been waiting impatiently to turn this over to you. I wouldn't have touched anything at all except the wind moves things and covers them with dust and dirt, and what if it rained?"

Darcy smiled at her. "It sounds like you've done an excellent job of protecting the evidence."

"I hope," said Charity. "Anything you need from me, let me know."

As Darcy approached the blast area, she saw that

the damaged side of the building gaped open like a devouring mouth. "Any chance we can get tarps over the side of the building? After I have a chance to get up top and make sure they wouldn't conceal anything. But not tacked to the side of the building until we've examined it."

Charity turned toward the two men. "Think so?"

"I'm sure," said Alex "We have a storage room at the school still full of roofing tarps from a tornado that went through a few years ago."

"FEMA roofs," Darcy said.

Alex laughed. "I've heard them called that."

"Thanks for the tarps," Darcy said. "We need to make sure any evidence inside is protected as well as you've done outside."

Standing near the edge of what appeared to be the blast circle, Darcy took in the damage to the cinder block wall, and the spread of debris, many of the larger pieces lying on the ground still, but carefully tucked into clear evidence bags for protection.

"I'm glad you didn't start gathering it up yet," she said to Charity. "I'll get a very clear picture this way. I'm going to walk around the perimeter and take some photos."

Charity nodded. "Do what you need to. Jeff and Randy and I will get back to scouring the area. We started at one edge and have been working our way slowly and carefully across so as to disturb as little as possible."

Darcy nodded, both impressed and pleased. Of course, as an investigator, Charity had plenty of knowledge of how to protect evidence.

She started walking around the edge of the

yellow tape, aware that Alex stayed nearby, but not concerned about it. With every step she took, she studied the ground in case something had blown farther out than the gridded area that the fire people had laid out. While they appeared to have properly designated the blast area, she'd long ago learned that some things flew a much greater distance than you'd expect. Some things that might appear innocuous when removed from all the surrounding evidence. Like a shiny building nail she'd found forty feet from the blast radius two cases ago.

She stopped and took another photo toward the center of the blast. "Do you suppose," she asked Alex absently, "we could organize a search of the area farther out?"

"I would think so. I could probably get a bunch of my students…"

She shook her head. "Sorry."

He sighed. "Yeah."

She faced him then, her heart skipping a surprised beat as she was struck again by his attractive features. "I shouldn't have to explain to you."

"You don't. But I don't have to like it. My students are all good people, but I understand you have to figure that out for yourself. The problem is, Darcy, how are you going to form a search party if you don't know who to trust?"

"Uniforms," she said shortly, then stopped. A young man stood at the edge of the no-man's land, his hands in his pockets, his gaze intent on the work around the bombed area.

"Who's that?" she asked sharply.

Alex swiveled his head. "Jackson Castor. Jack. He's in my cabinetry class. Great guy."

"Hmm." Darcy said no more but continued to slowly follow her circumnavigation while studying the ground far beyond the area where the firemen worked. When the opportunity arrived, she included Jackson Castor in a couple of shots.

Perps often showed a great deal of interest in the crime scene. She knew of numerous cases where a bomber had returned to watch the investigation while admiring his handiwork. Before she said anything about it, however, she was going to find out more about this Castor person.

She suspected Alex knew what had crossed her mind but she'd already sensed how protective he was of his students. A broody mother hen, she thought with amusement, but still one who had been an FBI agent and therefore probably knew how often the perpetrators showed up at the crime scene. Nope, better not to say a word. Maybe let him think the young man's presence had just slid right by her because of her focus on the ground.

The grasses were beginning to green with the spring, which didn't make her search any easier. What was the likelihood there'd been any metal in that bomb? Nobody had mentioned a pipe bomb or nails, so they surely hadn't discovered any nails and not enough debris to know the type of bomb.

Then she spied something odd. A green blade of grass had a hole in it. Squatting, she looked more closely. The edge of the hole was blackened. Something awfully hot had passed through it.

She set her tablet beside her, and pulled on a pair

of gloves so she could comb through the grass. Something had to be here unless it was nothing but a cinder. She couldn't take that chance.

She sensed Alex squat beside her, but he didn't say anything. Gently she moved blades of grass, drawing a line in her mind. The blast had come from over there. Anything flying from it would have come from the same general direction. That told her where to concentrate her efforts.

Then she spied it: a three-inch piece of slender wire. A little melted at one end, but otherwise surprisingly unaffected. It might be nothing, or it might be a part of the triggering device. Certainly not to be left behind. She took a photo of it and the blade of grass.

Then she tugged out an evidence bag, used a pen from her pocket to write on it, then carefully sealed the wire in the bag. Looking up, she tried to decide if it would be safe to leave it here or if she should mark the spot and take it.

Take it, she decided. This area hadn't been cordoned off. "I need some evidence markers from the back of my truck, or from the fire department."

Alex straightened. "I'll get you some from them. Might as well keep the numbering the same."

"Thanks." She quickly scrawled the GPS coordinates on her pad and waited for Alex to return with the plastic tent-style markers. When he did, she placed the numbered yellow piece and took another photo before adding the number to her description on the pad.

Painstaking work. Every bit of it.

"Any thoughts on what it could be?" Alex asked. He didn't sound as if he expected an answer.

"Too soon," she said anyway. All she knew for

certain was that it had been blown out here by the explosion.

She straightened up and looked around. "I need to change into some decent work clothes. And ask Charity to widen her cordon considerably. How's the motel?"

"It's clean but it's old," he said. "Wish we had something better to offer."

"Clean is good enough. How do I find it?"

Alex watched her talk to Charity, who agreed to bring the cordon out another thirty or forty feet. He wondered if she ever softened or if she was always so businesslike.

Then he saw her walking toward Jack Castor. Immediately he jogged over. He knew Jack well and was absolutely certain he wasn't capable of doing something like this. Yeah, he understood why Darcy was probably looking askance at the youth, but...

He caught himself. He'd learned a long time ago not to make those assumptions about anyone. Your own mother could be the murderer. Living with that kind of knowledge, borne out in his work, had driven him to a more peaceful life. Reality could be ugly. Oddly, he found himself recalling a quip he heard from reporters: if your mother says she loves you, check it out.

Darcy was doing her job. Ugliness had penetrated his new life, and he needed to squash urges that could hinder this investigation. Whoever had done this might move to larger bombs, bombs that could take a life. No time to be overprotective.

He reached Darcy and Jack in time to hear her say

pleasantly, "Alex says you're in his cabinetry class. So this bombing interests you?"

Jack grinned. "A whole lot. I never told anybody because I'm just a ranch kid and might not be able to go to college, but I always wanted to work for ATF."

"Yeah?" Darcy smiled. "It's fascinating work. What draws you to it?"

Jack's smile faded. "I have a friend... Well, his grandfather was killed in the Oklahoma City bombing. He wasn't even born yet, but his mom talked about it a lot for years and I heard about it, and every time she did I just wanted to do something useful about it. I know that's over and done with, but it wasn't the last bomb."

"No, it wasn't." She turned and indicated the school. "You have any ideas about this?"

"Who'd do this, you mean?"

Darcy simply waited.

"No." Jack looked almost crestfallen. "I wish I did. I mean, I can listen around and see if I hear anything, but I haven't yet." He looked down, then back at Darcy. "That's the weird part."

"What is?"

"You'd think someone would brag about it."

"Why do you think that?"

"Well..." Jack shifted from one foot to the other. "If it was some kid at the school...he'd tell someone. Most of us can't keep a secret that exciting."

Alex was surprised when Darcy laughed. "You make a good point, Jack."

Jack's smile returned. "Anyway, whoever did it would probably want to tell at least one person, someone he trusted, right? But that person would probably spill the beans to someone else…" He shrugged. "Or not. I guess some people must be really good at keeping secrets."

"Some are," Darcy agreed. "But your thinking is good. Keep it up. You're going to have to move back soon. We're extending the perimeter."

"Can I help with anything?" Jack asked eagerly.

Darcy shook her head. "Officials only."

"Okay, I'll stay out of the way."

"You do that."

Then she continued toward her truck. Alex followed, still concerned. "What are you thinking?" he asked as she opened her truck door.

"You mean about Jack?"

"Of course about Jack."

"Nothing yet," she said with a shrug. "Keep your pants on, Alex. It's early days."

He watched her drive away and half wished he could shake her out of her detachment. Then he remembered what had happened when he'd lost his. Divorce. Nightmares. End of career.

Aw, screw it, he thought and headed for the undamaged part of the school to check on those tarps. *Let the agent do her job.* He'd stay as far away as he could because he didn't want the nightmares to come back. And he sure as hell didn't need any new ones.

At the motel, which was clean albeit seriously outdated, Darcy showered away the travel grime, then changed into her gray working overalls and black boots. On her way back out to the site, she stopped long enough to grab another latte to stave off the fatigue from the long drive and added more tall cups of black coffee for the firefighters working out there.

She was surprised when she pulled into the parking lot to see that a small crowd of onlookers had appeared. Either word had got out that the ATF was here, or the firemen had found something exciting.

If they were curious because of her, they were in for a serious disappointment, she thought wryly. One agent in overalls was hardly the show they'd be hoping for. And they'd be right. Most explosions drew a bigger response, but at the moment too many cases had investigators pretty tied up. If she needed some backup, she would get it, but right now hands were tied.

She pulled in between two dusty pickup trucks, then retrieved her laptop and evidence case from the back of her truck.

Almost at once Jackson Castor appeared. "Let me at least carry the coffee," he said eagerly.

So he was still here, still interested in the goings-on. Might be a flag, might not be. So far nothing was setting off her internal warnings except his presence.

"Thanks. Make sure everyone working gets a cup," she said. Relieved of the extra coffees, she could handle the other items better. "Is Alex still around?"

"Yeah. He's been inside the school a lot. I guess you wanted some tarps?"

And just how did he know that? Was Alex talking to him? And what if all these people were here because something important had been found? The ATF preferred to keep evidence to themselves until they had the most complete picture possible. Dribbling news out to the public could only create problems and possibly false expectations or, worse, appear to accuse innocent people.

Not that her organization was completely without stains and mistakes. Like any organization, it was made up of people and people weren't perfect.

The cordon had been extended as she had asked, creating a much-wider area for investigation. She asked Jack to remain at the edge of the yellow tape and told him she'd tell everyone he was holding coffee for them. He seemed pleased by his job, however humble.

Well, she thought, it was possible he was just a kid who was interested in a career. It didn't *have* to mean anything that he was hanging around so eagerly. She discovered she was honestly hoping he was as innocent as Alex believed him to be.

The crowd, such as it was, showed a lot of interest in her, but she could feel their repressed disappointment that she was just one small woman and she didn't have a brawny team marching with her.

Not a very impressive display for the ATF, she thought with grim humor.

As she approached the most obviously blackened area, she caught up with Charity Camden. "Jack Castor. You know him?"

"The high school kid? Sort of. I seem to remember him from a talk I gave at the school about arson last fall. Eager and full of questions. Good questions."

How interesting, Darcy thought but kept the thought to herself. "I left him at the cordon holding coffee for you and your guys, and anyone else working on this. Maybe you're used to it, but it feels chilly to me out here."

Charity smiled. "Coffee's always welcome. Thanks."

"What brought the crowd? Did you find something?"

Charity laughed. "Not what, but who. They heard ATF was here. Enjoy your celebrity, if you can. I experienced a bit of it after I married Wayne. Good people, but curious as hell."

She called to her two helpers, telling them Jack had coffee for them. That cleared the zone briefly for Darcy, who set her equipment down, pulled on her gloves, made sure her loupe was in her pocket along with some evidence bags and started to walk through the grid laid out by the firefighters.

She squatted often, examining the contents of a bag more closely and checking the ground beneath it. Once, she lifted her head and sniffed the air. It still contained the faintest tang of fuel oil after nearly two days. It must have soaked the ground.

She added that tidbit to her increasing list of tidbits. She needed to find out what kind of fuel it was, because she needed to know its burn characteristics but also because she needed to know why she could still smell it. Fuel oil evaporated quickly if it didn't burn. It was the benzenes and xylenes that made up the gasoline that created most of the familiar smell. Those evaporated relatively quickly, so a lot must have leaked out of that bomb without burning at any point.

That brought her head up. Still squatting, she thought about it. That much fuel oil? In a closed container, why add the fertilizer? You could just make a great Molotov cocktail.

She looked toward the building. But it wouldn't have caused that kind of damage. She closed her eyes again, sniffing and thinking about it. Apparently the bomber hadn't perfected his method. He'd left far too much gasoline residue behind. Way too much.

Had this been a practice bomb? The notion chilled her deeply. One accident might well become a string of bombs if this had been a trial run.

Good God!

"Can I join you?"

Darcy turned her head a little in response to Charity's voice. "Yeah. Don't disturb anything." She almost winced as she heard herself. Charity certainly didn't need that warning.

Soon Charity was squatting beside her, saying, "I figured once we move everything we can see out of here we'll need to look again."

"Yeah, with a rake. It's hard to be sure we haven't stomped something into the dirt." Then she pointed toward where she'd found the wire. "We have all that to cover, too."

"You're sure the wire came from the explosion?"

"Unless someone was soldering out there, yeah."

Charity sighed. "I've seen some bad fires, Darcy, but nothing like this. You'll have to tell me what to do."

"I don't seem to have a problem with that, huh?" Darcy's voice was dry.

Charity chuckled quietly. "That's okay. There can never be too many reminders. By the way, Alex said you needed a place to spread all this out. He's talking the principal into turning the gymnasium over to you. I don't get why that would be a problem. We haven't even been able to determine if the rest of the building is structurally sound yet. We have an engineer coming from Gillette on Thursday. Meantime, no school. And thanks again for the coffee." She raised her foam cup as if in toast, then sipped.

"Darcy?"

"Yeah?"

"You've been squatting here an awfully long time. Is something bothering you or do you need help getting up now?"

It was such a relief to just laugh. Darcy let it out, along with a lot of tension. "I was thinking. You're the arson person. Do you still smell fuel oil?"

"Yeah, I do. Some didn't burn off. The ground must be soaked. It's driving my guys crazy because I won't let them smoke anywhere around here."

Darcy turned her head. "Your guys smoke?"

Charity shrugged with a half smile. "The chief, my husband, hates it, but it's as if these guys just can't get enough smoke. They're not allowed to do it in public, but it's no secret, really."

"Criminy," Darcy remarked.

"Yeah. You'd think they never saw the results of careless smoking. Anyway, fuel oil. I gather it's bothering you, too."

"If the bomb was precisely made, the residue of the fuel oil, the volatile chemicals in it, should be pretty much gone by now. The fact that I can smell it here in the open air after all this time…" She shook her head a little.

"You're thinking this guy didn't know what he was doing?"

"I'm thinking he knows what he's doing but hasn't quite got it right."

Charity drew a sharp breath. "I don't like what that might mean."

"Me neither. Say, you know Alex, right?"

"Fairly well, I guess. He's a friend of Wayne's."

"Well, he worked for BSU, but from what he said I gather he left some demons behind. Do you think I'd disturb him if I asked him for an evaluation?"

At that moment, Darcy's knees decided to raise an objection. She straightened and Charity was right beside her. The two of them stood sipping their coffees while Darcy shook her legs a bit and waited for Charity's answer.

"I honestly don't know what his instinctive reaction would be," Charity answered finally, drawing the words out as if she were still pondering. "I know this school matters a lot to him, and his students even more. He's the kind of teacher we'd all have liked, you know? He takes a personal interest and, from what I hear, is amazingly even-tempered even when provoked by some teen. You know how teens are. Or you can remember."

"Smart mouths."

"Yeah. And they push each other into stupidity sometimes. But he's never criticized one of them in a way that anybody complains about. Gifted with dealing with testosterone, I guess. But for the rest?" She looked at Darcy. "I've never talked with him much about his FBI days. Wayne's given me the sense that Alex would prefer to forget them. But given that his school has been struck by a bomb…and more specifically his shop facilities…" She trailed off. "I dunno, Darcy. He's a grown man. He knows how to say no.

My guess is that he'd like to do something constructive about this mess, but I can't guarantee anything."

"I'm not asking for a guarantee. I just want to avoid hitting a raw nerve, but I'm not trying to put you on the spot or deprive him of the right to speak for himself."

She was good at figuring out the mechanics of the bomb. Good at tracking evidence back to its source. Not so good at trying to evaluate the psychology of a bomber. Other than that they were usually cowards, she didn't know a whole lot. Once she'd amassed enough evidence, the FBI would probably assist in this investigation. They often did, having their own skill sets and people. But she didn't want to wait that long. She wanted to know if her nose was misleading her. Literally.

"Have you been inside the building?" she asked Charity.

"Sure. Fortunately, the blast didn't escape the shop rooms in there. Stopped dead at the corridor wall."

"More cinder block?"

"I believe so. I'm sure we have all that info back at the department. The paint is blackened but I was mostly looking at the containment. You can probably tell a lot more. Let's walk around to the door, though. I don't want to disturb the ground out here any more than necessary."

"Agreed," Darcy answered, surprised at how glad she was to have Charity as a teammate in this. Someone to show her around, someone who could answer questions because she knew the area and the people. Alex could do as much and in some instances more, if he was willing. She wished she knew what had happened to him in the BSU. She had no difficulty imagining the ugly minutiae he must have dealt with in that job, but something had pushed him to a breaking point. One that had cost him a whole lot.

She walked with Charity, ignoring the twenty-five or thirty people who'd gathered, nodding briefly at Jackson Castor, who still held the bag of cooling coffees that hadn't been claimed by the workmen.

"Have a coffee, Jack," she said. "No point letting it all cool down."

He grinned and nodded.

And if she were him, she'd probably have wandered away in boredom by now. He was what, seventeen or eighteen? Most people that age wouldn't want to stand around being bored, because sure as heck nothing exciting was happening right now.

Which caused a quiet ping on her internal radar.

Just as they rounded a corner of the building to face large steel doors with small windows, one of the doors opened and the Viking appeared. Well, it was Alex, but he still reminded her of a beardless Viking, one that reminded her she was still very much a woman. She wondered if that reaction would wear off. She hoped so because she'd spent a lot of effort developing a cool, professional persona in a career field dominated by men. Now that she was leading an investigation, it would be a bad time to mess that up by giving in to a sexual attraction.

Alex greeted her with a nod and a pleasant smile, and eyes that slipped over her body like a caress. "All set. You can use the gymnasium as long as we spread some of those tarps on the floor. I can get some help doing that for you. Gotta protect that finish, you know."

Darcy smiled. "I get it. That gloss on a basketball floor is expensive and essential."

"Oh, yeah." His smile widened a shade. "Going to look around inside?"

"Charity's showing me."

"I'll come along. I promise not to touch."

He said it humorously. She was quite sure he knew all about preserving evidence. Still, he was offering friendliness. He was also sending signals that he didn't want to be left out of this. Good. She didn't need him to take over, but she was sure his brain might be worth picking. A complete 180 from her initial reaction. She just hoped it wasn't hormone-driven.

The shop rooms were at the back of the school, in what appeared to be a separate wing. As they turned into the corridor leading to them, she stopped. From this vantage point, it appeared that farther down, near some doors on the right, the wall had bulged outward.

"What?" Alex asked.

She pointed. "Look down the right wall. What do you see?"

Alex drew a breath. Charity muttered something. "It's bulging," Alex said. "Good God. What kind of force would be needed to do that?"

"I need to do some calculations," Darcy answered. Her gaze swept down along the wall, then to the ceiling overhead. A drop ceiling, it should have showed some sign if it had been affected, but it appeared to be perfectly all right. She'd need some measurements to be sure, but her eyes were telling her it was still square.

Then she looked at the bulge again. "The bomb was fairly low. Right now I'd guess it was outside of the building when it detonated. Look what it did to the exterior wall. If it had been inside I think we'd see more than some bowing on that wall."

Alex nodded. "I think you're right."

"I still need to see inside the rooms. I'm just guessing." But a picture was beginning to build, and it didn't include access to the school when it was locked up overnight. Another piece to the puzzle perhaps.

They continued down the corridor and Alex pulled out a key ring. "This seems ridiculous now," he said as he slipped a key into the lock on the nearest door. It turned easily. "Well, I didn't expect that," he remarked. "I thought it would be busted."

It turned out, however, that the door was out of line and didn't want to open easily. "I imagine," he said, "that you don't want to take an ax to this."

"I'd rather see the original damage. Then I want to measure that bulge and how far it is from the bomb opening." She glanced at Charity. "Can I get a surveyor out here?"

"I'm sure you can get anything you want."

Alex spoke. "I know just the guy. He'll be able to tell how deformed the wall is." He leaned into the door while holding the latch open and pushed. It moved just a little. "Okay…" He gave another shove, harder, a grunt escaping him this time, but the door opened four inches.

"We're on our way," Charity remarked. "Should I get a pry bar from the truck?"

"Let me give it one more try. It feels like something is behind it."

He leaned backward into the door, this time using his entire body for leverage, and slowly, scraping every inch of the way, it opened wide enough that Darcy could slip inside.

There the story was very different. Not only were shop machines and tables twisted and tossed everywhere, but the ceiling had also burned and collapsed, leaving exposed wires dangling. "Circuit breakers off?" she asked.

"Absolutely," Alex said, easing his way in beside her.

"Surprise," Darcy muttered. "It looks like a bomb went off."

"No kidding," he answered. "Do you know what I'm seeing?"

She turned her head toward him, curious. "What?"

"A lot of opportunity smashed. A lot of really good projects my students were working on, destroyed. We might be able to get this shop up and running by next fall, but there are a lot of seniors who had some really fine stuff underway here, and it's gone. Son of a…" He stopped himself, but while his face remained emotionless, she could feel anger seething in him. Then he looked at her. "They don't get their dreams back. Their excitement over all they were achieving."

"No." Her answer might have been flat, but she felt her heart squeeze. He'd hit on the part she tried to avoid thinking about. "Collateral damage." There was always collateral damage.

"Yeah," he agreed. "*Collateral.* Such a cold word."

No point standing here and grieving. Tucking her hands into one of the many pockets on her overalls, she passed him some disposable booties, then donned a pair over her work boots. "Less contamination," she remarked out of habit. God, was she becoming one of those people who persisted in telling others what they probably already knew? But Alex didn't take it amiss.

"I'll stay out here," Charity said. "God knows what's on my boots and you don't have any of those that'll go over these things."

It was true. Darcy tossed her a smile, pulled a couple of high-intensity penlights out of another of her pockets and began to scan what she could see without moving from top to bottom. Alex took the other flashlight and followed suit. "Anything unusual?" he asked.

"Anything. Just point it out to me if it catches your eye."

"Got it."

"Charity? I don't smell the fuel oil in here. It's all outside. It wouldn't dissipate in here, not as fast, so…"

"I read you. Excessive fuel oil was used, so there ought to be some scent in here. Definitely seems like the explosion was just outside."

Darcy nodded. "I suspect that what we'll find in here will mainly be blast debris, not much from the device itself. But we still have to look."

And what a job it was going to be, she thought as she looked around. She'd seen plenty of scenes like this; she had no illusion about the painstaking work facing her. No illusion, either, about the fact that she'd get on-site help only if some were freed up elsewhere. Conard City, Wyoming, was kind of off the map and radar with so many other important things happening. Unless she found some kind of indicator signifying militants or terrorists in the area, she was pretty much on her own. A vanguard without follow-up.

"Damn," Alex said emphatically.

"What?" Darcy immediately followed the beam of his flashlight. He wiggled it over some blackened heap that seemed to have at least one thick leg attached.

"Chuck Ingram was working on that. A butcher-block island for his mother. She'd wanted one for years, but they were out of reach, so he saved up money for the last two years from his part-time job to buy the best, hardest wood. Glued the wood together, braced it, tooled the legs... He was going to give it to his mom for Mother's Day. He was almost done."

Darcy stared at what was now a charred lump and felt a growing flame of anger deep inside. This was about a lot more than a bomb, how it was built and who built it. This was about lives, hopes, dreams. "Hell." She usually avoided swearing, but that word seemed mild right now.

"There are other projects like that in here," Alex said grimly. "We gotta get this guy. That's the only way I can help these kids now."

With that, he passed back the flashlight and eased out of the room. Darcy saw Charity watching him as he left the building.

Then Charity leaned her head through the door. "It's probably too late to clean up this mess," she said. "I mean, we could get more wood for Chuck, but we can't give him back the hours he spent on that. Even if we could arrange for him to work in the shop at the college."

"No." Darcy scanned the room some more. "Okay, I'm going to need to take a lot of photos before I even start looking around. Then the tarps."

"My guys can help you on the roof, when you're ready to check it."

"Thanks. I'm definitely going to need some help with this."

She eased back out of the room and pulled off her booties, folding them inside out in case they'd picked up something that might prove useful.

"I'm surprised you're alone," Charity said.

"I wouldn't ordinarily be. Bad time. The bureau is overtaxed right now. Hopefully that'll change soon. Either that, or I find a lead to the bomber. Meantime, preserve the evidence." The endless mantra. *Preserve the evidence.*

And try not to think too hard about all the students who'd just had their work blown up by some jackass.

Chapter 3

Two days later, all the debris that had been bagged and tagged had been moved into the gymnasium, laid out in a duplicate of the grid outside, preserving positions. Off-duty firefighters and cops had volunteered to comb the ground outside, many of them on their hands and knees, gently raking over soil that had been trampled. A tarp covered the hole in the building. Surprisingly little had been found on the steel roof, arguing that the bomb had indeed been placed low.

With Alex's help, Darcy had taken measurements of everything: the size of the hole in the building, the blast radius, the area of damage in the shop. A surveyor had accurately measured the bulge in the interior cinder block wall.

Diagrams had begun to sprout on her computer—vectors of force running outward until she was fairly certain she'd localized the center of the explosion. All of this she'd sent back to the field office for analysis along with carefully preserved samples of the ground, the burned wood, the soot. Soon they'd be able to tell her more about the bomb's force and content.

But the smell of fuel oil outside still bothered her. A couple of evenings later, Alex asked her to join him at the diner for supper and she agreed, even though she knew she should feel wary of the attraction she felt for him. Boy, it was getting bad, so bad that she couldn't even think of him without tingling in her most feminine places. She couldn't remember the last time any man had made her feel that way just by virtue of existing.

She desperately turned her thoughts back to business and ordered her body to shut up.

Maybe she'd get the opportunity to talk to him in a more speculative way than she could allow at the scene. There she had to be the ultimate science expert, relying on proof, on actual evidence. That would be Alex's trained inclination as well, which is why she trusted him not to misunderstand if she discussed her thoughts tentatively. Brainstorming was something you could do with a colleague.

But Alex's thoughts were headed in a different direction, so she let him lead the conversation. Her opening would come and maybe she'd stop trying to imagine that spark she saw in his blue eyes reciprocated her growing desires.

"So how'd you get into the ATF?" he asked as they ate a delicious beef stew accompanied by fresh crusty bread.

"Probably the same way you got into the FBI," she said humorously. "A recruiter came to my college."

He laughed. "Uh, yeah. Same here. Except they didn't want to snap me up right away. I had a double major in criminology and psychology. They suggested that there'd be a job waiting for me if I did well in civilian police work."

"I guess you did."

"So it would seem. Three years into my work with Miami PD, they came knocking again. I thought they'd forgotten me."

She shook her head. "Now you know they never forget."

He laughed again. "You?"

"I majored in chemistry and physics, and the way they explained the work intrigued me, made me feel I could do some actual good. They snapped me up just before I graduated and sent me for intensive training. They wanted a scientist more than a law enforcement officer. I've been working with explosives ever since."

He slipped his fork back into his bowl. "Do you ever wonder how they settled on you to begin with? I wasn't the only double major in criminology and psychology."

"And I wasn't the only one majoring in chemistry and physics. I don't know about you, but I poked my head up. They had an interviewer on campus and I was just curious, so I went. I walked into their field of attention. But you didn't?"

He shook his head. "I still don't know why I was approached, and I doubt anyone could even tell me now. It was a while ago. Then, like you, I went through a whole lot of training and testing and wound up in the BSU."

"Not a good thing, I gather?"

He shook his head a little. "You know, it's ugly. That kind of work is always ugly. But for a long time I was able to live with it because we were helping take some horrible people off the streets. It seemed like a fair trade-off. I was proud every time we could provide information that helped narrow the search and bring a creep to justice. For a while that was enough."

She hesitated, eating a bit more stew before taking a dangerous step. "Then it wasn't."

He pressed his lips together before speaking again. "No. It wasn't." He forgot all about his meal and stared into space, seeming to be lost in memory. Then he shook his head. "You hear of the bicycle killer case?"

Oh, she had. She drew a sharp breath. Even the bits she'd heard had been sickening. Little girls, a murderous serial pedophile, torture. "Alex, I'm sorry."

"Anyway, that was my last case. I had a daughter that age."

He didn't need to say more. He probably saw his own child in every victim profile that crossed his desk, in every bit of suffering and torture. She didn't even want to try to imagine it. She was sure he'd learned to keep a certain level of detachment, just as she had, but having a daughter the same age as the victims? Her own detachment would have shattered in the face of that, too.

He probably carried scars and nightmares that would never go away.

"Your daughter?" she asked presently.

"She lives with her mother. I tipped off the rails for

a while. Anger, not sleeping, nightmares... I wasn't good for either of them. Hell, I wasn't good for myself. But I don't want to get into that."

"Of course not." But she couldn't quash the ache in her heart for him. God, she hoped none of her jobs ever brought her to that precipice. She lowered her head, giving him privacy, appreciating the honesty he'd just shared with her. He needn't have been so frank with her, a woman who was nearly a complete stranger. What did they have in common, after all, except a background as federal employees?

Eating halted conversation for a while and then Alex spoke again. "You probably don't want me in the middle of things, since I'm so protective of my students."

She hesitated again, putting down her fork and dabbing her mouth with a paper napkin. "Depends on how you want to help."

He raised his head a bit from his intense study of the bowl in front of him and smiled faintly. "I know next to nothing about your technical end of it. I couldn't intervene or interfere in any way. But I know quite a bit about human psychology."

She didn't doubt it. Aberrant psychology mostly, but still useful. "Well...I was disturbed by something. I wanted to mention it to you, if you don't mind."

"Sure, go ahead."

"When I arrived, the smell of fuel oil was still evident. The smell, as you must know, comes from the volatiles in the fuel—benzenes and xylenes for the most part. The fact that the odor was still apparent outdoors two days after the bombing means an awful lot of fuel soaked into the ground, rather than burning, and too much to evaporate quickly. Today the smell was gone, but I wouldn't have expected it to be there as long as it was."

"Meaning?"

"Too much was used. It never burned. It soaked the ground so that it evaporated more slowly."

"So an inexperienced bomber."

"Maybe." She pushed her bowl to the side and lowered her voice. "Maybe an experimental bomb. Maybe a test run."

His face hardened into expressionless stone. "Let's get out of here. We can talk privately at my house."

She thought that was a pretty good idea.

The sun had long since disappeared behind the western mountains, making the light flat though it was far from dark yet. Nothing cast much of a shadow if it cast one at all.

She drove behind Alex to his house, a small two-story near the high school with a well-tended yard. When she stepped inside, she knew what he did with his spare time, and to work out the demons. The place gleamed with loving care, the woodwork was amazing and classic. The oak floor beneath her feet in the entry didn't creak even a little bit.

"Did you do all this?" she asked as he closed the door behind her.

"I bought it for a song and gutted it. It was bad, but the basic bones were sound."

"Beautiful work," she remarked, touching the handrail on the staircase, then turning to admire the fine-looking wainscoting in white oak.

"Let's go to the kitchen. I didn't get my usual coffee from Maude and I can make you a latte if you want."

The kitchen was as up-to-date as any she'd seen. "Let me guess, you made the cabinets, too."

He nodded while he tossed his jacket over a chair and turned to the coffee maker. "Old houses didn't have a lot of cabinetry. I built more than I need, but I enjoy the work so I just kept going."

"Well, it's gorgeous," she told him frankly. Then she spied the kitchen table and pointed to it. "You made that, too?"

"Yeah," he said offhandedly.

"You sure keep busy, and you do wonderful work."

He smiled as he switched the coffee maker on and faced her. "It's nice to be able to do what I love. Grab a seat. Did you want that latte?"

"Regular will be fine. Thanks for the offer."

He leaned back against the counter, folding his arms and studied her. "You've got an uneasy feeling with little to pin it on."

"Very good, Dr. Freud."

A snort escaped him. "I don't think that way. No Oedipus complexes for me. No, it was pretty obvious from what you said. No kudos for me. So tell me."

"That's the thing," she admitted. "I want to pick your brain about the psychology of the bomber, because that's not my area. How the bomb was built, yes. That's what I do. But since I don't have a whole team out here, what with everyone so busy on other cases…" She paused. "I don't know if you've been paying attention since you left the bureau, but violence is on the rise. The kind of violence ATF deals with. Guns. Bombs. I don't know whether it's just a growing population or a genuine change going on."

"Change," he said succinctly. "People are getting

bolder about expressing themselves in deadly ways. Just as hate crimes are on the rise. I'd like to be able to point to one thing as the causative agent, but I think it's a whole bunch of things, so I'm not going to trot out the list. It is what it is, and it's getting worse. That's all we need to know right now."

"Bad enough that's it's happening," she agreed. "There are probably a whole lot of different motives anyway. Not one size fits all."

"No." He turned and pulled out two mugs from a cupboard. "Black, milk, sugar?"

"Black's fine, thanks."

He put the mugs on the table and joined her. Facing each other once again as they had at the diner. "So the excess gasoline is bothering you?"

"Yes, it is," she acknowledged. "Of course, the spill could have been a deliberate attempt to spread any fire in the hopes that evidence would be destroyed."

"Maybe." He frowned, leaning back and cradling his mug in both hands.

"The thing is, the concussive force of a bomb often snuffs any fire in its immediate vicinity, like blowing out a candle. You need debris that's hot enough to start a fire when the concussion passes or it lands somewhere. Now it happens all the time, but not every time, that we get extensive fire away from the blast. Anyway, the smell of that gasoline was obviously too close. It didn't burn."

"Or too far away, which doesn't seem likely given the hole in the side of the building. So you're thinking this was a mistake of some kind?"

"Possibly." She sipped coffee, running bits and pieces through her mind, trying to fit them together.

She'd know more tomorrow or the next day as she examined the debris and received evaluations from the field office. "Our bomber could always stop with this one. Maybe it said all he wanted to say. On the other hand, what if this was a trial run? He'd be learning nearly as much as I am."

Then she leaned forward, her full attention on him. "Ponder something for me, Alex. What would make that corner of the school a better target than any other? Assuming it wasn't just someone with a—what did you call it?—a hatred of band saws."

He set his mug on the table and his gaze grew distant as he thought. She let him be. He was coming at this from a totally different perspective than she could: the psychology.

"Not easy to see back there at night from the street. Pretty secluded, actually."

"No security lights?"

"We've never needed them. Some in the front of the school near the entrance, but back there it's not a good place to break in regardless."

"No garage doors?"

"You saw the only two. They're on the shop wing, facing the street. The auto shop is up there on that end of the building. The back…that's all wood and metalworking. If we need to bring in something large, it's delivered out front to the garage doors. Access between the work areas is good, but…" He shook his head. "If I wanted to break in to steal something, that would be the place, except that the risk of being spied by a patrol is high. But bombing? The back, definitely."

She nodded. She'd already seen what he meant.

It was a wonder the damage hadn't spread farther. "Okay. Why not someplace else?"

"Almost anyplace else would get you a classroom. The interior doors are all fire doors and locked. So if you want to get into the building, a classroom wouldn't be the best route. If all you want to do is destroy something, you'd get thirty desks and a whiteboard," He paused.

"The administrative offices are in the center. Hard to get to except from inside. The gym...well, you saw for yourself. It would have made a good target on the back side, but there are fire doors back there. I don't know if they'd cause a problem. Reasons this guy would pick my corner? No really good ones other than what I've said."

Now he rubbed his chin. "There had to be a reason other than not being spotted if all you want to do is bomb something. Why not blow out a classroom? Or try the gym..." He paused. "Unless my corner of the school resembled another target..."

Their eyes locked. Darcy's heart began to race like a horse in a steeplechase. "I was afraid that you might say something like that," she murmured.

"Yeah," he said after a moment. "I was trying to avoid that idea."

For a long time, neither of them said a word, lost in their own lines of thought. Alex rose once to freshen their coffee, and part of Darcy's mind once again noted how much he looked like a Viking, except that he wasn't shaggy at all. He ought to grow his hair out.

Her mind snapped back. She had to cut this out. Mooning over the shop teacher was well outside the parameters of anything she was here to do.

She was looking at what might be the first act of a serial bomber. No rhyme or reason, evidently, but a person who'd successfully created an ANFO bomb could not be ignored, even if he'd messed up and spilled fuel oil at the site.

"You need a break," he said, surprising her. "I learned the hard way that thinking about something else for a while not only refreshed me, but allowed my subconscious to churn things. Have you thought about anything but this bomb since you got here?"

You. But she wasn't going to admit that. "Yeah, a bit. I pay attention to other things but it keeps pulling me back. Your young friend Jack has been hanging around, too."

His face darkened. "Darcy..."

"You know the profile, Alex. Do you really need me to remind you? Excessive interest in the scene along with a desire to join the bureau. Those two things together... Well, you tell me how else Jackson Castor could get to watch ATF in action. He also said he didn't think he'd get to college, so any federal agency is going to remain a pipe dream for him. He's walking around wearing warning flags."

Alex's expression remained grim, but he didn't argue with her. Like it or not, he knew as well as she that Jack's behavior was putting him in the crosshairs. He wouldn't be convicted based on it, but he had to be watched and even investigated.

But what could you investigate with a kid that age? His whereabouts early on a Sunday morning? Whether he had the tools at home to put something like this together? An extraordinary interest in chemistry, maybe?

Darcy pushed her coffee away. "Sorry I'm upsetting you."

"No, you're being honest." Some of the stoniness left his face. "I don't like it, but I'm not dismissing it, okay?"

"Fair enough. You being his teacher and all, you can probably clear him easier than I could."

Finally, the stone chipped away and he smiled again. "Yes, I could. And you don't have to look so unhappy for mentioning it. It's a legitimate point, and much as I like that young man, I've been aware of the same flags you mentioned. I'm not going to overlook them."

She returned his smile then, inexplicably relieved. She hardly knew the man, so why care what he thought of her? "And we still have the issue of whether this was a trial run."

He nodded. "That we do. Unfortunately we can't know unless there's another one."

"I hope there's not," she said honestly. "It might make it easier to find the perp, but I'd rather not see it happen. Not at all."

Just then Darcy's cell phone began to vibrate in the breast pocket of her overalls. She pulled it out and answered the call.

"Agent Eccles, this is the sheriff's office. We've picked up an intruder in the school gymnasium. Do you want us to keep him here or take him in for questioning?"

Her gaze leaped to Alex's face. "Intruder," she said. "Any ID?" she asked the deputy.

"Jackson Castor."

* * *

Alex rode along with her in her black truck. He kept drumming his fingers on the window ledge, and his tension was almost palpable. He didn't say anything, but Darcy had a good idea what he was thinking. Jackson. The kid he'd defended. What the hell was he doing poking around the evidence they had sequestered in the gym?

She was wondering exactly the same thing herself. Could they have really caught the bomber this easily? Experience had taught her that it wasn't always difficult, and dealing with a kid Jackson's age might make it a whole lot easier.

But strangely enough she didn't want it to be Jack, even though she'd refused to let herself or Alex give the young man a pass. Warning flags. He was wearing them all.

She drove into the parking lot near the gymnasium end of the school. Several police cars were there now, lights swirling. "Jackson got himself into a mess," she remarked as she parked and turned off the ignition.

"Sadly" was all Alex said. She glanced at him. Night had begun to deepen but the glow from the dashboard illuminated his face. *His game face*, she thought. *Hard as granite*. She wouldn't have wanted to sit across an interrogation table from him right then.

They climbed out. Automatically Darcy carried her small evidence kit, which contained a digital recorder, among other smaller tools of investigation. She discovered she was hoping Jackson Castor had a really good explanation for this trespass.

She displayed her credentials to a deputy she didn't know and was waved on through. Inside, two deputies sat on the bleachers to either side of a very chastened-looking Jack.

"Hey, Beau," Alex said. "Hi, Cadell."

The middle-aged deputy whose name tag said he was Sergeant Beauregard stood. "Lots of excuses, no real answers," he said. "Jackson Castor. Age seventeen. But I guess you know him, Alex."

"That I do. Is it all right if Agent Eccles and I question him ourselves?"

Beau nodded. "That's why I called before I took him in. Hate to mess up a young idiot's life unnecessarily." He nodded to Darcy. "Agent. You need anything, let me know."

"I certainly will, Sergeant Beauregard."

"Just Beau. Nobody calls me anything else except my wife."

"What does she call you?"

He flashed a grin. "Mostly nice things." He and the other deputy, Cadell Marcus, moved around the edge of the gym.

Which left Darcy and Alex with a shamefaced Jack.

"Well?" Alex asked.

Darcy let him take the lead willingly at this point. Since he knew Jack, he might get further. Right now her insides felt as tight as an overwound spring.

Jack looked down. "I was curious. I saw all the stuff being moved, and I wanted to see how it was all laid out. How it works. I should have known there'd be a guard."

Well, thought Darcy, that sounded naive enough to be believable. "How'd you get in?"

"I work as a trainer for the basketball team. I have keys."

That caught her attention instantly. Forgetting that she wanted to look intimidating, she sat down beside Jack. "Keys, huh?"

"Yeah."

"Why are you the trainer?"

"'Cause I'm not good enough to be on the team, but being the trainer gets me to all the away games for free." He shrugged. "I was stupid, huh?"

"You could say that," Alex replied, still standing, still looking intimidating.

"I just wanted to know." Jack looked up. "I'll never get to do this for real. Nobody will talk to me because I'm just a civilian. This'll probably be my only chance to get up close to the ATF." He flushed. "Darn, I sound like a girl with a crush."

A remarkably astute observation, Darcy thought. She sighed. "How much do you know about what I do, Jack?"

"What I can read online."

"Okay. Have you ever read what we look for around the scene in terms of people?"

"Profiles, you mean?" He glanced up at Alex as if seeking confirmation. "Oh, man. It's me, isn't it?"

"You how?" Darcy asked.

"Hanging around, showing too much interest, wanting to be in ATF and then this." The young man jumped up. "But I didn't do it!"

"I'm afraid," said Alex heavily, "that Agent Eccles is now going to have to check you out. Thoroughly. Sorry, Jack, but even I can't explain this away."

Jack paced a few steps, then clenched his fists and closed his eyes. "Damn, I didn't even think about that. I was just curious."

"Maybe so," said Darcy. "Did you notice anyone else who was interested?"

Jack's eyes popped open. "I wasn't paying attention to anyone else. Oh, man…"

Darcy wished he'd had a different answer. "Do I need to get a warrant to check out where you live?"

Jack shook his head. "Not for me. Come look. I'll just tell my parents, I don't think they'll object because they won't want me to be under suspicion. You can look at anything you want. When?"

"Now," said Darcy, standing. "Sergeant Beauregard?"

"Yes, ma'am?" He came striding over.

"We're going to need a few deputies to help us out. We need to investigate the Castor homestead."

"How many?"

Darcy looked at Alex. "Are you familiar with the Castor place?"

"Been there several times."

"Big?"

"I'd bring at least six deputies."

She nodded and looked at Beauregard. "Six, maybe a couple more."

"You got it. It might take an hour to pull it together."

"That's fine." She returned her attention to Jack. "You sit right here, young man. Turn your phone over to Deputy Marcus. No calls until I say so."

"Yes, ma'am."

"One more thing." A small flicker of anger was trying to get started. "Did you touch anything in here?"

Jack shook his head. "I wouldn't have anyway, but the deputies were already in here."

She looked at Marcus. "He's yours. I need to step outside."

Marcus nodded and pressed Jack back down onto the bench.

Alex decided to accompany Darcy outside. She'd been very controlled with Jack, which he appreciated professionally, but he wondered what she was thinking. He knew what *he* was thinking: Jack was up to his neck in trouble now, although he still didn't honestly believe his student had a role in the bombing. But it sure didn't look good, and it couldn't be ignored.

Outside, Darcy thrust her hands into the side pockets of her overalls. "Keys?" She repeated. "He had *keys*? He could have got into anything. Why didn't everyone have to turn them in as soon as the bombing happened? I never thought just anyone had access to that building." She kicked the earth. "Damn, I should have verified that."

"It didn't occur to me, either," he said reassuringly. "I just assumed that would have been one of the first things the police did when sealing the scene."

"I guess they never thought the entire building could be the scene."

"I need to find out who was the scene commander. Someone needs a talking-to."

"Probably a simple oversight," she said grimly. "Otherwise everyone did a spectacular job. I shouldn't be so angry. Besides, they clearly had a good guard set on the gymnasium, and there are still guys watching the blast area both inside and outside. Sorry." Then again, she said disbelievingly, "Keys?"

"Sometimes the small oversights can really get to you."

"And cause huge problems."

He waited, admiring her restraint. He wouldn't have blamed her for giving in to at least a small explosion of ire. She was right, the entire school should have been locked down, but he wasn't accustomed to actually working crime scenes of any kind, and it had never crossed his mind that maybe it wasn't a good thing that administrators were still able to get to their offices. After all, he'd gone in and asked for use of the tarps and the gym.

Darcy had probably thought he'd passed some kind of gatekeeper to do that. Instead he'd walked in as easily as if he were going to teach a class. Admittedly, there'd been a deputy at the door, but he hadn't been restricted.

But maybe that's because the deputies keeping watch pretty much knew everyone who should be able to access the school. Maybe they figured that going to talk to someone in administration was a necessary access.

It had been, but it shouldn't have been so easy.

"I wonder how contaminated the scene is now," Darcy said quietly. "My fault. I should have noticed when you led me inside to show me the wall of the shop. It should have occurred to me that I needed to check if there was a lockdown on the building."

"Why would you imagine there wasn't? First, that end of the building *was* locked down. Remember? Tape and two deputies. It's not like the inside of the building was crawling with gawkers. Besides, we were really concerned about the structural integrity. We didn't want anyone in there unnecessarily. So the lock-down wasn't perfect, but it was good enough."

"Until tonight."

Well, yeah, he thought. *Until tonight.*

She faced him. "You need to know something. I've worked on a number of these cases but I've never been the lead on one. Now I'm out here on my own and I just made a potentially critical error. I wonder how many others I'll make."

Man, that must have been hard for her to say. She hardly knew him. He hesitated, wishing he dared to clasp her shoulder reassuringly but concerned about his roiled up feelings. Touching this woman might remind him of just how desirable he found her. Some lines were better not crossed.

He spoke, determined to keep this professional. "I don't think you've made a critical error. Part of what you're dealing with here is that darn near everyone knows everyone else. Maybe we aren't being as careful as we should be since everyone is familiar, but we ought to be more cautious. Anyway, I don't think you made any unjustified assumptions. I think we were a little more lax than you imagined. And I doubt there was a critical error, certainly not on your part."

"I guess we'll find out." She looked out over the area away from the school.

"I did want to ask you, though. No criticism intended. But does the ATF usually send only one agent?"

"Depends on what's going on, what local resources are available and how many we have tied up. We don't have any slack right now. I was pulled off another case to come here. I guess everyone was thinking it was probably some kind of accident."

"Is ANFO ever an accident?"

She surprised him. "Believe it or not, it *does* happen. It's like anything else. A bomb is next to impossible to make deliberately, then a factory worker inadvertently spills something while smoking an illicit cigarette and *kaboom*." She sighed. "You've read about it in the papers. Usually involving a chemical plant. So yeah, it happens, and that's kind of what I was expecting to find here, but I'm not going to make that assumption without proof. And now that I'm here, I'm pretty sure this was deliberate, however sloppy."

He nodded. "Tonight I wish I hadn't quit smoking."

That brought her face around to eye him. "You used to smoke?"

"Yeah, in college. I quit, obviously, but right now I wish I hadn't."

"I get you." Then she shrugged. "Okay, so we go out to the Castor place, upset his family, going over every square inch inside and out, and hopefully by tomorrow night we've cleared him. I'm going to take one extended look out there, turn it over to the locals, then come back here. I need to go into that gym and start looking for any sign of a detonator. That might be our only clue to the perp. Everything else is off-the-shelf. Your sheriff hasn't found record of a detonator being sold?"

"I'm sure he has. We've got all kinds of uses for them in this state. Checking them out is going to take time, especially when we don't know exactly what we're looking for. But if he finds anything suspicious, you'll be the first to know. Not me."

"Yeah." She rubbed her eyes. "Okay. I need to make a quick sweep through the Castor homestead. Look for things that could have been used to make this bomb."

"You'll find them. Bags of fertilizer. Fuel for tractors. Pieces of pipe for repairs."

She eyed him again. "Just about any ranch around here, right?"

He nodded, hating how tired she suddenly looked.

"Well, we've got to keep our eyes out for any indication that he might have been able to measure quantities carefully. That'll be the important thing. He might have the ingredients, but putting them together takes real care to make a bomb."

Alex agreed. "Unless it's a chemical plant."

He was happy to hear a small laugh escape her. "Yeah," she said. "But this was a reasonably controlled and directed blast. Not an accident. Sorry, Alex."

That surprised him. "I didn't think it was an accident. I just don't think it's one of my students."

She nodded. "And we're about to eliminate one of them. I hope."

Chapter 4

The Castor family proved eager to comply with the search. Younger children were pulled out of bed and dressed to sit in the family van while the deputies and Darcy examined the house, the basement and the barn.

Alex kept the family company, since he had no official purpose here, and tried to be reassuring. He listened to Jane Castor scold her son for poking his nose where it didn't belong, but he had to admit he felt sympathy for Jack.

The young man was extremely curious. Apart from being a nice kid, Alex had always noted his wide-ranging curiosity. He had to admit, however, he'd never dreamed Jack was interested in a career with ATF. But why would he mention it, given that he believed it to be impossible for him.

Alex was less inclined to believe Jack couldn't go

to college. He could start here at the community college, and if he did well enough, a four-year school would snap him up. Unless Jack felt his family's ranch was hanging around his neck like a lead weight, which was entirely possible.

As for Darcy, he found her fascinating. Over ten years with ATF, this was her first lead, and she was out here all alone. Made him wonder if someone was trying to limit her advancement potential. This was an awful lot to ask of anyone.

But maybe she was right. ATF had a limited number of agents, and right now most of them might be busy swarming over really big cases. A minor explosion all the way out here hardly seemed like a big deal... Unless something else happened.

Then there was Darcy herself. She was doing a fine job, but her quickness to criticize herself was something he wasn't used to. On the one hand, he really did believe it was natural for her to assume local authorities had locked down the whole building and taken away nonessential keys. On the other hand, who around here would do that without an obvious reason? And why should she even begin to suspect that matters around here might not always operate by the book?

No need for her to be so hard on herself. The fact that she was self-critical told him a whole lot about her. Exacting. That would apply not only to herself but to the work she did. So maybe her being sent out here solo was a mark of her bosses' belief in her. It was likely they thought she could tie the whole thing up into a bow by herself.

He himself thought she could. He just wished she wasn't so damn attractive. He didn't need that kind of mess again, he didn't trust the peace he'd finally made with himself and he knew how easily he could turn into poison. As for Darcy, she struck him as the type who never mixed business and pleasure. Very much career oriented.

He smiled faintly, then turned to look into the van again, speaking to Jack. "What made you decide you wanted to be in the ATF?"

The young man, who was holding his three-year-old sister on his lap while she slept against his shoulder, answered quietly, "I'm not sure exactly when I truly got interested. I told you about my friend's grandfather. Somehow it just kept growing in me that it sounded like important work. I was maybe ten when I really started thinking about it. It hasn't gone away, not that I'll ever get the chance. So…" He shook his head a little. "It's embarrassing to admit it, but when I heard there was a bombing at the school I got excited. A chance to see it all play out."

Alex nodded. "Don't be embarrassed. I'm sure you weren't the only one who got excited about it. It's not an everyday thing around here. And since nobody was hurt, just an expensive hole in a building…well, I'm sure a lot of people are fascinated."

"And some are probably scared," Jack said forthrightly. "Honestly, nobody can be sure there won't be another one."

Alex leaned in a little. "Maybe not. So people are talking about another one?"

"Everyone is. Most are wondering why anyone would do it in the first place, but if they did it once, why would they stop?"

Alex was fairly certain that was the question Darcy

kept dancing around although she hadn't asked it out-
right. She mentioned the possibility of another bomb
but if she was seriously concerned, she had yet to say
so. "So how do you feel about it, Jack? Think there'll
be another?"

"No." His sister stirred and he lowered his voice
again. "They're hard to make from what I read, unless you have everything you need exactly right. The
guy is probably thrilled he got *one* to work. But nobody's heard anything about someone experimenting
and setting off explosions."

"There's an awful lot of open land out there."

"True. I guess it's possible but nobody seems to
have heard anything."

"You talk to a lot of people?"

For the first time his mother, Jane Castor, spoke.
"He talks to everyone, Mr. Jansen."

"Alex, please."

"Alex. I don't know how much of it you get to see
in the shop classroom, but Jack knows nearly everyone, and he's always asking questions. Not rude questions, but he asks about their jobs, what exactly they
do, what do they think about things. People seem to
like it."

"I'm sure they do." Everyone liked to be asked
about themselves. Well, almost everyone. And nearly
everyone's favorite topic of discussion was themselves.

He paused, then said, "Jack, I'm going to have to
ask you to stay away from all this. Once Agent Eccles
clears you, just stay away."

"But why? Once she knows I didn't do it..."

"Then you might be concealing evidence without even knowing it."

Jack's mouth opened, then snapped closed. "The profile," he said after a few seconds.

"Exactly. She asked you if you'd noticed anyone else hanging around. We noticed you, but we wouldn't have noticed anyone else because—"

"I was a distraction." Jack interrupted with understanding. "Okay, I'll stay away if you can just let me know what's going on."

"Later," Alex said firmly. "We don't discuss ongoing investigations. You know that."

"He's watched enough TV that he ought to," Jane said drily.

"Okay," Jack said. "But I want to help!"

"Do us a favor," Alex said. "Don't get yourself into any more trouble. Someone out there is a bomber. You don't want to come to his attention. Not in any way."

He heard Jane draw a sharp breath, saw Jack's eyes widen. "Okay," the young man said again. "Okay. I'll hunker down."

A half hour later, Darcy came striding up. "The house is clear, Mr. and Mrs. Castor. You can take the children back to bed. Thank you so much for your cooperation. But we'll be poking around the outbuildings for a while. Just ignore us."

Then she looked at Jack. "A few words with you, please."

Jack turned his sister over to his mother and climbed out of the van. The rest of the family drove closer to the house, then began to go inside, three sleepy youngsters complaining a bit.

Alex felt a bit of amusement as Jack squared his shoulders, ready for a dressing-down.

Instead, Darcy smiled. "Nothing obvious to link you to the bomb. The search will continue awhile, but I'm inclined to think you're in the clear."

"Thank you," Jack said soberly.

"Do you understand what happened here?"

"Mr. Jansen explained to me. I not only made myself look guilty, but I might have distracted you from a real suspect."

"That's true. You were fitting a profile too obviously to be ignored. Someone else might not have fitted as well but because of you…" She shrugged. "But I don't need to repeat what I think you've already understood. You seem like a bright young man."

"Not bright enough," Jack said, his voice low.

"Blame it on your age. And your curiosity about what we were doing. Neither is a crime. But, Jack, you need to stay back. Far back. Let us do our jobs. Keep yourself clear of the whole mess. There's really nothing you can do to help and if you manage to draw the wrong person's attention your way, that could turn out very badly. Okay?"

He nodded. "But if I happen to hear something…"

Darcy tilted her head, studying him. "Tell me you're not going to try to play detective now."

Jack just shook his head.

"Good. If you *happen* to hear something of interest, that's fine. Tell me. But don't be asking questions. Not of anyone. Maybe you're not afraid—God knows, few seventeen-year-olds know what fear is—but if you ask questions you might make the bomber very nervous. He might be scared away before we can catch him. Got it?"

Jack's head jerked up. "I didn't think of that."

"Of course not. You've rattled the bars quite enough. Now what I need most from you is for you to lie low and stay away."

"I will," Jackson said seriously. "I didn't mean to mess everything up."

"So as far as I know, you haven't messed up anything except a few people's otherwise quiet night. Let's keep it that way."

Jackson walked away and Alex watched Darcy push her hair back from her face where it had fallen loose. "Tired?" he asked.

"Frustrated more than anything. I think Jack just saw a side of this job he'd have preferred not to. Anyway, I'd kill for some coffee and something to eat. Then it's back to work."

He glanced at his watch and was surprised to see how much time had passed. "It's nearly eleven. How about getting back to work in the morning? You must need sleep like everyone else on the planet."

"Right now I'm too frustrated to sleep." She paused, and then even in the dim light of the stars he could see the rueful expression appear on her face. "It's too early in this case for me to get frustrated."

"Oh, I don't know," he said. "You just took a trip down a pointless rabbit hole because some kid couldn't mind his own business."

She laughed then, and he could see her entire body relax. "I've been down rabbit holes before and probably will again. Nature of the job. Let me drop you off at your place."

"And then?" he asked as they started walking toward his car. "You'll go back to the gym? Or back to the motel and stare at the water stains on the ceiling?"

"How'd you know about those water stains?"

"I stayed there once, when I first moved here. Come on. I can at least make you that coffee. Maybe I'll even reveal some of my deep dark secrets just to distract you."

She stopped and faced him. "Alex? Don't use your secrets to divert me. Everyone has private places, and they shouldn't be shared lightly."

Then she resumed her walk to the truck. After a moment, he followed. She might think of herself as a scientist, but she'd just proven she understood human nature pretty well.

Remarkable woman.

Darcy knew she was growing tired. Very tired. It was silly of her to think she could press through without getting at least some sleep. The urge to get to the root of this bombing was strong; she hated the idea of taking even a few hours off, but she knew the reason the drive was growing in her.

There was going to be another bombing. She couldn't have written it in a report. She had no actual information to substantiate it, but something in her gut... Instinct was speaking. The bomber wasn't done yet.

Her thought that the bomber might be learning as much as she was struck her as highly likely. Yes, his first obvious attempt had worked, but it hadn't worked perfectly. Too much fuel oil had spilled possibly exposing the bomber to danger himself. And maybe the results weren't what he was hoping for in terms of the blast's power.

Worse, she could think of absolutely no good reason why someone would do this only once. Out in an empty field somewhere for a kick? Yeah, one might be enough. But to damage property this way?

No, she didn't think this guy was done.

Every time that crossed her mind, her stomach plummeted. Next time the building might not be empty. Next time someone could get killed or maimed.

So did she want to sleep? No. Did she need to? If she wanted a brain to work with, she was going to need to grab at least six hours.

Damn.

At Alex's house, however, she accepted the offer of coffee. She wasn't by any means ready to unwind yet. She'd told the deputies at the school to let absolutely no one inside before checking with her. And make sure that every external access was being watched so that another Jack couldn't enter through a door.

She believed they'd take extra care now, since none of them had appeared happy that someone had slipped inside.

So she had a building full of evidence, very little of which had told her anything useful. Anything that might take her beyond simply knowing the type of bomb and its size had either been destroyed or still hadn't been found.

But she needed more time to review what they had. Tomorrow. Right now she'd probably skip over something without realizing it.

Alex brewed a fresh pot, saying very little while she sat at the table, her eyes closed as she considered how very little she knew about any of this. Sometimes it all came down to the smallest bits studied under a microscope in the lab. By their nature, bombs didn't leave much behind unless the bomber wanted it or screwed up. A little shrapnel that survived, bits and pieces that might or might not be part of the bomb.

"Fuel oil," she remarked slowly as she opened her eyes in time to see Alex join her with two mugs of coffee. "A lot of it has additives that might identify a source. But out here, probably everyone gets their diesel and gas from a limited number of places."

Alex nodded. "Welcome to small towns. We have two gas stations. When the tanker truck arrives, it fills both. So much for brand identification. I thought it was amusing when I first moved here that the prices at each pump were different. Then we've got the dealer who fills propane tanks for household use and delivers diesel for heavy equipment. Plenty of fuel around, very few sources locally."

"Okay, so that's probably going to tell me nothing except our bomber is either inexperienced or messy." She closed her eyes again. "How'd you wind up here? In this town, I mean."

"I knew someone who came from here. So when I started looking for escape hatches, I applied here. They took a look at my portfolio and decided I'd be an adequate shop teacher."

"So it was always your hobby?"

"I learned it at my father's knee. He was a master carpenter and cabinetmaker."

She smiled faintly. "You learned well."

"Thanks. He had his own business. These days it's

not so easy with all the cheap ready-to-assemble furniture you can buy. So I teach, which I actually enjoy."

She didn't say anything, feeling an unusual twinge of envy for the life he had chosen. Of course, once she started really cracking this case, she'd probably feel a whole lot better about how she'd chosen to spend her life.

But she needed a breakthrough. Anything that would expose the bomber in some way. The first bread crumb that could turn into a trail. So far, she wasn't sure she had a single thing.

On big cases being worked by multiple agents it was much easier to ignore the passage of time. It almost always took time to start unraveling the threads, but, being solo, she was acutely aware it was taking her longer. Of course it was. Didn't mean she had to be happy about it.

"Don't push yourself so hard," Alex said unexpectedly.

"What do you mean? We've got to find this guy so he doesn't do it again."

"I get it, Darcy. BSU, remember? Do you have any idea how many cases I worked on where time was a pressure? Knowing that someone else could die if we didn't pull together useful information for whatever agency we were assisting. But you can push too hard. You can lose your detachment. Your clarity. That helps no one."

"Tell me about it," she said slowly. "The way you worked."

"Well, I didn't spend time in the field the way you do. Imagine a bunch of people in small offices who occasionally get asked to develop a profile when some local

LE agency can't catch anyone. We get their report of all the evidence they have. Sometimes we interview the lead detectives on the case. Then we sit and think and spitball. Not very exciting. Not like TV or the movies. If we're lucky, we might come up with something that's sixty to eighty percent accurate. Then it's up to local enforcement to decide what's useful."

"Sounds dull."

"It could have been except we were trying to walk the corridors of some seriously sick minds. Sometimes. Occasionally they turned out to be garden-variety creeps, but…other times, not so much."

"Like the bicycle killer." As soon as she said it, she realized how tired she must be. He'd already let her know that case had affected him too deeply, that it had driven him from the bureau. "Sorry. I shouldn't have mentioned that."

"Why not? I told you I'd tell you about it."

She shook her head quickly. "I already know that some cases can leave you with nightmares. I don't want to stir up yours."

"They started stirring the minute you arrived. I never thought I'd have anything to do with a Fed again."

At that, she cracked a weary smile. "Sorry about that."

"It's okay. After all this time, I think I've managed to achieve some separation. But that leads me around to you. I couldn't keep my detachment. I not only worked to get inside that bastard's head, but I stayed there even when I wasn't working. No breaks. I couldn't afford them, or so I thought. I needed to know how his twisted mind was functioning before he snatched another little girl."

She had to admit it. "That could mess you up."

"It did. Sitting here listening to you, I'm concerned you might do the same thing. No one's died yet, no one might die, but you're pressuring yourself into thinking that only you can prevent a death. That's not true, Darcy."

Her eyes felt gritty and hot as she looked at her FBI Viking. Oh, yeah, she was tired. "Meaning?"

"Meaning that we're not responsible for what others do. Yeah, it's great when we can stop them, but if we do our best and they still act again before we can find them…it's not our fault. We're mortals, not gods. I had to face that finally. And another little girl died before that profile actually fleshed out enough to be useful."

"Oh, my God," she whispered.

"Yeah. That was it for me. I nailed his profile, over eighty percent accurate, with things the others hadn't even thought of, and you know what? I couldn't find one little bit of solace in that, especially after weeks of living in what I thought was that SOB's head. Don't do that to yourself. Don't feel guilty. Don't feel dirty. You're not the perp and you never will be."

Her mind recognized the justice of what he was saying, and he'd certainly know, but her gut had a rather different take.

Sighing, she closed her eyes again, realizing the coffee wasn't going to help, either. She was dead.

Jack took quite a scolding from his parents. They hadn't been happy about having their home searched because of him, and they sternly warned him away from anything else to do with the bomb.

Jack knew they were right. Standing at his bedroom window, he watched the lights in the barn as the deputies finished looking for any potential bomb-making apparatus. He knew they'd find nothing because he hadn't even thought of making a bomb, let alone building one.

But it seemed to him from his online readings that ATF wasn't taking this matter seriously enough. Only one agent? She seemed like a smart woman, probably an excellent agent, but how was she supposed to do this alone? From everything he'd read, the bureau sent out teams of agents. Usually. Maybe they considered a single small bombing in a small town in the middle of nowhere to be of no real importance unless critical information was discovered.

Of course, there were the local sheriffs to help her, but what did they know about bombs? Probably not a whole lot more than he did.

Frustration filled him, not for the first time in his life. Ranch life didn't exactly hold his interest although it kept him busy. He dreamed of bigger things, and maybe he was a fool.

As his parents kept reminding him, he hadn't even finished high school yet. He was young. He was too young to know what he really wanted. Sure, they'd let him take a few courses at the community college…

They weren't trying to stop him. He was sure of that. They wanted the best for him. But they thought the best was right here, and now he'd gone and proved to them that he could still be a stupid kid.

Darcy was right. He might have concealed evidence

just by being so obvious they didn't notice anyone else who was watching the goings-on. Somebody with a lower profile, maybe hanging around in the distance.

Or not hanging around at all.

That was a possibility, of course. Darn near everybody with even a vague interest had come to look at the hole in the high school. How much would the bomber have needed to have seen? That the bomb had worked and a huge hole had resulted? He didn't need to come back to see that if he wasn't interested in the investigation.

But someone around here had decided to crack open the building and he couldn't see any reason for it. Like he'd told Darcy Eccles, if some student had done it, they wouldn't have been able to keep the secret this long. They'd have blabbed to someone they trusted.

So who did that leave? Someone not a student with a grudge against the school? Because obviously it hadn't been an attempt to kill anyone.

He kept watching the men working around the barn, thinking as hard as if he were taking a math test. Who? And why?

But even as he tried to figure that out, another thought occurred to him. Maybe this had been a test.

Maybe there'd be another, bigger one.

He couldn't just stand aside; he needed to do something useful. Without getting in the way.

So maybe he could listen around and ask a few innocent questions. Nobody would think he was a threat. Just a curious kid.

Now all he had to do was figure out how to manage it without alerting anyone to his doings.

Especially his parents. He figured by tomorrow morning they might be talking about grounding him.

And that would prevent him from doing anything at all to help.

Just then the cell phone in his pocket buzzed. Out here on the ranch it wasn't always reliable, so sometimes he received messages that were hours old.

This one was from his sort of girlfriend, Abby Clark. He thought of her as sort of since they hadn't been able to do much together yet, because of the restrictions of ranch life. He believed she'd meet someone else, someone who wasn't all bound up by chores. He supposed he should consider himself lucky that his parents allowed him the time to work with the athletic department.

Abby had sent a text: What you up to, big man? I hear the cops are all over your place.

Oh, great, Jack thought. Now that would get all over the world and his parents would be even angrier. His dad worked hard to keep a reputation for being a solid, honest and reliable man, sometimes costing his family in the process. How many times had Jack heard the words "A man is only as good as his reputation."

Jack could have argued with that, but he figured pulling out the lessons he'd learned in his logic class wouldn't win him any points with his father.

He debated whether to answer Abby. He didn't have a big investment in a relationship with her, and after this it would probably all blow away. Besides, Abby knew how unreliable his cell service was out here.

He looked from the phone out the window again. It seemed to him that the deputies were finishing up.

They'd be gone in a half hour or so, unless he'd calculated wrong.

Then he looked past the barn into the endless Wyoming night, a night where the mountains hulked like dark sentinels, visible only because they blocked the stars. They'd lost their snowcaps early this year, a bad harbinger. Less water, for one thing. His dad was already fussing about it, wondering if the wells and livestock ponds would be enough. Jack looked at it and saw the coming of climate change. He figured they'd be worrying a whole lot more about water and grazing in a few years.

In his mind, he could see the havoc that was beginning to be wrought by the pine bark beetles. Trees were dying, trees that provided important food for bears. It wasn't bad here yet, but without some really cold, extended winters, the destruction would grow.

He leaned his forehead against the glass, shoving his phone back into his pocket, Abby forgotten.

There were more than enough problems for a young man to be worrying about, but foremost in his mind right now was the bomber.

It seemed too stupid to be believed that someone had gone to all that trouble to put a hole in the side of a building. No, it had been a trial run.

And while Darcy Eccles was busy examining the detritus for a key to the bomber, he could put his ear to the ground. Better than she could, because no one knew her. Better than almost anybody, come to that, because he was just an invisible teen. Most adults hardly paid him any attention.

That was his advantage, one he could put to work for the ATF. To prove he wasn't just a kid with outsize dreams. And it was something he could do without getting into any more trouble, even with his parents.

As long as they didn't ground him. He sighed. For that knowledge he'd have to wait until morning. God, sometimes time moved just way too slow.

Fifteen miles away as the crow flew, a man sat in the back bedroom of his ramshackle farmhouse and soldered, liking the smell of the smoke. He'd always liked the smell of smoke, whether on a battlefield, a firing range or in his own small bedroom. He also liked the *whoompf* of an explosion, so different from gunfire. So much more powerful.

Sometimes when one of the medical helicopters flew over, he fell back in time. The Huey had a very distinctive rotor sound, one he would never forget. It had brought him into fights and carried him out of them. It had brought support when it was needed.

He was rather fond of the damn old birds. Last year he'd ventured out to one of those events where the emergency services opened up to the public, to let taxpayers see what they were paying for when it came to medical evacuations and mountain rescues. Very impressive. Also very tiring for him, sick as he was now.

But he'd been drawn to the Huey. It was roped off, kept in meticulous condition with huge red crosses painted on its sides and tail. Not that those had done much good in the war.

The door guns were gone, and even from behind the rope he could see the gleaming medical equipment, the Stokes basket, the winch. Ready for anything.

Then Billy Joe Yuma had wandered over. Both were vets, though they weren't well acquainted. Yuma had flown medevacs during the Vietnam War. The man figured he probably had as many nightmares as the ground troops.

Yuma had noted him, then asked if he wanted to get closer. Next thing he knew, he was past the cordon and sitting in the wide-open side hatch of the chopper. Where the door gunner would have sat, hanging his legs out and maybe bracing against the skids.

"I can wind her up for you, if you want," Yuma had offered. "Not too fast, though. We can't fly right now."

The man had nodded. "You hear those rotors in your dreams, too?"

"Yeah." Simple answer. A look of understanding.

"Thanks for the offer, but I hear you when you fly over sometimes." He'd slid to the ground and had begun to walk away.

"I didn't catch your name," Yuma had called. "Hicks?"

The man hadn't answered. He didn't give a damn anymore whether anyone knew his name.

Later, no one would forget it, but for right now he was the invisible man. They'd made him invisible, and he had every intention of taking advantage of that.

Shaking his head a little, he bent again to his soldering. The Army had taught him a lot, and he remembered most of it. For example, he knew how to build a low-residue detonator.

That woman from the ATF could look until her eyes went blind, but she wasn't going to find enough to tell her anything. All she'd ever know was that the trigger had been homemade, probably with a timer or a microwave signal to set it off. That wouldn't tell her a whole lot.

It bothered him that he hadn't got the fire he'd expected. He'd poured enough gas around that place that there should have been a great fire.

He wanted a fire. Bombs were destructive, but fire consumed a whole lot more over a larger area. It also consumed evidence.

Not that he was going to care for long. All he needed to do was complete his mission, strike his objectives. Then if they caught him...well, he was already a dead man walking.

Thanks to the good old US of A and its army.

Chapter 5

Darcy fell asleep right at Alex's kitchen table. By that, he judged she'd been shorting her sleep since her arrival.

Shaking his head a little, wondering what drove this woman so hard, he rose. He couldn't let her drive back to the motel if she could fall asleep sitting upright. She could have his couch. It would make a comfortable bed.

He tried to wake her, but she simply sighed and leaned into his hip, a nice sensation he tried to ignore. Okay, she was well past exhausted. Giving in to what he knew could be a dangerous move, he scooped her up off the wooden chair, one arm beneath her knees, the other around her shoulders.

Well, that got her attention. Sort of, he corrected with amusement.

Her eyelids fluttered. "Wha…?"

"Shh. I'm just putting you on the couch. You're too sleepy."

He half expected fire to light her green eyes, full consciousness to return and a fight to begin.

But it didn't. Instead she let her eyes close again and sighed softly. By the time he placed her carefully on the couch, she was sound asleep once more. He grabbed the throw that hung over the back of the couch and spread it over her.

She was done. Cooked.

Amusement followed him back to the kitchen. Past midnight. He ought to be turning in, himself. Instead he dumped out the coffee and got himself a glass of ice water.

Darcy Eccles was something else. He really didn't know a damn thing about her except that she was driven. He'd like to know what was behind that. He knew what had once driven him, propelling him into the BSU, into an unending nightmare that would never depart; he even understood what was driving him now. But Darcy? He couldn't begin to guess. Surely, it had to be more than simply doing a good job.

Hell, he understood what Jack was up to better than he understood Darcy, and he'd been working fairly closely with her since her arrival. She seemed glad to have another Fed around, glad to hear what he had to say as a result of his experience with aberrant psychology. Not that he'd given her a whole lot.

Mainly because he didn't like to jump the gun, but if he were to be perfectly honest, right now he'd say that bombing didn't look like a one-and-only. Other than getting some attention, it had accomplished nothing beyond a disruption of shop classes for the rest of the year and the burned-up dreams of some students.

He had the feeling whoever had set that bomb hadn't even thought of the students, except to make sure none of them got hurt. He supposed he ought to be very grateful for that.

Well, if he couldn't figure out yet what was driving Darcy, he supposed he could apply his much-vaunted knowledge of psychology to the perp. After all, he was apparently more comfortable with sick minds than healthy ones.

Hell, that was some commentary on the man he'd become, he thought with a distinct lack of amusement. He'd gained understanding of teens over the last few years, but nothing like he'd gleaned from serial killers and rapists.

What he understood about himself, however, was that he'd fled. He wasn't proud of it. But once the nightmares and rage had become an almost-permanent part of his personality, he was good to no one, not even his colleagues.

He'd shattered his detachment and distance because he got a real taste for catching the bicycle killer. He'd broken the rules.

It wasn't as if the agents of the BSU felt nothing for the victims. They were human. You couldn't hold up a photo of a tiny torn, bloody pair of underpants without feeling something. Rage, yeah. Fury, of course. But then you had to let go of it and focus in on what those tears meant with every other piece of evidence. You couldn't hang on to it.

With the bicycle killer it had been different for him. He hadn't been able to back out once he started to enter the sadistic mind of the killer. That time, not all the practice in the world, all the years of carefully developed walls, had saved him. He'd gone where he wasn't supposed to go.

He'd been consumed then subsumed. No more clinical statements about the killer, what he might be thinking, what he was revealing through his actions. There'd been nothing clinical left in him.

That he'd been largely responsible for taking the guy down was small solace. He'd lost his wife; his own daughter looked at him with fear, and he'd become a man alone with part of himself forever entangled with a sick mind. The years here hadn't quite erased the stains.

Now he needed to put those skills to work again. Darcy hadn't exactly asked, except once when she'd wanted to pick his brain, but he could tell she needed him. She was a technical specialist. His specialty was very different.

Right now every finely honed instinct from his old job was telling him that this bomber had just begun.

He cussed under his breath and paced the kitchen. Darcy might have lost the battle against fatigue, but he doubted he would get any sleep himself tonight. His mind had latched onto a problem, and it wasn't about to let go.

His initial response to the bombing probably hadn't been far different from Darcy's. A student pulling some kind of prank that had probably gone awry.

He knew kids, and they were capable of amazing stupidity if only because they were incapable of considering consequences. Larks gone awry were common.

But he knew the kids in his shop classes well

enough to be fairly sure none of them would have thought of doing any such thing, certainly nothing that would have damaged their achievements over the past years. So at first he thought maybe the explosion had been bigger than anticipated. Maybe some kid had bound together too many heavy-duty fireworks...

Nah. Those hopes hadn't lasted long, not when he really looked at the damage. Then Charity Camden, the arson investigator, had discovered chemical signs of ANFO.

At that point he had known it was no gag gone wrong, and he'd become certain it had not been one of his students, easy as it would have been to point out that the shop appeared to be the target.

But he'd been looking and thinking since the first shock, and certainties were beginning to settle in him. No accident. A lot of preparation and study. Not necessarily directed at the shop rooms. ANFO bombs didn't just happen. They had to be carefully and deliberately executed. No one would do that without a purpose.

He retrieved a few more ice cubes and refilled his glass with water.

Darcy's attention to the corner of the building the bomber had chosen also interested him. Poor view from the street was probably the least of it.

No, external, reinforced cinder block walls. A type of construction found in many places. No windows on that end of the building, just some exhaust vents to keep down the sawdust.

Sawdust. He straightened a little, thinking about those flammable properties. The exhaust fans worked constantly to keep the dust down so an errant spark didn't cause a conflagration. It was an extremely well-ventilated area even without doors and windows. What if the bomber hadn't known that? What if he'd expected the sawdust to ignite?

It would have been a disappointment. Not only did his students use shop vacs throughout the day, but those exhaust fans never quit. It was almost clean enough to perform surgery in there.

Well, okay, not quite. But safety was paramount.

Maybe the choice had nothing to do with the shop, simply with the construction as Darcy had remarked at some point, which he was getting too tired to recall.

Maybe the perp had a different target in mind and this was indeed a test run. He knew the thought had been running around in Darcy's mind—and his as well—because building that kind of a bomb didn't seem like something anyone would do just once, unless they'd made a mistake.

This didn't smell like a mistake.

He leaned back against the counter once more, closing his eyes to think.

A purpose?

Another bomb?

Not enough yet to give him a line on anything, but enough to make him uneasy.

He strode down the hall and turned on his computer to look up bombers. He wanted to know something about the profile, about how often they struck again. He wanted some facts on which to base the suppositions he felt he was going to build, want to or not.

He was back in the game.

Damn it.

* * *

Darcy woke in the morning to gray light streaming through a window. It took her nearly a minute to realize where she was. Sometime during the night she had been put on a couch and covered with an afghan.

She sat up quickly, a little confused but mostly embarrassed. It must have been Alex, and to think she'd fallen asleep in the middle of their conversation...

She remembered being at his kitchen table with coffee. She had the vaguest memory of being carried. Oh, my God, had he carried her to the couch? Had she done that to him?

Sheesh, she owed him a huge apology. How rude.

But she smelled toast and coffee and possibly bacon, so she tried to organize her hair into its usual neat bun, then gave up before dropping the blanket and standing.

She felt icky, but from the aromas she guessed she wasn't going to be heading back to the motel immediately for a shower and change.

Alex must have heard her footsteps. "Darcy? Bathroom's down the hall, first door on the left."

"Thanks," she managed, surprised at how much her own voice croaked. Gads, she hoped she hadn't been sleeping with her mouth open and snoring. Or at least she hoped he'd gone to bed before he learned any such thing about her.

The bathroom was a full bath, which she hadn't expected. Fresh towels hung from a rack. Inviting, but she'd have to climb back in her dirty clothes.

A look in the mirror told her that death probably had an edge on her this morning. Alex had been right. She'd been pushing too hard. Her watch said she must have slept about six hours, but she didn't feel like it. She suspected that if she let her eyes close, she'd drift off standing here at the sink.

She forced herself to clean around the edges, freshening her face, finger combing her hair so she looked a little less like Raggedy Ann. Then there was nothing more she could do. It wasn't as if she carried lipstick in her overalls, and she'd need more than that to conceal the circles under her eyes.

Almost reluctantly she went to the kitchen, where she found Alex looking reasonably fresh and busy cooking breakfast. "I hope you're not a vegetarian," he said, "because I'm making bacon and eggs."

"You know I'm not," she reminded him. She'd eaten a steak sandwich with him on the day of her arrival.

He flashed a grin. "Just making pointless conversation. There's a fresh mug by the coffeepot. Help yourself."

She was grateful that he didn't try to wait on her. He must have been the one who had got her to the couch and covered her last night, and that realization made her feel a touch fragile, this morning. Nobody had ever done that for her, at least not since early childhood, and it felt like a weakness.

"How much rye toast?" he asked.

"Two slices," she answered as she carried her mug to the table. "Can I help?"

"Probably not," he said lightly. "I'm used to doing this by myself. I'd need retraining to share my kitchen again."

"Thanks for the couch," she offered, feeling almost tentative.

"Hey, nobody else was using it." He looked over

his shoulder and smiled. "Next time I tell you you need some sleep, maybe you should listen." Then he winked and returned his attention to the frying pan.

Despite the oddity of the situation for her, she laughed. He had a morning sense of humor. Kudos to him. She wasn't sure she did and hadn't spent much time trying to find out. She almost never talked to anyone before her second cup of coffee.

There was probably a good reason for that, she realized as the words popped out of her. "You should let your hair grow out."

That stopped him midmovement and he turned. "Answer quick. That bacon needs to come out of the pan. Why?"

She flushed. "You'd look even more like a Viking," she admitted.

At least he laughed, apparently taking it as a joke, thank God. He went back to cooking and she downed the first cup of coffee as fast as she could without burning her mouth, then grabbed another.

The stack of bacon was growing. An open carton of eggs sat near the stove. A loaf of bread was ready beside the toaster and two slices popped up as she watched. She really felt as if she ought to help, but at that moment didn't trust herself.

How had those words popped out of her? Dang, she was probably still too tired. What if she screwed up today because she'd been shorting her sleep?

What if she'd already screwed up? Horrifying thought. She stared down into her mug, her hands growing tight around it, and hoped that she hadn't already made a mistake too big to be corrected.

"I was up a little late last night, too," Alex remarked

as he dropped more bread into the toaster and brought plates with scrambled eggs and bacon for each of them to the table, plus two slices of buttered toast for her. "Dig in. My timing's off. No point letting the eggs get cold while I wait for my toast."

She was happy to pick up a fork. There was cheese in the scrambled eggs. Yummy. "Why were you up late?"

"Thinking. I may as well be honest. Since you arrived I've been fighting old instincts. I swore I'd never again get into a sick mind. So I've been avoiding doing what I'm most qualified to do. That's not right."

Her chest tightened for him. Already she cared this much? "You don't have to do that."

"But I do. You're the tech expert. I'm the mind expert. And last night I could no longer pretend to myself that I don't think this is a test run."

Her heart stilled. "I'd love you to tell me you've changed your mind."

He pulled out the toast and began buttering it. "Sorry, can't do that. I ran myself around the Maypole last night and kept reaching the same conclusion."

Her stomach began to sink. Eating became difficult, but she forced herself to continue. She'd already cheated sleep enough. If she stopped eating she'd become a royal mess. "So you're expecting another one?"

"Afraid so. Although at this point I couldn't begin to tell you when and where. Not enough information. Assuming the bomber didn't get the results he wanted, we might have some time while he fiddles with his recipe."

She swallowed more coffee, trying to wake her brain up the rest of the way. This was important; she needed her wits about her. All of them. When a guy with Alex's training and experience voiced an opinion, it would be irresponsible to ignore it.

She waited while he ate a bit before asking the paramount question while ignoring her own concern about the excessive fuel spill. That wasn't irrelevant, but she needed to hear his reasoning. "Why would you think he didn't get the results he wanted? It was a fairly good blast."

"Right." He reached for his toast. "But you saw the inside. Unless this guy is hell-bent on blowing down walls, he accomplished remarkably little. Some fire inside. Almost none outside. His blast didn't escape the shop rooms and get into the rest of the building. In short, it was a stab, not a bullet."

She froze, forgetting everything—her plate, the man across from her—everything except the blast site.

It arose vividly in her mind, and she felt the truth of what he was saying in a place she usually ignored when it came to her work: her gut. She always tried to rely on evidence and scientific knowledge. Heck, that was a large part of her job. Estimating whether a bomber would strike again was not. Yet she felt the truth of what Alex was saying. Had even suspected it, though she'd pushed it away to deal with what she already had on her hands.

Heck, she could remember speaking those words herself her first day: *Maybe this was a test.* A trial run. Mistakes had been made. She'd even thought that the bomber was probably learning as much from this blast as she was. Maybe more.

The suggestion had been there all along. Hearing it

confirmed by a man with Alex's background brought it into the harsh light and made it impossible to ignore.

"You mentioned it yourself early on," he remarked, almost as if he were reading her mind.

She had indeed. She clearly remembered the moment when the idea had struck her. And how quickly she had dismissed it. There had to be more proof.

Which was pretty much what he was saying. Without further evidence, he couldn't assess and predict. Neither could she.

Yet something about the entire bombing was wrong. Something had grated on her at the outset, and apparently it hadn't stopped grating on him.

"I'm afraid you're right," she said finally. She looked at him, into eyes the blue color of the North Sea on a sunny day, and felt some spark of understanding leap between them. At least she thought it was understanding. "I need to get back to work. We need clues, and so far all I've got is a lot of detritus that isn't adding up to much except that somebody made an ANFO bomb. Nothing to trace it back to anyone. No answers to any questions, except that I would almost be willing to testify under oath that he made a big mistake with the fuel oil spill. It didn't go off the way he thought it would. Which means—"

"*May* mean," he corrected carefully.

She nodded. No time for imprecision. "May mean. May mean he's not satisfied, and if for no other reason he'll try again."

He nodded. "Now, eat. Damn it, Darcy, you need to be at the top of your game, and you don't need me to tell you that. You've got a plate full of protein. Brain food. Swallow it."

She complied, although what had tasted so good when she started now tasted like dust. Her body was shifting into high gear, her mind beginning to race with ideas about what she needed to look into.

"What's your propellant?"

The question startled her and she raised her gaze from her plate. "What?"

"What drives you? Because you're pushing way too hard. The fact that you're alone out here? Or do you always operate in hyperdrive?"

Maybe she had a morning sense of humor after all because she felt a smile twitch the corners of her mouth. "Hyperdrive, huh?"

"Sure looks like it. You've been pushing past your physical limitations. Not your mental ones, I'm sure, but you're wearing yourself out awfully fast."

"Mainly because my mind won't stop working," she admitted. "I want this solved, yes, but I'm not alone out here. The fire department, the sheriff's department... I've got lots of help."

He nodded and used a serving fork to put two more slices of bacon on her plate. "If you don't want them now, we'll make you a bacon sandwich for mid-morning."

"Who made you my mother?" she asked, half-jokingly.

"Me." He smiled and for an instant, just an instant, she felt as if there were no air left in the room. Wow.

"I need to go back to my room to clean up and change."

"Okay. I'll make that sandwich. See you out at the school."

She rose and left and wondered why she felt as if

she were fleeing. And if so, from what? An attraction to the man?

It hardly mattered. This would get wrapped up one way or the other and she'd be gone.

Boy, she'd taken off as if someone had lit a fire under her tail. With a private smile, Alex set about cleaning up from breakfast and making her the bacon sandwich he'd promised. Two, he decided, because he'd watched her work through lunch more than once.

He knew she'd been considering the possibility that the bomb was a trial run, but had put the thought aside without evidence to confirm it. All very proper.

And maybe he'd been wrong to share his suspicions with her. After all, he had nothing to go on, not really, except that when he thought about it he couldn't begin to imagine what the bomber had hoped to achieve.

That was all he needed to get his own mind into overdrive. He was used to considering cases from this angle, from little hints and clues. He didn't know how it worked for her, but he knew how he operated, and his mind wouldn't let him overlook what might appear irrelevant to others. He'd too often seen those seeming irrelevancies turn into something important.

Ah, hell.

He cleaned himself up for another day of poking into places he really didn't need to go, places where he might not be especially welcome for all he knew. He had no credentials, no authority. He'd chosen to be a small-town shop teacher. He supposed he ought to be honored that Darcy hadn't simply told him to butt out.

She'd have had every right to. In fact, the first day, when she learned what he used to do, he could almost have sworn that she'd have loved to tell him to get out of her way.

But she hadn't. Whatever instinctive reaction she'd felt had been swiftly overcome and she'd made him a sort of sidekick. Even so, given his past, he should have known better than to stir his own emotional pot.

Now he was in it up to his eyeballs—he'd ventured an "authoritative" statement he knew she wouldn't ignore, and he couldn't back out now.

Although he wasn't a quitter by nature. The only reason things had turned so bad in his personal life was because he didn't know how to quit. Well, this was different, he assured himself. No little girls. No torture, no rape. Just a serial bomber who so far hadn't hurt a human being.

He ought to be able to deal with that and help. Why else had he stuck his neck out?

He'd started with an urge to protect his students from needless suspicion, but it had grown past that. Suspecting that this bomber would strike again made it about much more than protecting his students from the relentless eye of a federal agent.

Because sooner or later, a life would be struck by this madman. He wasn't just about blowing up walls. Alex knew that with sickening certainty in his gut.

It was drizzling—a light rain. Cops in yellow slickers stood around the building with an eye for anyone who approached. Darcy stood at the edge of the cordon, staring straight into the maw the bomb had opened in the building.

Carrying two coffees, Alex joined her. She hardly

looked at him, but she already had a tall coffee in her hand.

"You ready for a hot and fresh latte?"

She turned and looked at him almost blankly. Then she looked at the cup in her hand. "How long?"

"How long what?"

She tipped her cup to her mouth, then grimaced. "Cold. Thanks for the fresh." She pulled the lid off the cup she held, dumping mere dregs on the ground before accepting a fresh cup from him. "I was just wondering how long I've been standing here."

"I couldn't tell you that. I thought I'd be right behind you but if your coffee's cold…"

She nodded, her gaze returning to the hole in the school building. "I texted my bosses."

"And?"

"I shared my suspicion—*our* suspicion—that this was a test run."

"Okay." He waited while she sipped coffee. Her slicker gleamed. She must have been standing here awhile, given the drizzle wasn't that heavy.

"They're checking the samples I sent them, the fuel oil soaked into the ground was standard diesel fuel, and if I get any *proof* that this guy will move again, let them know. They're swamped, Alex. It's been a great couple of months for militia problems, gunrunning and bombers, I guess. Some terrorist activity. I was working on that, you know."

"So this is a step down."

Her gaze trailed back to him again. "No. I may have thought so at first, but I'm not buying it now. You don't have to be a terrorist, or even a terrorist ring, to be dangerous."

"No." He sipped his own coffee, then remarked, "If you ask me, anyone who sets off bombs qualifies as a terrorist."

"Maybe. I guess folks around here are worried."

"You know it. How could they not be? Bombs don't exactly happen every day, and parents are especially worried that the school was a target."

"I would be, too."

He joined her in her study of the blast site. "What are you seeing?"

"That nothing is right."

That statement intrigued him more than anything she could have said about it. The profiler in him came to attention. "How so?"

"There are easier ways to make a hole in a wall. Unfortunately those ways are easier to trace. Have you ever tried to buy a stick of dynamite?"

"Not lately," he answered drily, grateful he had the coffee to drink. It was getting cold out here.

"Exactly. Which brings me around to the choice of ANFO. Lots of bang for the buck, as they say, but so fussy to make. Anyway, detonators, dynamite, blasting caps…everything you buy gets recorded. You're limited in what you can buy and how much without a special permit, unless you have a hookup on the black market, and a lot of that is traceable back to military sources. But ANFO is virtually untraceable. Possible to make with items you'd find on almost any farm in the country."

He was sure they'd covered this. Where was she going? He sipped more coffee and kept silent, waiting, certain she must be working through something. After all, he'd run around the same Maypole dozens of times last night.

"I'm looking at that hole and thinking nothing went right for this guy. Yeah, he got his explosion but he really didn't get much else. Like you said, unless all he wants to do is blow down walls, it's a failure."

She raised her cup to her lips, drank deeply and continued to stare at the hole in the wall. As if it were speaking to her.

Maybe it *was* speaking, he thought as he stared at it, too. After all, it had his mind running down an avenue that said there would be more.

"A learning experience," he remarked.

"So I fear. And I keep thinking about his choice of target. The school is isolated enough to make it easy to set up his bomb. Easier than in town. But the structure…"

She faced him. "I'm getting out of my bailiwick here, but I think he wanted to know what the impact would be on exactly that kind of wall. Problem is, millions of buildings have the same kind of construction. Probably dozens or more even around here. Cheap modern construction basically. Sturdy, durable, but cheaper than wood framing and drywall."

"You're right. I know something about that."

"I thought you might."

"It's not just materials, it's labor. It's maintenance later. You don't usually have to patch cinder block walls because someone bumped into them, for example. That's the reason you see it in so many institutional buildings."

"So…" She drew the word out. "Is he after an institutional building?"

The question went a few steps too far, and she knew

it. He could tell it by the way she sighed, sipped her coffee and resumed.

"Anyway, Alex, I don't like what I'm seeing. I've seen all kinds of bombings. I've even seen some accidental ones. This is no accident and everything about it says it was a trial run."

Then she started walking. "Come on. Let's go to the gym and give what we've got another look over."

He followed willingly enough, although he was sure he wouldn't be able to tell much himself from the detritus. But you never knew, he reminded himself.

Another glance at the hole in the wall, before they rounded the corner, gave him a sudden chill.

No, this wasn't over. By no means.

Chapter 6

Jack wasn't grounded, thank goodness. His folks weren't feeling quite so angry this morning, and then they'd decided that nailing him to the ranch might look like he was in real trouble—an appearance they didn't want making the rounds, not after last night.

So with no school, he was free to drive the old Chevy that he kept running with his auto-shop skills into town and wander around.

Briefly, he ran into some of his friends, who wanted to hear all about what had happened last night.

For the first time he wondered how that news had got out. He doubted the agent or the deputies would have gossiped about it, but last night his sort of girlfriend had even texted him about it while the search was still ongoing.

Clearly someone had blabbed, and he wasn't exactly happy to find that a lot of suspicion was being directed his way. Most of his friends just thought it was cool, but he couldn't miss the way some of the adults were looking at him.

Oh, man, his parents were going to be upset if this continued. He had to find out something about the bomber. Anything to direct the suspicion away from him.

Taking a risk, he drove out to the school. The deputy out front, Sarah Ironheart, stopped him. "You know you can't go in there, Jack."

"You must be cold," he remarked. He hated slickers. Sooner or later they made him just as wet inside as they got on the outside. "I know I can't go in, but I need to talk to Agent Eccles."

"Why?"

He liked Sarah a whole lot, so he just told the truth. "Because the whole town thinks I'm the bomber. Because the ranch was searched. Deputy, somebody talked."

Sarah's cool expression turned into a frown. "That shouldn't happen. But what can Agent Eccles do about it?"

"Maybe not her. Maybe you. *Somebody* needs to clear me publicly or my folks are going to ground me until I die."

That brought a smile to Sarah's face. She had kids of her own. "Hang on, kiddo. I'll see if I can talk to her, but she's really busy right now. We may have to turn to Sheriff Dalton."

"He'd be good, too," Jack agreed.

So he waited. Sarah didn't leave him hanging

around alone, though. Nope. Deputy Conroe replaced her as guard.

Damn. Who would have thought so much trouble could come from a bit of curiosity?

Darcy was sitting back on her heels with a length of wire in her hand, maybe four inches long. One end had a small blob. "Alex?"

He made his way to her side, walking carefully between the gridded squares that had been laid out to match the outdoor locations where everything had been found.

"Yeah?" He squatted next to her.

"I found one of these the other day about forty feet from the blast. Now another one. At first I thought the end of the wire had been melted by the blast, especially since it burned a hole in the grass it passed through."

He nodded. "I seem to remember."

She passed him the wire. "You work with this stuff. Has this been soldered or just melted by heat?"

He pulled on a pair of latex gloves, like hers, and held the wire up, then surprised her by pulling a pair of wire-rimmed glasses from his breast pocket.

"I didn't know you needed those."

"Usually no. Nonprescription reading glasses. Magnifiers. For small things like this."

He turned the wire, studying it carefully. "Soldered," he said finally, then pointed to the melted end. "See the discoloration of the metal right next to the bulb? Only one end of this wire was heated, most likely by soldering."

"Bingo," she said and gave him a smile. "We have struck gold."

He passed the wire to her and watched her seal it in a sample bottle. "How so?"

"Someone made their own timer. No other reason to solder a damn thing, unless it was blown out of your shop."

He shook his head. "We don't do a lot of soldering in there. We're working with wood, which means a whole lot of flammable dust. Anyway, any soldering we do happens in the other shop. Plus, I'm a real devil about everything being spotlessly clean."

"Good habit to have," she said almost absently, turning the bottle in her hand and peering at it. "Well, since the whole wire didn't get heated, my guess is the detonator was some distance from the bomb itself. I can confirm that by finding more wires. Or... He might have had some det cord."

"Explain," he said. What he knew about this stuff would fit in a thimble.

"Det cord, short for detonating cord, is a plastic-wrapped, high-explosive cord that can be used as an explosive itself or used to send a detonating wave along its length to set off a bomb at a distance. Highly flexible, and it can detonate multiple explosions. But that wouldn't be any easier to get than a blasting cap. Damn." She shoved the evidence bottle into one of her pockets.

"Unless he had some lying around for some reason," Alex said.

Her head turned sharply toward him. "What are you thinking?"

"You'd be surprised what someone can bring

home in a backpack from a military exercise. Det cord would be easy to conceal from the way you describe it."

"Yeah, it would. It also has a good shelf life, in some cases up to ten years. But let's not limit our suspects to a certain group. Not yet. Too many unanswered questions."

He agreed with her. It was just that the thought had arisen and he'd naturally shared it. Ignoring any sense of what might be meaningful could hamper investigations. Especially this kind.

"I also need to find what kind of container he used for his device. ANFO doesn't explode well at all in the open air. It needs to be contained in something. A pipe, a metal box, a barrel, depending on how much ANFO you're using. We've got some pieces of PVC pipe—splinters, really—but I guess you had water pipes in your shop."

"Yeah, we had sinks. Overhead piping." He paused. "Darcy?"

"Yeah?"

"The ceiling was fairly undamaged in the shop. That pipe could easily have come from outside. We need to check the damage to the sink area."

"Yeah." But she didn't immediately move. He felt as if she were taking a mental picture of the debris before her. He wondered if she could actually do that, or if she was scanning for anything that stuck out.

Just as she straightened to her feet, Sarah Ironheart's voice reached them. "Darcy. You wanna give Jack Castor a minute? Unexpected complication."

Darcy appeared taken aback by the request, a reaction that didn't surprise Alex. She was here to do a job, not maintain relationships or solve other problems.

But without hesitation, she wiped her hands on her overalls and began to pick her way toward the door where Sarah waited. Alex followed because he was useless when it came to the shattered remains scattered on the floor. Might as well see if he could be useful in some other way.

"What's up?" Darcy asked Sarah as she reached her.

"Seems news about the search has made the rounds. Jack wants some help if you can provide it."

Darcy blinked, seeming to drag herself back into the present. "Me?"

"For starters. I'm not exactly full of ideas myself, but at least hear him out. He did get a bad deal."

"What deal?" Darcy asked as she pushed through the door. Alex already had a pretty good idea what might be going on.

Jack stood waiting on a spring day that felt more like approaching winter, a ball cap protecting his head from the ceaseless drizzle. "Thanks for seeing me," he said.

"What's up?"

"The town thinks I'm involved with the bombing. Somehow word has got around that our ranch was searched last night."

Darcy frowned. "That shouldn't have happened. Nobody's supposed to talk, and it wasn't even official. No paper trail, no warrant."

Jack nodded. "That's what I thought, but word got out pretty fast. At first I didn't make the connection, but my girlfriend texted me last night and she already knew about it. My folks are going to hit the roof." He looked down. "All because I got curious. This isn't fair to them."

"No it's not," Darcy agreed. She looked at Alex, then at Sarah. Alex shrugged. He had no idea how to stop a rumor. In his experience, very little could.

"I wonder who blabbed," Sarah murmured. "I suppose I could tell Gage, the sheriff, and he could have us pass the word somehow. How maybe we were looking for something that had nothing to do with your or your…"

Darcy's head snapped up. "I have an idea. You wanted to help, Jack?"

He nodded.

"Guess who might get annoyed if you're getting credit for his bomb. Guess who might actually let something slip."

Jack looked at her, wide-eyed. "You think he'd talk to me?"

"I think he might talk to someone. Just go about your ordinary life. I'm sure Sarah will confirm the cops have every ear to the ground."

"We sure do."

"Darcy." Alex had to object. "This could put Jack in danger."

She shook her head. "If anyone asks him about this bomb he's going to deny he had anything to do with it. He's not the one the bomber would want to convince."

Alex was having a problem with this. "If Jack's not the one he's going to want to convince, then what? How can this possibly be useful? We ought to clear him publicly and save his family from all the grief."

Darcy chewed her lip and he could almost see the

wheels spinning in her head. "Okay," she said. "You're the psychologist, not me. But suppose Jack goes out there and denies the bombing himself without any heavy-duty backup. What are people going to do?"

He didn't think she was being perfectly clear, but he was getting a sense of what she was trying to drive at. Something. Useful. How?

He stared off into the distance, muttering a mantra he'd used often in his work. "No man is an island." It was true. Somehow, some way, someone always knew *something*. The idea was to kick it out of obscurity and put their attention on it.

"Let me think about this. Jack, we'll call your parents and settle them down, but this idea of Agent Eccles's... I'm not sure it would do any good."

"I just want to help," Jack said again. "If I have to look guilty for a while, that's fine as long as my dad isn't going to ground me and give me all the worst chores to do my every waking moment."

Serious as all this was, Alex couldn't smother a grin. "I'll make sure they understand you're being helpful and we need you."

"Okay, then." Jack looked from him to Darcy then to Sarah. "I did want to help," he repeated, but not with as much confidence.

"You'll be safe," Darcy said. "He's not going to have anything to do with you if you just keep denying any involvement. But his ego may force him to brag to someone he trusts. Once you start doing that..."

This was clearly something Jack understood. "Yeah. If more than one person knows, everyone is going to know eventually. I get it. Look at the mess I'm in. Someone gabbed."

Sarah spoke. "We're going to find out who, I promise."

Jack shrugged. "Could have been a neighbor, I guess. You guys sure came out to the ranch with enough vehicles to make someone wonder what was going on. Right after the bomb…" The young man shrugged. "Small leap, I guess."

Darcy smiled at him. "You hang in there, Jack. Don't ever let yourself believe you can't follow your dreams. I mean it."

Sarah walked Jack back to his battered Chevy that was more covered in rust preventer than paint.

Darcy looked at Alex. "Who's calling his parents?"

"I will. They know me." He faced her, making sure no one could hear. "I hope you're right."

"You're the psychologist. Would the bomber have *any* reason to speak to Jack?"

Alex blew a long breath between his lips. "In theory, no. But what if he gets the mistaken idea Jack is taking credit?"

"God," she said.

Her next words slammed him hard. They hurt.

"You live in an ugly world, Alex. Why on earth would anyone think Jack would *want* credit for this?"

His back stiffened. He waited a minute to take charge of his roiling, angry emotions before he spoke again. "I know aberrant psychology, Darcy. What in God's name makes you believe this bomber might think like a sane person?"

Then he turned and strode to his car. Enough. Absolutely enough. He had plenty to deal with, including Jack's family and his own resurging nightmares. He didn't need to deal with that woman's judgment.

And now he had to worry about Jack. He should have put his foot down. Immediately.

But Jack wouldn't have listened. That boy wanted to help. He'd got into a whole peck of trouble because he wanted to help, and now he'd get into more. He'd choose to fulfill his dream of being an ATF agent if only for a week or two as a shill.

Damn, Darcy. Didn't she *understand?*

He didn't get all the way into town before he pulled over and leaned back, seeking more internal calm, seeking the steel behind which he had once shielded himself. The effort didn't much help. He couldn't risk letting Jack become another victim.

Then he slammed the car into gear again and headed for the sheriff's office. If there was one man in this town that Alex had come to fully respect in his few years here, it was Gage Dalton. Another former Fed. A guy who'd dealt with the ugly side, too.

Darcy stared after Alex's departing back, able to read his disgust in every step. Maybe he was right. Maybe she was exposing Jack. But somehow she couldn't believe the bomber would approach him in any way, not if Jack persistently denied he'd had any part in the bombing. No reason for the bad guy to show any interest in him. If he talked, it'd be to a buddy, not a falsely accused kid who claimed no responsibility.

Alex must be going over the edge. His nightmares must be returning. She felt badly for him, but what could she do about it? Her first duty was her job.

Still feeling uneasy, she turned to go back inside, deciding to take a look at the shop room for damaged

PVC, then walk through the debris again. Somewhere there had to be evidence of the container, of the detonator. Maybe not a lot but some. Enough to start piecing together a solid picture of the device.

Often enough, finding out those details would lead to a suspect or two. It was as Locard's exchange principle said, "The perpetrator will always leave something at a crime scene, and will always take something from it." That held true for bombers, too. The problem for the investigator was to find those things and make links.

She needed to start putting the pieces together. And she needed to stop thinking so much about Alex.

Alex stopped at the diner to pick up some strong coffee for himself and Gage. He knew the reputation of the coffee at the sheriff's office: awful. It was usually made by the lead dispatcher, Velma, a woman as old as the hills, who ignored the no-smoking laws as if they were meant for others. She also made famously bad coffee, which deputies drank only to avoid offending her. No one wanted to get on Velma's bad side, he gathered. He also gathered that no one could figure out how she made such lousy coffee. The department had been suggesting a commercial drip coffee maker for years, but according to Gage, Velma always objected.

It was one of those stories he loved about this place. Maude, who ran the diner, was a dragon; and the police dispatcher, who loved all her deputies like her own children, violated the law openly and made the worst coffee ever.

Velma was apparently out to lunch when he entered because she wasn't there to cast a dark eye on his two foam cups of coffee. Her substitute merely grinned and winked. She was new. Theresa, he thought. He wondered what it was like to work with Velma, then moved on as he passed down the hall to Gage's office.

The sheriff was in, as he usually was, studying a computer screen while eating a sandwich off a big piece of butcher paper. Must have got it at the diner. He accepted the coffee with a smile.

"Thanks. So how's the ATF doing?"

"Working." Alex sat in the chair across the desk. "You know something about bombs and the underside, Gage."

Gage's hand instinctively lifted to the shiny skin graft that covered most of one side of his face. When he'd been an undercover agent for the DEA, his targets had found his home address. The bomb intended for him had also taken out Gage's first wife and small children. Gage had suffered serious burns and back damage that left him in constant pain and limping, but he never complained.

"I know something," Gage said. "Mostly about what it's like to be the target of a bomber. As for knowing the underside...mostly drug types, Alex. You know that. Not like the people you dealt with."

"Not usually," Alex agreed. "But I still want your opinion on something. Or maybe your help. You know Jackson Castor?"

"I do now." Gage reached for his sandwich again. "Mind?"

"Don't stop eating on my account."

But Gage didn't immediately take another bite. "The kid got too curious, set off alarms as I understand, and we cleared him last night."

"I wish it were that simple." Pulling the tab back on the lid of his own coffee, he sampled it cautiously. Hot. "Jack came round, looking for some help this morning. It seems gossip is going around because his ranch was searched last night."

Gage sat up a little straighter, wincing as he did so. "That shouldn't have happened."

"But I guess it did. Anyway, he came out to see if Darcy could help quell the rumors because of his family. She decided not to. She decided to ask Jack to work for her."

"Okay, this is sounding convoluted and I already don't like it. Jack's underage. Why do I think we're headed for trouble?"

"I can't say for sure we are, Gage. I'll explain and you tell me if you think I'm going over-the-top."

"Fair enough." Gage resumed eating, pausing to sip coffee while he listened to Alex's rendition of events, Darcy's reasoning and Alex's concerns.

"And that's it. So am I overreacting?" Alex asked.

"A colleague of mine became involved with the sister of a drug lord and got her pregnant. When the bastard found out my colleague was DEA, he killed his own sister. I'm hardly inclined to quickly dismiss anything as overreaction. Let me think."

Well, that was a chilling enough description, Alex thought. Maybe he ought to share that one with Darcy. He couldn't believe that she was so convinced no harm could befall Jack. But then she was thinking as a rational person.

Unfortunately, Alex knew all too well that not everyone was rational. Or even remotely sane sometimes.

He sat sipping his coffee while Gage ate and drifted away in his thoughts. All the while, he felt his own nerves tightening again, as if they were being wound around a screw. If anything happened to Jack, he didn't think he'd be able to live with himself. Especially if he could have prevented it.

"Okay," Gage said finally. He sighed, rolled up the remains of his sandwich in the paper and tossed it into the trash can. "I don't like it. I can see why it's got you so unhappy. But I don't think Agent Eccles is completely offtrack, either."

Alex kept silent, prepared to listen. The only reason Darcy's comment about the ugly world he lived in had hurt was because it was true. He was too ready to assume the worst, a tendency he'd been battling since he left the bureau. Usually, with his teaching job, he was able to suppress it.

Today had wakened his alerts with shrieking alarms.

"My guess is," Gage continued, "that nobody knows enough about the perp to even guess what kind of person he is. You're worried about the worst type, and Darcy's worried about the ordinary type of jackass, and neither of you have enough to guide you yet."

"That would be true," Alex agreed. "But it seems safer to me to assume a bomber is the worst type, not just some idiot who wanted a big bang."

Gage nodded. "Safer, yes. Useful? Maybe not as much. Jack got himself all wound up in this, didn't he?"

"Yeah." Alex rubbed his chin impatiently. "The thing is, he's a total naïf. All he knows is what he's read online, and who can say how accurate it was?"

"But Darcy's dealt with bombers before. She knows that not all of them are careless about who they kill. Take the Unabomber. He had a specifically selected group of targets and he was very careful not to hurt others. At least he tried not to. Then you've got McVeigh. He didn't care about the day care center at Oklahoma City. That's quite a variety of psychologies, I think you'd agree."

"Of course." It wasn't as if the sickos he'd chased with the BSU had all come out of the same mold. "Okay. So what you're saying is that I don't know enough to intervene."

Gage smiled faintly. "What I'm saying is that either one of you could be right at this point. Darcy needs some way to link the perp to the bomb. You don't want to see anyone get hurt. Me, I'm going to have my department keep an eye on Jack. Discreetly."

Alex started to relax. "That leaves us with the problem of who talked about the search last night."

"I'd bet a year's pay it wasn't one of my people, but I'll be careful. We'll probably find it was some nosy neighbor who drove by last night and saw the activity. Anyway, I've got a dozen or so people I'd trust with my life, not all of them in the department. I'll have them nose around."

"Thanks, Gage. Maybe all my klaxons are blaring for no reason."

Gage frowned faintly. "I wouldn't say no reason, Alex. You've dealt with things Darcy can't even imagine and you know it. Maybe the two of you can find a way to balance one another. Regardless, she strikes me as a straight arrow, not a cold fish at all, and if you see something that truly worries you, she'll listen."

"Probably." What little he knew of her from the past few days hadn't made him believe she'd steam ahead at any cost. She just didn't see there could be a real cost here. And she might be right.

"All right," he said eventually. "I'll tamp down my reaction and between you and me maybe we can stop any trouble for Jack before it happens."

"Right." Gage sighed, leaning back. "There's going to be another bomb, you know."

"We're talking about it. Too much like a trial run."

"But what do you know about bombers?"

"Not a whole lot. Not my area. I believe most seem to have a target of some kind."

"A high school shop hardly seems like a target. Does it?"

Darcy had gathered some pieces of bent, burned, twisted metal and, after marking their locations on the grid, she put them to one side. A deputy came over. "Something specific you want?"

She looked up and realized she saw a strongly Native American face, a tall broad-shouldered man with dark gray-streaked hair. "I've seen you around."

He half smiled. "I'm hard to miss. Micah Parish. Sarah Ironheart is my sister-in-law. Anyway, you seem to have focused in on something."

"Yes." She squatted, placing another piece of twisted metal by the others. "I'm trying to figure out what kind of container held this bomb. There had to have been a container. I was thinking maybe PVC, but I checked the shop and saw that some of their water pipes to the sinks had shattered during the explosion. Then I saw this. Remind you of anything?"

He pulled on one of the requisite rubber gloves and picked up a larger piece of the metal. "Pretty sturdy," he remarked. "It could contain something heavy."

"That's what I was thinking. But there's hardly enough left. Can't even guess what color it might have been. It's so twisted I'm not sure that's a corner, there."

"So help you find some more?"

"Please. I'm still looking out for pieces of the detonator, too."

"Well, I know a little about that. Former Green Beret. I built a few improvised bombs in my day. I'll start looking."

"Thank you." She gave him a warm smile. *What a find!*

By late afternoon, she hadn't seen Alex again. Much as she had tried to ignore it, she realized she had been needlessly harsh with him. Maybe even cruel. His work had been important, essential. Yes, it had obviously been ugly. He'd said as much himself. But to accuse him of living in an ugly world?

What had come over her? She wasn't usually a thoughtless person. At least she hoped she wasn't.

She looked around the gymnasium. A few firefighters and deputies were helping with a search for slender pieces of wire and anything else that seemed like it might belong to something besides the school. She wasn't alone with this search.

But she was missing Alex. A ridiculous feeling, she supposed. Yeah, he was great to bounce ideas off, and he had some insights that were useful, but this was so far from what he was trained to do she was probably doing as well with the volunteers. In terms of work, that was.

But what she had said to him… Hell. It had been unkind and was probably untrue. She'd been so eager to glean information she hadn't listened to a man who probably had a better view of what went on inside the human head than she did. Far better.

If she were to be honest with herself, unless they were dealing with some young prankster, they were dealing with someone with a twisted mind. How could the bomber be certain no one would be hurt by that bomb? There were no guarantees.

She remembered a case from Denver years ago where a couple of children had found an unexploded homemade bomb under a Dumpster. When they caught the perps, some stupid twentysomethings, they learned that the bomb had never been intended to cause harm. They'd just wanted to have a thrill. Instead a young boy had died.

So yeah, it happened. But usually with a stick or two of dynamite. Not with ANFO.

The ANFO was a real hang-up. It was a far cry from someone finding a couple of sticks of dynamite and seeking a thrill. The time and effort that went into it was a clear case of serious intent.

So she should have listened to Alex. At least taken his concerns into account. It seemed incomprehensible to her that the bomber would do anything to Jack when he denied all responsibility. It seemed far more likely the bomber would tell a friend somewhere, "Hey, I did that." Or say nothing at all. Jack should be safe.

But Alex wasn't sure of that. Why had she been so quick to dismiss him?

Because she was tired. At last she admitted it. Alex was right about pushing herself too hard. Trying to prove something? That she could finish this task as quickly as a whole team? Absurd. But the fact remained, being a woman had often made her feel at a disadvantage among so many male colleagues.

Glancing at her watch, she realized that it was almost supper time. After five. She hadn't stopped once since this morning except to eat a bacon sandwich Alex had left for her.

Not good. Sighing, she rubbed her eyes with the backs of her hands and stared at the debris. Little by little, it was being grouped into piles of similar items. They'd get there.

In the meantime, she stepped out into the wet late afternoon and walked around the school again to look at the site. Such a strange target.

Likely practice.

But practice for what?

Micah Parish came round the corner. "Agent? I've gathered all the pieces of that metal. It doesn't look like anything I recognize."

"Not anymore," she admitted.

"But there's still something about the way it feels when I heft it."

She faced him, her heart quickening. "And?"

"I'm not sure. Something is familiar but I can't nail it. Maybe we need the lab to look at it, but it's awfully burned. I'd almost bet it was the container, though."

She nodded. "I agree. I'll send what we have to the lab. Maybe they can get something off it. Paint color. A letter."

He nodded. "I've got patrol tomorrow, but I'll come back in the late afternoon. In the meantime, I'll call if something jogs my memory."

"Thanks. I really appreciate it, Deputy."

"Micah. Just Micah." With a nod, he strode away.

Darcy stared down, hardly aware of the continuing rain, feeling like she was getting nowhere at all.

Chapter 7

A while later, Darcy saw Alex approaching across the sodden ground.

Oh, hell, she thought. Not now. Not when she had just decided she was going to grab dinner and burrow into her room at the motel. The deputies on guard would protect the evidence overnight; she could close her eyes with reasonable confidence that nothing would happen before she opened them again, rested and ready to deal.

But there was Alex, and this morning's conversation hung over her like a heavy weight. She couldn't pretend she hadn't said something awful, so she was going to have to face it now.

"You look bushed," he said when he got nearer.

"I am." So easy to claim fatigue and just walk to her truck, but she knew that would only harden her earlier words as a permanent judgment. She didn't

"4 for 4" MINI-SURVEY

We are prepared to **REWARD** you with 2 FREE books and 2 FREE gifts for completing our MINI SURVEY!

FREE
Value Over
$20!

You'll get...

TWO FREE BOOKS & TWO FREE GIFTS

just for participating in our Mini Survey!

Dear Reader,

IT'S A FACT: if you answer 4 quick questions, we'll send you **4 FREE REWARDS!**

I'm not kidding you. As a leading publisher of women's fiction, we value your opinions… and your time. That's why we are prepared to **reward** you handsomely for completing our mini-survey. In fact, we have 4 Free Rewards for you, including 2 free books and 2 free gifts.

As you may have guessed, that's why our mini-survey is called **"4 for 4".** Answer 4 questions and get 4 Free Rewards. It's that simple!

Thank you for participating in our survey,

Pam Powers

To get your 4 FREE REWARDS:
Complete the survey below and return the insert today to receive 2 FREE BOOKS and 2 FREE GIFTS guaranteed!

"4 for 4" MINI-SURVEY

1 Is reading one of your favorite hobbies?
[ ] YES [ ] NO

2 Do you prefer to read instead of watch TV?
[ ] YES [ ] NO

3 Do you read newspapers and magazines?
[ ] YES [ ] NO

4 Do you enjoy trying new book series with FREE BOOKS?
[ ] YES [ ] NO

YES! I have completed the above Mini-Survey. Please send me my 4 FREE REWARDS (worth over $20 retail). I understand that I am under no obligation to buy anything, as explained on the back of this card.

240/340 HDL GMYJ

FIRST NAME

LAST NAME

ADDRESS

APT.#

CITY

STATE/PROV.

ZIP/POSTAL CODE

READER SERVICE—Here's how it works:

Accepting your 2 free Harlequin® Romantic Suspense books and 2 free gifts (gifts valued at approximately $10.00 retail) places you under no obligation to buy anything. You may keep the books and gifts and return the shipping statement marked "cancel." If you do not cancel, about a month later we'll send you 4 additional books and bill you just $4.99 each in the U.S. or $5.74 each in Canada. That is a savings of at least 12% off the cover price. It's quite a bargain! Shipping and handling is just 50¢ per book in the U.S. and 75¢ per book in Canada*. You may cancel at any time, but if you choose to continue, every month we'll send you 4 more books, which you may either purchase at the discount price plus shipping and handling or return to us and cancel your subscription. *Terms and prices subject to change without notice. Prices do not include applicable taxes. Sales tax applicable in N.Y. Canadian residents will be charged applicable taxes. Offer not valid in Quebec. Books received may not be as shown. All orders subject to approval. Credit or debit balances in a customer's account(s) may be offset by any other outstanding balance owed by or to the customer. Please allow 4 to 6 weeks for delivery. Offer available while quantities last.

▲ If offer card is missing write to: Reader Service, P.O. Box 1341, Buffalo, NY 14240-8531 or visit www.ReaderService.com ▲

BUSINESS REPLY MAIL
FIRST-CLASS MAIL   PERMIT NO. 717   BUFFALO, NY

POSTAGE WILL BE PAID BY ADDRESSEE

READER SERVICE
PO BOX 1341
BUFFALO NY 14240-8571

NO POSTAGE
NECESSARY
IF MAILED
IN THE
UNITED STATES

want that, not for either of them. "Let me buy you dinner," she said impulsively.

His eyebrows lifted.

God, he was gorgeous. Too tired to bury her response to him, she just let it roll. Gorgeous. Attractive. Sexy. Viking. Cripes. Beneath his navy jacket she could see the outline of powerful shoulders, maybe from all the carpentry and construction he did. Inevitably, like dawn following the night, she wondered what it would feel like to have those arms wind tightly around her. She had only the vaguest memory of him carrying her to his couch, and now she wished she had been more awake.

"Darcy?"

She blinked, realizing she'd remained silent as she drifted on her crazy thoughts. "Sorry. I'm having trouble concentrating."

"Dinner," he said. "Yes. Are you okay to drive?"

"I better be or it's going to be a long walk to the motel."

He snorted a laugh. "Like I'd let you. Seriously, are you safe to drive?"

"I'm sure. I can't leave my truck out here anyway. Everything is in it, including all my gear and my suitcase."

He shook his head a little and grinned slightly. "Are you afraid your toes might grow moss if they hold still too long?"

He turned, starting them walking toward the cars, but she found herself wondering if he'd just hit on something important about her. Was she afraid to hold still? She knew she preferred to keep busy and often worked extra hours, but she'd put that down to having little interest in the regular activities of life. Keeping up her apartment, occasionally enjoying a lunch or dinner with another colleague, an infrequent movie… Gads, she'd become a hermit!

But she was aware, too, that there was a disadvantage to being a woman in her kind of position. No one would say it out loud, but while she might be able to manage a relationship, the men she worked with probably wondered how a husband would tolerate her being an agent, and if she married how would she balance that with being a mother?

Those things weren't supposed to matter, but she was well aware they did, however unspoken they remained. She was also aware that she had to work harder than her male colleagues, had to constantly prove herself. For her, advancement was much slower and more difficult.

So she was looking at this assignment as a good sign. Maybe she was getting ahead. Or maybe she'd just been sidelined from a more important investigation. Hell.

Gripping the steering wheel of her truck, she drove behind Alex to the diner and wondered what his reaction would be to her crazy thoughts. After all, he'd been in the FBI. He must have some idea of what she'd felt and whether it was true or imaginary. Of course, as a man, he might be blind to all this. Psychological wizard or not.

But first she had to clear the boards with him. Her comment had been inexcusable.

Maude's diner, as she'd learned the City Diner was called by locals, was blessedly quiet. The cold had to be keeping folks at home. Or maybe they were still nervous because of the bombing.

Regardless, she and Alex took a corner booth with plenty of privacy. Good, because she wasn't inclined to make her apology public. Wouldn't that cause tongues to wag?

After the inevitable coffee and menus had been delivered by a younger version of the gorgon she usually met—Mavis, according to the name tag—she broached the most important matter.

"Look, I want to apologize for what I said to you this morning. You were making valid objections to what I was doing with Jack, and I said an awful thing to you."

"About me living in an ugly world?"

"Yes." God, she hadn't wanted to say the words again. In retrospect they'd been hideous. She didn't know this man well enough to know what kind of world he lived in. Nor whether his judgments had been warped by his job. Yet she'd implied they had been.

"You might be right." He handed his menu to Mavis as she returned and ordered the steak sandwich. Ravenous, Darcy did the same. Today's cold had left her feeling as if she hadn't eaten in weeks.

"Why do you say that?" she asked when they were once again alone.

"Because I went to talk to Gage Dalton, our sheriff. You don't know about him, but suffice it to say in another life he was undercover for the DEA and it cost him everything."

Almost in imitation of Gage, her hand flew to her face. "A bomb?"

"Took out his whole family and left him mangled.

Anyway, he shares our perspective a bit, being a former Fed. But he also knows this county like the back of his hand. He thinks we're both right."

Her brows lifted and then a tired laugh escaped her. "You didn't say he was a diplomat."

"He's not. He's as blunt as he needs to be. He was blunt with me. He listened to my reservations and your decision with Jack, and he agreed we both might be right. So, ipso facto, anything could happen."

Tired as she was, she almost laughed again but without any humor. "Great."

"Well, he promised he had some really trustworthy people he was going to have keep an eye on Jack. I presume he means that nobody's supposed to know they're watching. Loose cordon."

"That makes me feel better," she admitted. "Because, nasty as I was to you this morning, I started having qualms. I still don't believe the bomber would be foolish enough to approach him, but my beliefs and reality haven't always agreed."

"Nor mine." He fell silent while their dinners were slammed down in front of them and Mavis refilled their coffee mugs.

Darcy reached for a fry, wondering where this got them. At least she had apologized, but the situation with Jack hadn't changed.

"I'll be honest," Alex said before he even touched his plate. "I'm not only worried that the bomber might come after Jack for stealing his thunder, as it were. I'm worried about Jack himself. Here's his big chance to work with the ATF, maybe the only one he'll ever have, and I don't trust him not to attack this in ways he shouldn't. What you asked of him was clear. But if he takes it further…"

Her heart sank a little and the potato stuck in her throat. She had to reach for the glass of water this restaurant still offered without being asked, something she'd long since forgotten had once been common. After she swallowed, she asked, "You don't think he'll follow instructions? I just told him to keep denying the story."

"Right. But you didn't really limit him any other way."

"Is he crazy?"

"No. Just eager and young. While you studied explosives and detonators, I studied psychology, Darcy. Young men his age have very little sense of consequences. Their brains are still growing. They're daredevils, and only with experience does that overgrowth of brain get trimmed by the experience of consequences. Why else do you think the military wants to get them at eighteen? They're damn near fearless and they don't worry about what's going to happen next. Ready to be molded."

Darcy looked down at her plate. She needed to eat. She *had* to eat. Funny how little appetite she suddenly had.

Alex sighed. "Look, we came for dinner. Eat. I'll shut up about all of this until you're so full you groan."

For once she didn't feel her hackles rise at being told to do something. Sighing, she took a bite of sandwich and began to eat indifferently. Fortunately for her, after a few mouthfuls both her appetite and sense of taste returned.

When they finished, Alex suggested she come over

to his place. "Better than that damn motel room, unless you want to fall asleep right away."

Full of good food, her desire for sleep had faded. Besides, she was discovering she liked talking to Alex as much as she liked looking at him.

At his house, he brought a plate of cookies into the living room and asked if she wanted a beverage of any kind. "Call it dessert. I have some Tia Maria if you like liqueurs."

"Tia Maria sounds wonderful. It's been years since I've had any." Indeed, she'd almost forgotten it existed.

"I keep a small stash for guests." He smiled. "Unfortunately, most of my guests opt for a beer."

She laughed, relaxing at last, and ready to enjoy some good company. An unexpected perk on this assignment. She settled on one edge of his recliner sofa, and when he returned and handed her a glass, he sat on a facing gooseneck chair.

She held the tiny liqueur glass in one hand, taking the smallest sip and rolling it around in her mouth. "Excellent."

His smile grew more comfortable. "So how do you feel about having been sent out here all by yourself? That doesn't seem usual."

"It's not. I think I told you we're overtaxed right now. They'll get me some help as soon as they can."

"They must have a very high opinion of you."

She sighed and stared at the delicious brown liquid in her glass.

"Darcy?"

"You're a man," she said. "Did you ever notice that it's not the same for women agents?"

"I heard about that ATF supervisor who was accused of sexual harassment. Is that what you mean?"

"Not exactly. Oh, there's still sexual harassment, but it's not the kind of thing you could make a stink about. And to be fair, most of the men I work with are scrupulous about trying not to make female agents uncomfortable."

He nodded. "How many sensitivity-training courses did we attend?"

She smiled. "Oodles. For the most part, I get treated like just another one of the guys, which is fine. And I don't mean locker-room banter. That stuff isn't professional in any job."

He nodded. "I couldn't agree more."

"So it's largely a comfortable environment for me."

"But?" He smiled faintly. "I hear a *but.*"

She hesitated. "I really don't want to sound like a whiner. And maybe there's a good reason for it, but… I feel I don't advance as rapidly as I might. As if I have to work twice as hard to get any kind of recognition. But maybe it's something I'm doing wrong."

Alex leaned back in his chair and crossed his legs loosely. "If you've got anything working against you, Darcy, it's not your mind or personality."

"Meaning?"

"It's the fact that you're a pretty woman. I may be a man, but I've noticed it. There's a strange kind of dynamic. I'm not at all sure it's conscious. Maybe it's an inherent flaw in the male psyche. No woman can be as good as me, and certainly not a pretty one. Pretty ones are supposed to be decorations."

She drew a sharp breath. "Wow, Alex. You're unsparing."

He shrugged one shoulder. "I haven't only studied the seriously ill. Human nature fascinates me. Men have a certain sense of entitlement, passed on to them by parents, by society or maybe just testosterone. Regardless, they're better than any woman. And they may not even realize that consciously."

He drained his glass and set it aside. "Anyway, for what it's worth, I don't doubt that you have to work twice as hard for recognition. You being sent out here on your own is probably a vote of confidence from people you impressed. But it's still a nearly impossible job for one agent. Take full advantage of the local facilities. I know Gage won't begrudge you a single deputy, nor will Wade begrudge you his firefighters if they're useful. Everybody in this county wants the threat identified and removed. We're not going to get hung up on jurisdiction or gender. Believe me."

"That would be refreshing," she admitted. "You'd be surprised how often we've been looked at as interlopers when we arrive on the scene. Even when we've been requested."

"Oh, that doesn't surprise me at all." He shook his head. "I've been resented by the very people who asked for our expertise. Feds aren't popular, most places."

Surprisingly, she felt her lips tilting into a smile. "Thanks."

He looked at her glass. "More Tia Maria?"

She decided she could do with one more. "Unless I need to drive right away."

"You don't need to drive anywhere. The sofa is always available. Just relax."

This time he brought the bottle and topped off both of their glasses.

Something else had been working on her, and the alcohol must have loosened her inhibitions a bit. "The bicycle killer. I'm so sorry he ruined your life, too."

"He didn't exactly ruin me," he said, his voice a bit steely. "I'm still here. Those little girls…" He let his voice trail off and closed his eyes.

"I shouldn't have mentioned it. I'm sorry."

"Ah, hell," he said quietly. "Why wouldn't you mention it? I worked on a lot of cases, but that one… that one was beyond anything. If I could have, I'd have probably killed the guy with my bare hands when he was caught. No, I do not exaggerate. I'm not given to violent impulses. Not before him anyway."

He rose as if he couldn't hold still. Moments ago he'd been relaxed. Not now. Darcy wished she'd zipped her lips.

All of a sudden he halted, reached into his hip pocket and pulled out his wallet. He flipped it open and showed her a photo of a little girl with blond ringlets. "My daughter, Hally, at the time. Same age as most of those victims. She fitted the profile, too." But then he flipped the photo over and she saw a young woman dressed in a formal gown. "That's Hally going to her first prom last spring. She's sixteen now."

"She's beautiful."

But then he flipped the wallet and showed her the little girl again. "She's the reason I couldn't keep my distance, my objectivity. The photos of the missing little girls would come in, and I saw Hally. When they found the bodies…I saw Hally."

"Oh, Alex…" She felt her heart beginning to rip

in two and her eyes heated with unshed tears as she truly began to comprehend the nightmare he'd lived.

"I drove my wife crazy. I wouldn't let Hally go anywhere alone, not even the trip to school. She used to ride her bike, just like the other little girls. I put a stop to that. I put a stop to a lot of things, like trips to the playground. My wife understood some of it, but it became a real burden, me inflicting my fear on them. Perhaps needlessly, because this creep was operating a couple hundred miles away. But I insisted anyway. Then there were the nightmares. Night after night, I'd wake up shouting. The last straw was when I grabbed my wife in the throes of a dream and left her bruised. She threw me out. Understandably."

"I'm so sorry," Darcy whispered. She couldn't imagine how terrible that must have been for him. Couldn't begin to touch upon the fears for his daughter that had haunted him, the crimes that had haunted his nightmares until he became violent in his sleep.

"*I* became the danger to my family," he said. "I have only myself to blame. I should have made them pull me off that case the instant I realized I was losing my separation. But I didn't. I wanted that guy caught more than I'd ever wanted anything. It was like a bloodlust. The fact that it worked, that I was a major part of stopping that guy… Maybe it was worth the price. No other parent had to lose their little girl to such horror. But maybe I could have achieved the same thing without crossing the line."

Suddenly he squatted before her and took her hand. "Darcy, don't ever lose your objectivity so much that nothing matters more than catching your bad guy."

His grip was warm, his palm and fingers calloused.

At first, as that simple touch began to seep through her like hot honey, stirring yearnings she'd kept buried for a long, long time, that's all she noticed. Then she realized what he'd just said.

"Do you think I lost my objectivity with Jack?" Fear ran icy fingers up and down her spine, dispelling the magical moment of growing desire.

"I don't know." He released her hand and stood. "But now you understand why I was so concerned this morning."

She nodded. "And then I said that horrid thing."

He waved a hand. "You were right to question me, even though I didn't like it. We can't lose track of the fact that Jack is now involved, whether we like it or not. Worse, that he *wants* to be involved. Maybe it's best that you gave him a relatively safe assignment. Who knows what he might have come up with on his own."

Her hands tightened. "Or maybe still will come up with on his own. Damn it, Alex, it all seemed so simple when I opened my mouth. I should have listened to you. Just found a way to make sure everyone knew he wasn't involved, that we'd cleared him."

"Easier said than done," he answered. Once again he settled in the chair facing her. "Time to look at this situation with Jack objectively. I give a damn what happens to that boy, hence my objections this morning."

"You think I don't?" she demanded, bridling.

"I'm sure you do, but not in the same way. You hardly know him. You saw an opportunity, and like a good field agent, you were happy to take it."

He held up his hand as she started to object. "Wait.

We're being blunt here. At least I am. Honesty requires me to admit that no matter what you'd done, that young man wants to be involved somehow. Maybe you gave him the safest means. Because I can almost guarantee you he'd have found a way to do something. Anything. He's probably figuring he'll never have another chance to work with the ATF. He doesn't want to blow his opportunity."

"Oh, God" was all she could say, worry growing in her. "You think he's that determined?"

"Jack's always determined. So I'm going to have a talk with him as soon as possible to try to settle him down. He *has* to understand that he's risking his neck."

"But we don't know that."

"Of course not. So far we have no evidence this bomber wants to kill anyone. But it doesn't matter, because we also lack any proof he *won't* kill someone."

She nodded. "He needs to understand that. Maybe I can come up with some cases that would make it clearer to him. Anyway, a good, long talk with him might help. If this was a trial bomb, we're in for worse. We don't want Jack in the way of the bomber's plans."

"Because that might be enough to tip the perp over the edge." Alex nodded, settled back into his chair and crossed his legs again. "Glad we're on the same page."

"Well, you know Jack. I don't."

"And I don't know *you*," he said bluntly.

More uneasiness began to stir in her. "What do you mean? Do you think I'm not an agent?"

He shook his head swiftly. "Not at all. Just…I don't know if you've got a boyfriend, if you've ever been married, if you have family somewhere. The kinds of things we generally casually mention to each other. You're very job focused, Darcy."

He was right. "There's a reason for that."

"I imagine so. When I'm at work…even when it was the FBI, we used to gab about personal stuff. Little things. The anniversary, the kid's birthday, the dinner plans, weekend outings. Things got mentioned. Watercooler conversation. You don't say anything at all."

She looked away. "I'm not good at casual conversation."

"Maybe. Some people aren't. But maybe you're afraid to say anything."

Once again she felt a flare of anger. "I'm not afraid!"

"Let me put it another way. Maybe you're afraid of casual conversation because you don't consider it professional. Or because you're worried you might let something slip that could be used against you."

She nearly glared at him. "I'm not paranoid!"

"Then who broke your trust?"

Damn, talking to a psychologist was dangerous. This guy made her feel like he could see right through her sometimes. "I'm not on your couch."

"Never had one. Other than the one you're sitting on anyway. So, do you have living family? Mine left me and there's no one else. I was a singleton."

She retaliated. "Do you still see your daughter?"

"Every summer and every other Christmas."

"That's good," she replied rather grudgingly. But then she wondered what the heck she was resisting. He was right. These questions of his weren't intrusive.

They were casual. Why should she resent answering any of them?

Because her trust *had* been broken in a big way during her first years with ATF. "There was a case," she heard herself saying even as some little voice in her mind told her to shut up. "Back when I was a rookie. I worked closely with another agent, Archie Westover. He was training me. Thing was... I guess I was smarter than him. I developed damn near the whole case, and then he took credit for it, never mentioning any of my input."

"Ouch," he said quietly. "How do you still manage to work?"

"Because after that I made sure more than one person knew what I'd figured out or learned. I don't care if the whole team gets credit. That's the point of a team. But no more talking only to the man in charge."

"Good way to handle it. So that made you more guarded about everything?"

"You worked in the BSU. You must have run into office politics and competition. I just refuse to provide any ammunition. It may seem small or irrelevant, but you never know."

"True." He leaned forward and took a cookie from the plate. "Help yourself. So, family?"

He seemed to want her whole life story, but she thought it was all pretty boring. All she'd done all these years was work. "Family. Check. Sister is a nurse in the army, presently in Germany. Parents retired to Guadalajara and these days talk to me on the phone half in Spanish. It can get interesting."

He laughed. "I bet. Any particular reason Guadalajara?"

"The place is full of retired Anglos, which makes it comfortable for them. Nice weather, nice lake and the Social Security checks are enough to live on and still have fun."

He was still smiling. "But they're happy."

"Very. I think they're living out a dream they never mentioned until they got their visas and moved. I'm thrilled for them."

"What about your sister? Do you see her often?"

"Not really. A few days here and there. It's not always easy because her husband is with a big construction company and he's traveling the world, too. Right now I think he's in India. With their kids."

His jaw dropped a little. "They're managing this with *children*?"

"I know. It's amazing. But Danny, her husband, loves taking the kids with him. They're nine and twelve now, and he always manages to find a good caretaker for them. For Judi it would be harder, especially since her hours are all over the place." She shrugged, smiling. "It works for them, and Danny brings the kids to visit her a lot. His ability to get away for a few days is a lot better, I gather."

"It must be. So you only get to see her when she can come Stateside?"

"Once in a while I get to Germany, and twice they have come to the States for a family reunion with our parents." Suddenly she laughed, feeling better than she had all day. "It sounds crazy, doesn't it? But they all seem happy."

"I think it's incredible, actually. Wonderful but incredible. So do you feel like the odd man out?"

The question startled her. "Why would I? I'm doing what I want to do."

With her career anyway, but she didn't say that out loud. Did she sometimes feel that she was missing a lot? Of course. But she loved her job and didn't want to give it up.

To her it seemed almost inconceivable that Alex could have given up the FBI to become a shop teacher... Until she remembered why. Fortunately she didn't have those nightmares. Not yet anyway. By the time ATF arrived at the scene, bodies had usually been removed.

So here they sat, she found herself thinking. A man who'd lost everything he'd loved, she who had gathered little to love, both of them alone in some very important ways. Yet both of them claiming contentment with the status quo. Then something else slipped past her lips.

"I don't want a relationship with a man because it might interfere with my work."

He arched one brow. "How so?"

"I'm away a lot. I work long hours when we're on a case. I don't need someone complaining about it. I don't need to be feeling guilty because I'm going to miss dinner or other plans."

"That was the one problem I never had with my wife," he said slowly. "Maybe she was a saint, but she never complained when I'd leave her in the middle of a dinner out or disappear in the middle of the night. It wasn't as bad as being a field agent, probably, but when a case heated up, it could get that way. Never a complaining peep."

"She must have been remarkable."

He half smiled. "I thought so. I doubt it was as easy on Hally when she was little. But later I didn't come home anymore except when I was allowed."

She bit her lip, surprised by the deep ache she felt for this man. He'd paid a high price. "Is it better now?"

"Lots. My ex married an orthodontist who has regular hours, and Hally has some beautifully straight teeth."

He said it humorously, so she laughed. "Very white smile, too, I bet."

"Oh, yeah. Bev and Hally gleam like diamonds when they smile now. The important thing is that they're smiling."

A very generous soul, Darcy thought. *Very generous.* She wondered if she'd be able to manage that herself, even after what was apparently a significant time. "How long since all this happened?"

"Hally was ten by the time Bev had enough. So it's been a few years. But as you might know, the case was solved a couple years before that. So I wasn't adapting well even after the fact."

"I hope you're doing better now."

"Obviously," he answered. "It's getting chilly in here. Are you okay, or do you want a hot drink?"

She ought to be heading to the motel and bed, but she also didn't want to leave. As much as he sometimes challenged her, Alex was good company. Very good company. "A hot drink would be nice."

"Hot chocolate? I don't want to keep you up all night with caffeine."

"I seriously doubt anything will keep me up all night."

"Then after I start warming the milk, let me get

some blankets and a pillow for that sofa. You don't need to go anywhere unless you want to."

In remarkably short order, he had a bed made up for her on the sofa, then went out to get her suitcase. Funny, she thought as he went to finish making the hot chocolate, how she'd put that suitcase in her truck this morning after going back to the motel to clean up. Almost as if she'd been hoping she'd spend the night here again.

She closed her eyes and leaned her head back. She couldn't afford to let her subconscious take over. She had a big job staring her in the face and almost no information at all.

And then there was Jack. After talking to Alex this evening, she was seriously worried about the boy. Would he really get himself into trouble somehow?

She didn't want to think she might be responsible for that. Damn, she'd been a fool.

When Alex called her to the kitchen, she had grown tense again. "Things aren't moving fast enough," she said as she pulled out a chair and sat. Alex poured a mug full of cocoa right in front of her, then filled another mug.

"I hate to be difficult," he said mildly, "but you've only been here a short time. What do you think should be happening faster? The cops are interviewing everyone associated with the school, and that takes time. You're still trying to piece together the remains of something that practically turned itself into dust when it exploded. What do you think isn't moving?"

"It's not that it isn't moving," she answered, feeling the tension in her jaw. "It's that we need it to move faster. The longer I look at all of this, the more convinced I become it was a trial run. Which means there's going to be another bomb, Alex. What if this time it kills someone?"

He pulled his chair around and sat diagonally from her, surprising her by reaching out to cover her hand with his. "We've been jawing about that from the start," he reminded her. "We've got next to nothing to work with. You're hoping the device will provide a clue. The cops are hoping that someone they talk to will say something that'll give them some direction. Even with my experience, I can't build any sort of picture of who would do this. What more can anyone do?"

That was the problem. His touch felt good, but it also worried her, so she drew her hand away and wrapped it with her other around the hot mug. Things were getting complicated, she thought. Alex and Jack. And the bomb. She'd been sent here to learn about the bomb, everything she could. No one expected her to solve the case. She had the aid of every bit of law enforcement in this county, and they'd probably do the solving, which was the way it often worked. They'd focus in on a group of people while ATF told them everything it could about the bomb and what was needed to build it. Sometimes agents would work on finding the perps, but, often enough, local law did the yeoman's share of the work on that end. Why? Because ATF came in as outsiders, not knowing the people, the area. Unless ATF had been following the case for a long time, they were left providing the technical information that could lead to a bomber or uphold his arrest and conviction. Yes, their investigators looked for a perp, but without a link to another bombing...

Well, it was as Alex said. Even he didn't have enough yet to build a profile. And he lived here.

Hand in glove cooperation did the job. Not one agent alone.

So what had she gathered so far? A pretty good picture of where the bomb had been set. Some indications of a homemade detonator. Some twisted metal that might have been the container because it didn't match anything around the school. The force of the explosion. The fuel oil that soaked the nearby ground.

Little pieces that needed to be put together somehow into a picture of the man who had built it.

"Give yourself a break," Alex said. "Drink your cocoa, get some sleep. You'll be fresher in the morning."

She nodded and did as he suggested. He was right. Battering herself was only wearing her out. Maybe morning would bring her a fresher mind-set.

Chapter 8

Jack didn't want to go home. He figured by now his parents had heard that he was a suspect as far as the rest of the town was concerned, and they were going to be very unhappy with him for sticking his nose where it didn't belong.

On the other hand, Darcy Eccles had given him an assignment: to let people think what they chose in the hopes that the bomber might get annoyed enough to say something to someone. But how was he supposed to hear about that if he was buried at the ranch?

He was excited that she was allowing him to help. For once in his life, he was a party to something more important than the ranch or a school project. Maybe the only time in his life, but he refused to think about that right now.

No, he needed to find a way to be even more useful than simply letting people think he was the bomber.

Jack never lied to his parents, but that night he did for the first time. He called and told them he wouldn't be home because he was staying with a friend. Before his dad could get really ramped up on the lecture, he disconnected. Sometimes unreliable cell signals were a good thing.

Then he turned off his phone and started driving slowly along back roads. He couldn't stop at the places where he might hear the best gossip, like the road-houses or Mahoney's Bar, because he was too young. That frustrated him.

But he knew a lot about the county where he'd grown up. Maybe driving around and thinking about the people who lived down those ranch roads would jog something for him.

Because, even though he didn't know much at all about bombers and stuff like that, he'd formed some opinions from his readings. Bombers would work alone unless they were terrorists. The idea of a ter-rorist having any interest in this place made him want to laugh out loud. Sure, blow up an empty school in a town in the middle of nowhere. That definitely sounded like an ideal terror target.

So a loner. It's not like they were rare around here. Some folks liked the wide-open spaces simply be-cause the emptiness meant they didn't have to deal much with other people. There were a number around. Jack didn't know much about them because they kept to themselves, but he knew who most of them were.

Maybe he could find an excuse to talk to some of them. Yeah, he could say he was working on a school project. Most people fell for that one. All he had to do was come up with some useful questions, ones that would sound like they could be part of a term paper and ones that might give him some information.

Whistling, he bumped along back roads and made his plans.

The bomber's disability check had been paid to his bank today so he'd made his monthly trip to town for groceries and odds and ends. His shelves were stocked with dried foods, canned foods, imperishable for the most part. He wasn't prepping for a catastrophe because he wouldn't live long enough to see one. It was just that he hated to go into town. Once a month was enough.

In his bedroom workshop, he worked on measuring chemicals that were going into his bomb. Making it with bagged fertilizer just made it a more challenging job. Like when he'd been in the field, in the mountains of Vietnam. He'd learned to make bombs with all kinds of things as part of his training.

But this time he wanted a big bomb. He needed to do more than collapse a man-size tunnel. Or blow the corner off a school building.

That bomb, he judged, had been a dud. Oh, it had worked, proof of concept, but it hadn't done nearly enough damage. This one had to do better or he'd never accomplish his mission.

He paused, closing his eyes against a wave of pain. The long-ago poisoning was making its final inroads. He didn't have long, but long enough to make them pay for what they'd done to him, not just back then when they sprayed the poison on him, but for so many years after when they denied they'd injured him.

That betrayal was worse than the poisoning to his

mind. The poisoning was an accident of war. Denying it had harmed him was a bureaucratic evil. It was the evil he wanted to avenge.

He opened his eyes and looked at the photo of his squad that hung on the wall. They'd been leaving the Nam for a rotation home. All of them looked like hollow-eyed skeletons, unshaven, rumpled and—unbeknownst to them—dying.

He was the only survivor remaining. The last one of them had died last year. Judging by the letters he'd received over the years, the same could be said for many of the Vietnamese who'd fought beside him.

The big lie. The big secret.

Anger flared in him again, but he tamped it down. These days, anger exhausted him, and he didn't have time for that. Right now he needed absolute calm for some very careful work.

One more test run, he hoped. Just one. Then he'd take care of the buggers who had betrayed them all.

Alex awoke to another rainy day. After a quick shower, dressed in work clothes, he went out to see if Darcy was awake and wanted breakfast.

She was gone.

He glanced at the clock and saw it was just after 7:00 a.m. He'd bet she was already at work at the school.

He understood the obsessive need to solve the problem. He'd shared it for years. It helped make a good investigator, but he also knew the toll it took.

However, he wasn't far from sharing her concern. Yeah, they'd talked about it repeatedly, but the conviction there'd be another bombing was steadily becoming more than speculation for the two of them. He was beginning to feel it in his bones, and when that happened he never dismissed it.

This guy had fired the first salvo in his rampage. He dreaded thinking of what the second move might be.

With his large insulated carrier in hand, he stopped at the diner and bought a bunch of egg-and-sausage breakfasts, as well as enough coffee for an army. Officers and firefighters were out there working, even at this early hour, and the day was inhospitable.

At the school, he saw nothing unusual. The police still kept an eye on the perimeter, and only a handful of cars filled the parking lot, most of them police vehicles.

He passed out coffees to everyone outside, then stepped inside with the chest and announced he had breakfast for anyone who wanted it. The coffee disappeared fast, the breakfast containers less so. In the end he was able to send one of the deputies outside with enough foam containers for the guards out there.

Darcy had given him a small wave when he entered, but she was deep in discussion with Deputy Micah Parish. Promising? He walked over with cups of coffee for each of them, hoping he could find out what was going on.

Micah greeted him with that faint smile. He remembered hearing about when Micah first arrived in town over two decades ago. He'd been a friend of the old sheriff's and was given a job as a deputy, but that didn't protect him from the local prejudice, at least not at first. Micah's Cherokee heritage was stamped plainly on his face, and he'd had a real showdown with

Maude, who owned the City Diner. Details had been blurred by time, but the animosity Maude had felt for him had apparently long since dissipated.

"Any news?" he asked.

"Micah called me earlier," Darcy said. "We'd been discussing these heavy metal fragments. I was going to send some to the lab this morning to see if we could find any clues as to what they came from. But Micah remembered something."

"That I did." Micah squatted and placed his coffee on the canvas covering the floor beside the pyramid of twisted, burned metal. "When I was in the Special Forces in Vietnam, we got a lot of training in bomb making. We used to joke we could make a bomb out of damn near anything…and we could pretty much. Big ones, little ones. The little ones were easier and had more uses. They were the kind we most often had to make. But…" He pointed to the metal. "Ammunition can."

Alex squatted beside him. "How the hell can you tell?"

"That's exactly what I asked," Darcy said, a tremor of amusement in her voice.

"The metal," Micah said simply. "It's not the first time I've seen it after it's blown up. It was the feel of it. Anyway, we used them often when we needed a container for a bomb. Unfortunately, used ones are available from lots of places."

"But for ammo storage I would think," Darcy said.

"Yeah," said Micah. "You'd think."

"But someone who knows they make a good container for explosives…"

Micah stood up with his coffee. "I can't guarantee

it was an ammo can. You need analysis to be certain, but I pretty much am."

"So the question becomes who would think of using an ammo can that way," Darcy remarked.

"Lots of people," Micah answered. "Probably most of them are vets. Most people would only see them as a great way to store ammunition. They're tight. They keep it dry, so long-term storage is a good use. The boxes most people buy ammo in won't keep it that long, depending on temperature and humidity. But there's a reason the military designed these cans. Until you open them, they're air- and watertight. They're also reusable and resealable. Easy to come by from surplus stores."

"How many do you think there might be around here?"

"Dozens, maybe more, easily. Lots of hunters and plenty of ranchers who need to protect their stock from vermin. So we have lots of guns, and I'd bet most people buy larger quantities of bullets and would probably want a place to keep 'em dry. Of course, you could use them for storing other things you want to keep dry."

Alex stood up as well, and let Darcy do the talking. Her job and not his place. He wondered if he'd stepped out of that place last night and that's why she'd left this morning without letting him know. Come to that, considering he had no official status, it was a wonder she hadn't told him to get lost and stay away.

And this was a doozy of a time to be thinking about how much he wanted a few quiet hours with this woman, about how much he wanted to hold her and learn her body from head to toe. What was wrong with him? More important things needed his attention right then. But he still couldn't prevent the quiet hum of hunger he was beginning to feel every time he saw her. Then her eyes met his just briefly, and warmth zapped his loins. Did he see his hunger reciprocated? But the moment was gone faster than an eyeblink.

"An ammo can," she repeated thoughtfully, staring into space. Then she looked at both Micah and Alex. "What's the likelihood only someone with military experience would think of using one for a bomb?"

Micah moved his head an inch to one side, almost a shrug. So Alex spoke. "Highly likely."

"Why do you say that?" Darcy asked, pinning him with a sharp look.

"Remember what you hear about on the news all the time. Pipe bombs, mainly. Hell, even in movies, it's pipe bombs. Yeah, pressure cooker bombs were used in Boston, but again, no reference to ammo cans. We're flooded with images of terrorists wearing belts of plastic explosives. There's no reason to think that someone who has never learned to use an ammo can that way would even conceive of it, Darcy. It's neither intuitively obvious, nor part of the mainstream culture. Not many people would even consider an ammo can for a bomb."

"That still leaves detonation."

Micah spoke. "Small hole. You can insert the detonator or the det cord, and seal it with caulk. You've still got the container you need for ANFO."

She compressed her lips. "I gotta get this stuff to the lab, fast. I need to know if it's from an ammo can."

"I'll grab a big evidence bag," Micah said. "Give

someone a call and let them know I'm coming, then tell me where to take it."

Five minutes later, the state crime lab said they were standing by and would start analysis immediately.

Darcy and Alex moved outside, watching Micah leave with a heavy-duty Tyvek bag full of the metal fragments.

"I still need to figure out the detonator," Darcy remarked. She turned once again to Alex. "How many vets around here?"

"I don't know exactly, but a good many. A better question is how many of them would have gone off the rails this way. And the person to talk with about that is the sheriff."

Jack was misbehaving again and he knew it, but he'd got near the school and was listening as Darcy and Alex stepped outside. He watched Micah take off with a big bag, then heard Darcy ask, "How many vets around here?"

A veteran? Jack's heart quickened. He might be just a kid, but he knew a few, including some who just plain didn't like people all that much. He wondered if they should head his list for questioning.

Yes, he decided. But he'd have to be careful not to be a nuisance, because sure as he was sitting here, they'd call his parents, who weren't very happy with him right now.

He eased back away from the corner and waited for Darcy and Alex to go back inside, aware that time was getting short. He'd been hearing that on Monday the high school would move classes to the college campus, where they'd been given room. Soon he'd be tied down again and limited in his excursions.

Once Darcy and Alex disappeared inside, Jack strode back to his aging Chevy as if he owned the world. Nobody questioned him.

Alex knew he was taking a leap about the ammo cans, but if it turned out that the metal debris was indeed a military ammo can, then it wasn't a huge leap. He was used to making assessments of this kind. His evaluation of who was likely to use such a container was indeed based on his knowledge of what would occur to most people.

Some things just weren't in the mainstream, and that was one of them. Yeah, it was possible somebody else conceived of it, knowing he needed a container, but it was easier to run to the hardware store and buy pipe and caps. No surplus stores in this town. He'd have to find out where the nearest was.

And that wouldn't rule out ordering the cans online.

"Darcy?"

"Yeah?"

"Can you get your colleagues to check for online orders of ammo cans in the last year or so?"

"Of course." She paused as she walked through the grid, seeking another clue. "Why online?"

"It's easy to find out where the nearest surplus store is. But if this guy doesn't want to be remembered, he might think he'd be safer ordering supplies online."

She pursed her lips and looked down a moment before raising a smiling face. "You know, when I first met you and heard you were former FBI, I was afraid of interference. Now I wonder what random chance dropped you into the middle of this because you're remarkably helpful with the human aspects."

He returned her smile but shook his head a little. "I could also be wrong. It's been known to happen, sometimes spectacularly. So don't close any line of investigation because of something I say. We've got so little to go on right now."

She nodded and resumed her stroll, examining the bits and pieces. "If a bomber only acts once, it's possible we'll never get him. We need a chain of evidence. But you know that. Anyway, without that chain to tie a person to the scene, we might never find out who did it. Fortunately, most people leave some kind of trail no matter how careful they are."

"Like the Atlanta bomber," he remarked.

"Exactly. Everyone lit on the security guard who found the backpack and literally saved people's lives by clearing the area. All because he was so damn obvious. Then we researched a little more and realized we've seen that MO before. Linking up cases from around the country. It took some time. I hope it doesn't take time here because people seldom build bombs just to blow a hole in the wall of a school in the middle of the night."

She squatted again suddenly and picked up a twisted, melted piece of plastic. "Det cord?" she asked herself, her voice barely a murmur.

Alex closed his eyes briefly. Det cord and ammo cans? The story here wasn't just the ANFO. His eyes snapped open. "Let's see if we can get together with the sheriff. I want to pick his brain."

"Me, too," she said, straightening with the short length of plastic in her gloved hand. She pulled out a small evidence bag and wrote on it quickly with a marker. "I wish I'd been able to send this with Micah."

Too late for that, Alex thought. He grabbed his empty insulated chest on the way back to the car, while holding his phone to his ear. Gage agreed to meet them right away.

Alex had become her sidekick, Darcy thought as she drove behind his pickup into town. All the initial resistance she had felt had vanished rapidly. Which reminded her, she needed to check in.

She got her boss on the phone quickly. "How's it going?" Vince Malkin demanded.

"Slowly. At this time I'm not sure having a whole team here would make much difference, honestly. I'm getting good support from local agencies, but right now I'm up against a barrier we're trying to break through. You've probably seen my reports. Small ANFO bomb, yes. Oddly placed... Have you seen my vector analysis of the explosion?"

"Just a sec."

She heard some typing in the background.

"I've got it in front of me," he said. "Compact explosion. Small container, bigger than a pipe bomb."

"That's my read, too. We think we've found the remains, but the evidence is on the way to the lab to make sure. It's been tentatively identified as a military ammo can. And I just found what I think is the first piece of det cord."

"That's interesting," Vince said slowly. "This guy isn't exactly inexperienced then."

"That's my thought right now. The sheriff's people are hunting for detonator purchases but they're coming up blank. Of course, det cord has a long shelf life. It could have been hanging around in someone's house for a long time."

"Ten years under the right conditions," he answered. "Okay. I wish I could send you more help, but I just sent four agents down to Georgia to assist with a string of bombs scattered around synagogues and churches. Ugly. Anyway, I'm still stretched. Can you manage?"

"So far," she answered truthfully. "So far we have one bomb, minimal damage and no dead or injured. However, we are concerned about a repeat."

"I would be, too," Vince said. "Damn bomb seems utterly pointless right now. So..." He didn't finish. "If you start feeling swamped, let me know. I'll find a useful body somewhere. I hope."

"Right now more help would probably be overkill. I've also got a former BSU psychologist helping me."

"Well, that's probably useful. I could use a few of them myself, but the waiting list is long. Take advantage."

She disconnected just as she was pulling into the angled parking space next to Alex outside the sheriff's offices.

Inside, Velma waved them to the back, hardly giving them a look. Gage sat in his office framed by a stack of files and a computer that was clearly old.

"You need a flat-screen monitor," Alex said to him.

"Why?" Gage asked. "It'd just make more room for paper. I'm still trying to figure out why I need both." He pointed to the stack on the corner of his desk. "Printouts. Why?"

Alex laughed and shrugged. "Electronic data can disappear."

"So why bother?" Gage shook his head, but he was smiling. "So what's up?"

Alex looked at Darcy, evidently waiting for her to speak. "We may have found the bomb container. An ammo can. And a piece of det cord."

Gage leaned back and rubbed his chin. "You're the bomb expert. What's that telling you?"

"Ex-military," she said. "Alex feels, probably rightly, that using an ammo can to contain a bomb probably wouldn't occur to someone who'd never been exposed to that use."

Gage's eyes shifted to Alex. "How so?"

"Gage, you know what most people see on TV or the movies and in the news. The most exotic container they've heard of has been a pressure cooker. The rest of the devices are all plastic explosives or pipe bombs. I just don't think it would occur out of the blue to someone."

Gage pulled his keyboard closer and typed briefly. "Well, it certainly doesn't come up among the top usages listed for ammo cans. And you'd probably have to search for it specifically. Searching for making a bomb... Well, no ammo cans. Okay, if that's what it is, very useful info."

He leaned back from his desk and looked at Darcy. "So what are you thinking?"

"That there are probably too many vets to check out around here. So do you have any ideas to narrow it down?"

"Good question." He rubbed his chin thoughtfully. "I might better ask some of my friends among the vets. They'd be the likeliest to know who might be that unhinged. I'm not going to guarantee any results, though. A lot of vets have problems and they try to help each other."

"I know," she answered. "I hate to focus in on them. But…" She shrugged. "Unless you can find me someone from the school who just wanted a week off…"

He nodded. "I haven't. It's not that we don't have our troublemakers. It's always possible that one of them conceived of this, but we're not getting any hints that it's school related. It's such a damn strange thing, start to finish." He leaned forward again and Darcy didn't miss his wince. "So we're thinking this might have been a trial run? Because I don't see any purpose in it otherwise."

"We are," Darcy agreed. "And I hope we're wrong. But we need to find some information about the perp that's useful. Anything. Right now we can tell you loads about the bomb, but not a damn thing about who or why. That worries me. An empty building? In the middle of the night? Give me a purpose that doesn't involve testing the device and I'll be thrilled."

"We briefly had some militants on a ranch in the middle of forest service land, but it turned out the owner was being pushed along by a sovercign citizen group. We cleared that out and I haven't heard anything along those lines since. Not a whisper. Which may be weird, I don't know. Militias seem to be springing up like weeds these days, but not here. Not yet." He drummed his fingers. "Okay, I'll put ears among the vets, see if anyone feels someone is capable of this. Sad thing is, when most of these guys can't handle it anymore, they take it out on themselves."

Most of the time, Darcy thought as she left the office. Veteran and military suicides were frighteningly frequent. But they didn't usually involve a bomb of any kind.

Damn, she felt like she was trying to pierce a dark veil. At this point, except for the original detonation device, she could probably rebuild the entire bomb.

How long was the det cord? How far away was the bomber when he ignited it? Being close could be dangerous. A remote trigger would involve skill and soldered wires.

She needed more pieces. Small pieces.

"You were right at the outset," she told Alex.

"About what?"

"About it not being one of your students. Gage is almost positive no one from the school was involved."

"So that leaves nearly ten thousand other people."

She gave a short, mirthless laugh. "Yeah. Small pool."

That night, Darcy accepted Alex's offer of his spare bedroom. He didn't flatter himself that she wanted to be closer to him. No, it was a business decision. He was closer to the school; he had great cell reception and a landline if that failed. Besides, by staying here, she could bounce ideas around with him whenever they occurred.

She told him about her boss having to scrape together four agents to send to Georgia to help with a serial bombing case.

"That must be a real pinch considering he could only spare one for here."

She smiled faintly at him over the remains of their meal. "Feeling dissed?"

"Not unless we find out we've got a serial bomber after all."

Her smile faded. "I hope we don't."

"You getting edgy?"

"Of course I am. If he's in a testing phase, maybe he's got another one ready to go. But what if he's not? What if he's making a whole bunch of them and we wake up some morning to the news? Anyway, once you get the method down, it doesn't take a whole lot of time to build a second bomb. I'm getting impatient because we need to find this guy before he hurts someone."

"Of course." He pushed back from the table. "Go on into the living room. I'll bring you some Tia Maria."

She didn't feel like arguing, so she did as he asked. It was a nice living room anyway. Perks of being a shop teacher, she guessed. She wouldn't be surprised if he knew how to upholster, as well.

But her mind was still racing like a hamster on a wheel and she accepted the liqueur gratefully. Maybe it would take the edge off. She needed something because her impatience to find a solution was growing apace with her investigation.

This time Alex didn't take the easy chair but sat right beside her on the couch. He lifted his glass toward her in a toast. "Take a night off, Darcy. Nothing's going to happen tonight that you can do anything about. Give your brain a break to freshen up."

She nodded reluctantly. "I'm one of those people, Alex."

"What kind is that?"

"I can't leave a problem unsolved. I worry it end-lessly. Letting go isn't my thing."

"Ah."

She almost heard amusement in that single sylla-ble. "What?"

"You're talking to someone who's the same type. Look where it got me."

She tilted her head and looked at him from the corner of her eye. "I guess I should take that as a warning."

"Maybe you should." All humor had vanished. "Look, you've got every law enforcement officer in this county out listening and looking. Did Charity tell you that the fire marshal is also poking around? She gets to go into all sorts of places to make sure codes are being observed. It's not usual unless there's been a problem, but she's ratcheting up their code enforce-ment. Off-duty firefighters are being tasked to poke around, too."

"She didn't mention it." Darcy bit her lip. Was she being cut out? Maybe not, but she might as well be. She wasn't feeling especially helpful.

All of a sudden, Alex astonished her by wrapping his arm loosely around her shoulder. She nearly stiff-ened at the unaccustomed touch, at the liberty he was taking. But before she could reject the embrace, she realized how achingly much she wanted it.

At last she gave in. For a little while at least, she was off duty and had the right to act like any other woman, especially when she'd be leaving here soon one way or another, case solved or unsolved. What risk could there be? And it wasn't as if she thought

Alex would want to cause her any problems with gossip.

Although there was probably enough gossip making the rounds with her truck parked out front the last few nights.

She sighed and leaned against his side, inviting a deeper hug. He obliged, squeezing her shoulders gently.

"Get off the hamster wheel for a few hours," he said quietly. "Right now we're dealing with an impenetrable wall. We need a break of some kind and soon. But until it comes, how many times can you turn the pieces around in your head?"

"An infinite number of times," she admitted. "A bit of obsession."

"I don't have to remind you I know all about that. But give this some thought, Darcy. Have you done all you can for the moment?"

"I think so."

"Then take a breather."

Good advice, she supposed, even though it ran contrary to her nature. "I'm afraid another bomb will go off."

"We all are. But what can you do about that right this minute?"

Not a thing, she thought unhappily. "Not a damn thing."

"Exactly." Then he cuddled her a little closer and she rested her head in the hollow of his shoulder, listening to his strong, steady heartbeat.

"Did you get past the nightmares?" she asked.

"Mostly. It's been a while."

"The thing is, Alex, I think I'll be living with

nightmares the rest of my life if I don't stop this guy before he hurts someone. It's on my shoulders."

"Not *just* yours," he argued. "An awful lot of people are working on this. But if it's going to keep you awake, let's go back to the school and look at the debris again."

She stirred, feeling her heart lurch. "Would you?"

"Of course, I would if it'll help you to feel better."

Amazing, she thought. Just amazing. Not many would make that offer. "No. I just need to learn to turn it off for a little while."

"I don't know about turning it off. I think you wouldn't be half as good if you did. But let it go to the background. I told you before, your subconscious can do a wonderful job while you're thinking about something else."

"So how do I learn this wonderful trick?"

He gave a husky laugh. "I have some ideas but you'd probably object. Just know that I find you incredibly attractive, and I'd have no problem distracting you for the rest of the night."

Her breath stuck in her throat. In all her life, no man had been so boldly honest with her. Her heart started thumping like a trip-hammer and all the oxygen fled the room.

"I don't want to get involved," she managed to whisper. No, she had a job she wanted to keep. She wasn't going to stay here.

"Who said anything about getting involved?" he asked.

The last of the wind whooshed from her. "Alex," she croaked.

He laughed, a deep, warm sound. "Told you I could distract you."

Irritation swept away the heaviness of growing desire. "Alex!" She turned her head and glared at him.

"Of course," he said, still smiling, "it helps that I meant it."

"Now, how am I supposed to take that?"

"Any way that pleases you. You're extremely attractive even in ATF overalls, and I'm a normal man. You've been dancing through my fantasies since you got here."

He'd been dancing through hers, too, she realized. Ever since she'd set eyes on him and thought he looked like a Viking.

"Then there's this whole thing you have about me looking like a Viking."

She flushed. "It just popped out. The way you look…"

His mouth curved a little more. "A very romantic thing to say."

"Romantic?" She didn't consider herself to be at all romantic. "It was just an observation. You *do* look like you descended from Vikings."

"Mainly, I guess, but not totally. Like so many in this country, I'm a mix." He gave her a gentle squeeze. "Distracted?"

She had to laugh. "You succeeded." Succeeded in more than that, though. The attraction she'd been feeling for him from the outset had been on simmer because she wouldn't let it loose, but now it was hotter than that. More demanding. She wondered if she had the ability to cut loose like that anymore.

And then she wondered if she should try.

Jack had pled the resumption of school next week as an excuse to stay out with friends again. He could tell his dad was getting a bit impatient.

"The chores still need to be done, Jack."

"I know, Dad. Promise I'll do them tomorrow when I get back."

"Kids," he said gruffly. "Just don't get into any trouble."

He understood what that meant. His dad was making a point but wasn't going to erupt if Jack skipped out. He always tried to make room for Jack to have a social life, even though it meant more work for him. He had a good dad.

So just as long as he didn't get himself arrested tonight, he was probably fine.

But despite Darcy's hope that someone might say something to Jack, no one had said a word. It was as if the county had a total blind spot about this bombing. As if no one honestly knew a thing. Even among his friends, who seemed to pick up tidbits of gossip from everywhere, there was nothing. An utter silence.

He might be only seventeen, but Jack had already figured how hard it was for anyone to keep a secret around here. So that meant someone who had no social contacts. Someone so far in the background that people didn't even notice him.

Back to the vets who'd been mentioned for some reason. There were a few who'd shoot before they said hello to the mailman. Or so it seemed. They kept away from everyone. True hermits. One of them might be able to keep a secret. But could one of them make a bomb like this all alone?

Probably, he decided. And something about the bomb had Darcy and Alex talking about vets.

Well, he didn't want to get his head blown off. He stopped to put more gas into his Chevy, then started cruising the darkened street. Nearly midnight. He didn't know what he hoped to see or find, but he drove past the high school again and then out to the college campus, where he tooled through parking lots, then decided to drive the outer perimeter. During the day, the pavement was blocked for maintenance golf carts and students to walk, but at night no one cared.

The few security guards on the campus were inside the buildings where they were most needed. At night, the place was like a ghost town. No dorms, no resident students. Those who came from long distances shared apartments in the complex that had originally been built for the brief period when they'd had a semiconductor plant on the edge of town.

It was quiet, however, and he was a night owl anyway. Listening to his favorite music quietly, watching the mist rise from the ground beneath the trees, the result of the earlier rain—it made him feel good. Alone time was hard to come by between family, school and extracurriculars. He savored it.

But driving in circles eventually bored him. He left the college behind and went out to the old semiconductor plant. Like so many things around here, it had brought a brief prosperity, and the temporary influx of high-tech workers, only a few of whom had remained.

It had also brought tension to the close-knit community. That many new people had stirred things up, but before it could all settle down and the two camps could find a way to join, the plant had closed. Microchips had suddenly become cheap.

Hardship had followed, not only for the people who had moved here. Many young people who lived here had found good jobs only to lose them. Promises of a resort in the mountains had been born only to die multiple times over the years. The talk was back, but so far the action was minimal.

Jack honestly didn't see much of a future here. Like others his age, he had bigger dreams and wanted brighter lights. He also knew how much his parents wanted him to stay.

Reaching the edge of the plant building finally, he pulled over on the shoulder and stared at the darkened hulk. So far it hadn't decayed much, maybe because the fences around it were high and a couple of men patrolled it at night. Or at least they had until recently. If those security guards never returned, Jack had no problem imagining that huge building becoming an eyesore, with broken windows and graffiti sprayed everywhere. The company's promises that they would return as soon as the market improved had never materialized. Jack wondered if the place could be retooled to make solar panels, which seemed to be the up-and-coming thing. Surely those semiconductors would share some of the same qualities as solar panels and could reuse some of the tooling. But who listened to him?

He turned off his music and rolled his window down to let the chilly night breeze in. It still smelled of the day's rain: fresh and clean. He figured sooner or later a patrol would pass by and ask him what he was doing here. He couldn't stay for long.

But he still hadn't come up with the interview questions he wanted to try out on some of the vets around here. Dang, he hadn't realized this could be so hard. Maybe he should think of another approach.

Just then, the night exploded. Jack's car rocked in the shock waves, and after his vision returned, he saw that a huge part of the plant had vanished in smoke and fire.

Then he saw a truck pull away farther down the road.

Without another thought, he followed, excitement building in him. Maybe he could solve this whole thing!

The tremors woke both Darcy and Alex from sleep. They met in the hallway—him wearing boxer shorts, her wrapped in a robe.

"Explosion?" they both said at once.

Darcy added, "It felt like an earthquake."

"We have them from time to time but not often and not very strong. That must have rattled the whole town."

Darcy bit her lip. "How can we find out?"

She'd barely spoken when sirens began to howl in town. Fire truck. Police. She looked at Alex, spared a wish they had time for her to enjoy the sight of him so scantily clad and then she turned back into her bedroom. "Let's go."

She dressed swiftly in her overalls and work boots, and grabbed her gloves. Her hard hat and other equipment were in her vehicle. Back out in the hall she met Alex once again. He'd chosen jeans, heavy boots and a thick flannel shirt. Out of his hip pocket hung a pair of heavy-duty leather gloves.

Neither of them said another word. Darcy felt her heart beating nervously, and all she could think was that if she were better at her job, this might not have

occurred. She was fairly certain it was a bomb, probably a bigger one. What if someone had died because
she hadn't been able to find the perp earlier? What if
she still couldn't find the perp?

Part of her felt like a total failure even as the rest
of her geared up into an intense professional mode.
Logically she knew they had almost nothing to go on
with the first bomb. Hell, they wouldn't even know if
the container was indeed an ammo can until the lab
responded. A few pieces of wire. A small piece of
det cord. The sheriff had been out asking questions
and checking everywhere he could for purchases that
might lead to this bomb.

Again she reminded herself that ANFO was nearly
untraceable. That was the point of going to all that
trouble rather than buying a few sticks of dynamite
and a blasting cap. Who knew how long this bomber
had been building a stash for this?

Well, she told herself as she drove as fast as she
dared behind an emergency vehicle, maybe this scene
would give her some really useful information.

"It sounded bigger," Alex remarked. "Bigger than
the one at the high school."

"So it was practice."

"It looks that way."

"God, I hope he didn't kill anyone."

"I guess we're going to find out." Then he surprised
her by reaching out and resting his hand on her thigh.
"Easy, Darcy. You've been doing the best job possible. We knew this was a possibility, but with all the
eyes and ears local enforcement has on the ground,
what were you supposed to do? Be a mind reader? It's

not like you find fingerprints on the stuff burned and heated by a bomb."

"No." That much was true. Fingerprints resulted from oil on the fingertips. They didn't usually survive a whole lot of heat.

Ten minutes later on the western outskirts of town, they arrived at the scene. Firefighters were busy putting out flames and cooling the ruins. Nobody would be able to approach anytime soon.

"Was the building occupied?" she asked Alex.

"In theory, no. The company moved out years ago. For a long time they had some security guards, but I think they were dropped a year or so ago. Apparently whatever was left in there no longer needed guarding."

"Except for the building itself."

Which was now a royal mess. From what she could see—hard to tell exactly with the bright flames, the geysers from the fire hoses and the night all around— it appeared that this bomb had taken out a huge chunk of the building.

Calculating upward in her mind, assuming it was ANFO, she figured a much-larger container had to have been used. Or several of them. She doubted it had reached oil drum size, although it was possible.

But this guy was being surreptitious. If he was trying out a bomb he intended to use elsewhere, oil drums could be a problem unless, like the Oklahoma City bomber, he meant to drive a truck up near a building and blow it all up.

This explosion hadn't been anywhere near that big, although allowing for the effect on structural elements, Oklahoma City had been exacerbated by the building's design. Here, however, she couldn't tell yet.

The one-story high school building had been easy by comparison.

If this bomber wanted big damage, he'd just created some. But another empty building?

Her skin was crawling. At some point, this guy meant to do more than blow up empty buildings. The question was what and where.

And how many would die.

Chapter 9

Jack's excitement buoyed him over the next twenty miles of back roads, some unpaved. He figured he was keeping a safe distance, and when he could he turned off his headlights. Unfortunately, the night was moonless and he couldn't travel very far that way.

But these roads led to a few ranches, so whomever he was following could easily assume he was headed to one of them.

Then he saw the truck turn into a driveway toward a ramshackle ranch. Figuring to be smart, Jack kept on driving. Who was it who owned that place? He couldn't remember but felt he should.

Farther down, he pulled over behind some brush, then backtracked on foot, keeping a quiet, slow pace. He knew this place, vaguely. Some old guy who lived alone. So old and sick he hardly seemed likely to be a bomber. But Jack wasn't prepared to give up yet. Each one he eliminated was one less to worry about.

When he reached the end of the drive, he could faintly pick out the truck parked beside the house. The guy was still there.

Deciding to stick to the edge of the drive, his figure blending in with the sage that had piled up in the ditches to either side, Jack headed toward the house.

Then his head exploded and everything went dark.

After a little more than an hour, the fire was out and smoldering ruins were all that could be seen under the floodlights. Darcy walked over to join the firefighters and connected with Wade and Charity. "What do you think?"

"Bigger bomb," said Charity. "And plenty left inside the building to burn. If we hadn't felt the concussion, I doubt there'd be much left of anything. Anyway, it's too hot to walk yet, so hold your horses."

"Fumes?"

"Your electronic sniffer is as good as mine."

Taking the hint, Darcy went back to get her unit from the truck. Charity was probably exhausted from fighting the fire in over fifty pounds of turnout gear and needed a breather.

She carried the case back with her to the edge of the burned area and brought out the detector. Turning it on, she began to sweep the sensor around. At first it looked like an ordinary fire, but then other things began to show up. Cadmium. Heavy metals. Jeez, this plant hadn't been cleaned up very well.

Then she got what she was looking for. "ANFO," she said. The signature for ammonium hydroxide grew stronger in certain directions, and she was sure that it would get even stronger as she was able to approach the building.

So the bomber hadn't tried a different type of bomb. He'd just built a bigger bomb and tried it on an empty building.

As she stood there, waiting to be able to move in and examine the blast area, she felt her stomach sink sickeningly.

This was just the beginning. This guy had no intention of stopping.

When Jack came to, his head throbbed as if a jackhammer worked on it. The room he was in was mostly dark so he couldn't tell its size. The most important thing at the moment was that he was bound around his ankles and he could feel his hands cuffed behind him. When he tried to move, the restraints barely gave a half inch, so he was cuffed to something. No way to move.

He tried to stifle a groan but, even so, a small sound escaped his lips. That was when he learned he wasn't alone.

"You're lucky I didn't kill you, boy," said a rough voice. A voice that cracked repeatedly. "But don't plan on going anywhere. You're here until I'm done. You give me any trouble, and you'll be done, too."

Jack tried to speak, but his mouth was so dry he couldn't. Suddenly a hand landed on his shoulder and urged him to sit up. With effort, ignoring his pounding head, Jack wiggled and managed to follow instructions. His legs straight in front of him let him know he was on a floor. The cuffs on his wrists tightened a bit at the change of position, but not enough to cut off all circulation.

Only then did he notice a single flame burning some distance away. An old lantern?

A cup pressed to his lips.

"Drink," said that ragged voice. "It's just water. Behave and I'll make sure you live."

Jack sipped the water, warm but welcome, and wondered if he was being offered a good deal or just a lie. Then the fear arrived. The grogginess from the blow to his head was easing a little, and other reactions were returning.

He was a prisoner. He was tied up. He'd just been threatened and he didn't believe the guy was telling the truth. He'd been taken prisoner. He was going to die.

His heart raced and anxiety ripped along every nerve ending in his body. Terror. For the first time in his young life, he felt true terror. It dried his mouth again, silenced him and sent his thoughts skittering around like crazed mice seeking a way out of a death trap.

The cup touched his lips again. This time he had the sense to guzzle it. Who knew when he'd get another drink?

"Guess I gave you a concussion," the voice said. "Hardly surprising. What's wrong with you, boy? Following people at night. What were you going to do? Kick an old man to death for the fun of it?"

"No!" The word escaped Jack's terror. Then his voice shut down.

"No, huh?" The creaky voice didn't say any more for a while. Jack thought he saw a shadow moving in the darkness. A bent man, not standing straight. Why? Was the roof too low?

Then something scraped and the shadow sat down, out of reach of the flame's light.

"So you weren't out to beat up an old man. What were you doing?"

Jack didn't dare answer. The truth might make the guy even madder.

"I knew you were following me," the voice continued. "Don't know why, but you're not good at it if you thought I wouldn't know. I've been followed by people with a whole lot more skill and I knew it. You crazy, boy?"

"Maybe," Jack said hoarsely. Right now he wondered if he was. All Darcy had asked him to do was listen in case someone around him said something. She'd never suggested anything as stupid as following a guy in the middle of the night, certainly not someone running from the scene of an explosion. Suddenly he wasn't at all sure he'd make a good ATF agent. Darcy spent all her time studying evidence and relying on local law enforcement to do the footwork of finding other clues.

But him? Oh, he'd thought he was a superhero who was going to catch this guy and solve the whole bombing. Sheesh, why hadn't it occurred to him to just call the cops and tell them what he'd seen?

Stupid!

"So, boy, what were you doing out there?"

Jack licked his lips. He doubted a lie was going to work here. He'd never been a good liar anyway. "I saw the explosion. Saw you leaving."

"So you thought I was the bomber and you were going to catch me?"

Jack didn't answer. It sounded even more stupid when this guy said it.

"Well, don't worry about it now," the creaky voice said after a few minutes. "You won't do me any harm here, and when I'm done, I won't care anymore."

"What *are* you doing?" The words burst from Jack and he nearly winced as a fresh spear of pain hit his head.

"Getting even," the man said. "Just getting even. I'm dying, boy. So you can trust me when I say I won't give a damn what happens when it's over. But you're going to talk to me a little later or you won't see another sunrise."

"Let's go home and catch a little sleep," Alex said.

Darcy didn't want to leave, but Wade chimed in. "That mess isn't going to be safe to walk on for hours yet. You can't do a thing until well after dawn. How about I give you a call when we're sure there aren't still fires burning under the rubble, when you won't fall into a weak hot spot?"

He had a point, Darcy thought. They both did. She nodded reluctantly, bowing to reality. She needed to be fresh when she started pawing through this mess.

"We'll make sure no one moves anything unnecessarily," Wade added. "If we have to move something, we'll keep track of where it was from, okay?"

Well, that settled it. Nothing more she could do here except kick her own butt for failing to solve this case sooner.

"But no one was in there?" she said for at least the tenth time.

Charity shook her head. "No guards in the last eighteen months. The fence keeps most people out. If a trespasser was in there...well, God rest them. We'll find out."

From the way Charity's eyes pinched in her smoke-stained face, Darcy guessed she'd found remains at other scenes. Never something you wanted stamped in your mind's eye.

She and Alex strode back to the road in silence. Vehicles lined the shoulders, the fire trucks had gone right through the fences that had once been topped by concertina wire. Yellow tape fluttered from metal poles around a huge area.

It had been bigger, all right. How much bigger only examination would tell.

She paused, looking back. "Wade?"

He turned in the midst of wiping his forehead with his filthy sleeve. It didn't help much. "Yeah?"

"You've got the blueprints for this place, right?"

"Everything we need for firefighting. I'll show you in the morning."

"Thanks."

Alex spoke as they reached the car. "Wouldn't the city have the blueprints, too? They had to be approved by Code Enforcement at the very least."

"The fire department will have a better version," she answered. "They make plans for having to deal with fires in every building in their area. Those are the plans I want. They'll have an idea of how the structure would respond to fire and what pitfalls to avoid."

"I didn't know that."

"Very useful to their job and mine."

When they got back to Alex's house, they simply walked in, dumped their jackets and began to head back to the bedrooms.

But Alex astonished her. He grabbed her hand and tugged her with him. "Not a night to be alone."

She didn't argue, although she supposed she should have. She let him draw her to his room and sit her on the edge of his bed. He knelt and pulled her boots off, then said, "Curl up." He drew the comforter over her as she lay back. Moments later, he'd dumped his own boots and came to rest atop the comforter beside her. He wrapped his arm around her waist and drew her close until she faced him.

She felt as if she were numb to her very soul, beyond the warmth or the cold. Just empty. Going through the motions. But with his arm around her, his comforting presence, her walls began to crumble.

"It's my fault."

"I knew you were feeling that way." He moved his arm, rubbing her back. "Thing is, I'm pretty sure you were with me this evening, so I don't remember when you went out there to place the bomb and detonate it."

"Oh, stop it," she said irritably. "You know what I meant."

"Of course, I know what you meant. I'm merely pointing out that you can hardly be responsible for what someone else did. Would it have been nice to catch him before he did this? Sure. But we don't have a whole lot to go on yet. It's not like you haven't been working the scene and trying to put the pieces together. Diligently, I might add. Everyone in this county is trying, too. Want to blame everyone? You can start with me."

She stirred, some of her irritation giving way to the comfort he offered, but nothing dispelling her sense of failure. "I'm supposed to be the bomb expert."

"And you are. But you're not also expected to find the bomber, are you? How many jobs have you worked where the FBI has come in to look for the suspects? How many where local LEOs help with that. And how many where ATF has been purely alone on an investigation?"

"Few enough," she admitted.

"You understand bombs. I don't see someone from ATF here to help you with the suspect part. Besides, you've been around long enough to know how hard it can be to find a bomber."

"I know," she said quietly. "But this bomber didn't leave anything behind to identify him. Nothing I've found yet anyway. Remember McVeigh?"

"How could I forget? Arrested by accident for not having a license plate and carrying a concealed weapon. Might have got well away except for delays in his hearing date. Then what, Darcy? What happened next?"

She sighed. "They found the truck axle. The serial number was still legible. The FBI did that."

"See? And you're here all alone. I hope they send you some help when you call your boss in the morning. This is getting bigger. If he doesn't have someone to spare, maybe the FBI will. Anyway, my point is obvious. Unless the perp leaves something behind at the scene, what have you got? Nothing. So quit kicking yourself."

"The ammo cans," she said after a minute. Hardly realizing it, she snuggled closer to the comfort he offered. At once his arm tightened around her and with the comforter between them he still managed to press her close enough to remind her she felt other things besides despair and failure. Womanly feelings.

"Yeah, maybe they'll turn out to be the something if they *are* ammo cans. Regardless, we're going to do a whole lot of looking tomorrow, right? We're far from done."

Far from done, she repeated to herself. Far from it. "Locard's exchange principle," she murmured.

"Exactly. The perp always leaves something behind or takes something away. Those cans may be forensically important. So might the det cord. You know something, Darcy?"

"What?"

"There's not a whole lot of need for explosives around here. Ask the sheriff sometime. No mining, whatever. There was an attempt to build a resort on the mountainside but an earthquake put paid to that before they built the foundation. As for the semiconductor plant this jackass just blew up…I seem to remember hearing it didn't have a basement. Placed on a floating slab. Don't ask me why, but the point is there hasn't been any need to blast anything around here in recent memory as far as I can tell."

"Meaning?"

"That you're not going to get confused by a whole lot of people in possession of det cord, for one thing. And if anyone around here knows of someone who has the wherewithal to make a bomb, sooner or later memory will nudge them into talking. Probably sooner than later after this explosion."

She hoped so, but his embrace was softening her, allowing weariness to emerge through the anxiety that had been driving her.

An axle with a serial number. Maybe an ammo can this time. It didn't always take much. Something always got left behind.

"Now, sleep if you can," Alex said, his voice deepening. She could almost feel the sexuality awakening in him, though he did nothing about it. "I'll be here, Darcy. I'll hold you all night."

Eventually she fell into a deep sleep with dreams made more pleasant by the strong arms that held her. Dreams about a Viking lover.

Jack was woozy, probably because he wasn't sleeping and because of the blow to his head. He kept pulling himself back to the present, however, because he couldn't risk missing a chance to escape.

His arms had begun to hurt from being cramped behind him for so long, and he used the pain as a focal point for keeping his mind as alert as possible.

Gradually he became aware that gray light had begun to filter into his prison. A huge room in an old structure of some kind. Light seeped between boards, but not much of it.

When his captor returned, he had his face covered. "Hungry?" he asked Jack.

"My arms hurt." It sounded like a whine but he didn't care. Maybe he'd get his chance.

"I knew boys your age who got tied up for a whole

lot longer and beaten while they were. Never heard them whine."

What was this guy talking about anyway? "Who were they?"

"Soldiers."

For some reason that made Jack's spine prickle even more than knowing this man was a bomber. A soldier. A vet like Darcy and Alex had been concerned about. But why would a vet do any such thing?

He didn't dare ask, however. His captor drew closer and even in the poor light Jack suddenly noticed he was carrying a pistol. "I'm going to untie just one arm," the man said. "You try anything and I'll pull this trigger. Read me?"

"I read you."

When the man moved behind him, Jack realized he was tied to a post, not to something buried in a wall. That ripped at any hope of being able to break loose.

In spite of every effort not to, Jack let a sigh of relief escape him as his right hand was freed. Aware of the pistol pointing at him, he moved slowly. His captor backed up and sat on the vague outline of a chair.

"I'm still aiming at you," the man reminded him. "Shake it out good. Then I'll give you something to eat. If you behave, I might free your other arm for a while."

Probably not at the same time, though, Jack thought sourly. At least the throbbing in his head was easing a bit. "My parents are going to notice when I don't come home."

"Don't matter. Nobody's gonna find you here."

Probably not, Jack thought grimly. When his arm

and shoulder stopped aching so badly, the guy threw some bars on his lap. Nutrition bars. Damn.

But he wasn't going to comment on the strangeness. He might have expected a plate of beans from this guy. He tore the wrappers with his teeth and began to eat ravenously. As energy began to return to his body, Jack started to think seriously about his situation. The thoughts that occurred to him didn't make him feel any better. So what if this man said he'd free Jack unharmed after he finished whatever it was he wanted to do? First of all, Jack wasn't sure he believed the guy. But even if it were true, it meant that he'd be tied up here, his head full of knowledge the ATF and Darcy could use, and he couldn't do a damn thing about it.

Dang, give him the award for stupidity. He should have just kept driving last night. What made him think he should try to creep up on this guy? If he'd just headed home, one phone call would have brought the whole of the county crashing down on this guy's head.

No, instead he'd had to go all comic book. God! It was almost enough to make him hope he didn't survive this, because he didn't want anyone to know he'd been an incredible idiot.

When he finished the four foil-wrapped bars, the guy gave him a paper cup full of water. No weapon there, not that he'd be able to do much with his ankles bound and one arm still tied to the post behind him.

As soon as he'd finished the water, the man approached again. "Gonna tie up your arm, son."

"I need to go to the bathroom."

"You can do that right there. It'll dry."

Jack closed his eyes, dealing with it. Now he wanted

a way to get even with this guy. Anger filled him, but he didn't struggle as his arm was cuffed behind him again.

A one-armed man couldn't do much right now. He had to start thinking about ways to deal with this guy. Ways to get loose. Not that that was looking too likely.

Then his left arm was freed and he shook it out with relief, aware that the gun always pointed at him, never wavering.

"Why?" he demanded finally. "Why are you doing this?"

"Because nobody's gonna stop me. And that means you."

"I can keep my mouth shut."

The man gave a small, crackly laugh. "Yeah? That's why you followed me? Tried to creep up on my house? Sure. I recognize a so-called hero when I see one. I knew enough of them in my life. Funny thing, heroes usually wind up dead. Maybe you'll be the lucky one who doesn't."

The words chilled Jack. He might be the lucky one? "You said you wouldn't hurt me."

"I won't if you just sit there and do as I say. But you wouldn't be the first kid I killed."

Jack stuttered. "W-w-what?"

"Spoils of war, boy. Spoils of war."

What kind of man was he dealing with? The guy was suggesting he might actually like to kill Jack. Stupid question, he supposed, given the guy was a bomber. But killing kids?

Then he froze internally. He might be only seventeen but he'd heard about kids dying in war. This guy was a veteran. Maybe… "When did you serve?" he asked abruptly.

For a long time the guy didn't answer. Then he said, "Vietnam."

The guy stood up and Jack watched his shadow leave the building. Alone again, he had plenty of time to realize he hadn't used his opportunities to glean more information very well. Or to gain the guy's sympathy.

Pinned, he had become totally useless to everyone. Even to his own family.

The dunce in all this was him.

Just as the first gray light of day filtered through a crack in the curtains, Darcy's eyes popped open and she realized she was wrapped in more than a comforter. Alex had wound himself around her, cradling her close, as if he would protect her.

Dawn was here, or near, and she knew she needed to get up, start her day, find out if it was safe to check out the new bombing. Call her boss and see if she could beg, borrow or steal some more help.

One minor blast at a high school that everyone had originally believed would be traced to a student who was either experimenting or angry about something, had proved to be anything but. Now a second bombing made a complete hash of anyone's attempt to dismiss the first, bad though it was, as an isolated incident.

Of course, she'd told her boss they were beginning to suspect something much bigger. But he'd just sent four agents he could not really do without to a serial bomber in Georgia.

But now they had a serial bomber here.

She didn't want to move. Charity had said she would call when the site was safe for examination. Surely she could steal a few more minutes here, comfortable and warm, with Alex so close.

It had been a long time since she'd even considered what she might be missing by keeping herself so attentively focused on her job, and by avoiding relationships beyond a few casual girlfriends. A long time since she'd last thought how wonderful it would be just to be hugged.

Boy, she'd been missing a lot. Almost unconsciously, she snuggled closer and felt Alex's arms tighten just a bit. God, so good to be held like this. Part of her never wanted it to end.

One of her arms had worked out from beneath the comforter during the night, and now she dared to wrap it around his broad shoulders. Powerful man, filled with strength of every kind.

Inevitably, she wondered how difficult it had been for him to leave his work with the BSU and start over again as a shop teacher all the way out here. She knew the level of tension and excitement that went with their kinds of jobs. Rarely a dull moment. Boredom was unfamiliar. What must a change of this kind be like?

Had he struggled with the quieter hours? With the lack of seriously important tasks? Or had it come as a relief to him to know that someone's life wasn't riding on his shoulders.

Right now she wondered if that might be a good thing for her, too. She already felt like a failure, and nobody had died yet. What if they didn't catch this creep before someone did? Because now there was no doubt he was escalating.

She sighed and a murmur escaped Alex. "Stop it."

"What?"

"Thinking so loudly. Nobody's called. You can't race out to the scene, so just give yourself a break until the phone rings."

"I need to call my boss."

"He can wait. Like a normal person he's probably having breakfast with his family."

"Are you saying I'm not normal?"

A sleepy chuckle escaped him, then he drove the breath from her by rolling on top of her. "You're normal enough to be driving me out of my mind," he said softly. His mouth was only inches from hers. She was staring into the amazing blue fire of his eyes.

"Alex…" She could barely find breath to force his name out. In an instant he'd set her entire body ablaze, and she cursed every layer of clothing and blankets that separated them. She wanted him. To hell with everything else.

"I should have undressed you last night," he muttered.

She couldn't have agreed more.

"A Viking would have," he said more lightly.

But then the talk was over, and she tumbled so far so fast that no further arguments arose in her. A few minutes. A little time, maybe an hour, for just the two of them.

He pushed himself off her and yanked the blankets away. They reached for one another, struggling with buttons and snaps, hands getting in the way, small laughs slipping out as they fumbled their way to nakedness.

"Just don't ring," she heard him say before he

pushed her naked body back onto the bed and began to kiss her from the top of her head all the way down to her ankles.

"Time," she whispered hoarsely. There might not be enough time and she didn't want this to be inter-rupted...

"I don't want to rush," he muttered.

Nor did she. But her body was already arching toward him, her hands digging into his shoulders. Later... Maybe later they could take the time to ex-plore, to learn, to savor...

Then it happened. Her cell phone went off from her pocket in the heap of clothing on the floor. An instant later his began to ring, as well.

He swore. They froze. But the moment was lost.

"Later," he said like a promise.

"Later," she agreed, not at all sure there'd be one.

Still aching with desire, disappointment almost overwhelming her, she let him go, then stood up.

"You shower first," he said, pulling on some shorts. "I'll get breakfast going."

The phones shrieked again. Darcy clambered around the floor, finding hers. She answered.

Charity Camden. "It's probably safe for you to come out here now," she said. "One of our men brought out our plans during the night. Wade said you wanted to see them so just come out when you're ready."

"You?" Darcy asked.

"I'm not going anywhere. I'm an arson investiga-tor, remember? I can help. Some guys went back to town to get us all food and coffee. We'll be waiting."

Alex had answered his phone as well, and apparently got the same kind of message. He looked over at her. "Shower. Then we'll grab some takeout at the diner."

"Sure. But I need to call my boss. You shower first."

He shrugged. "Good enough."

Like it mattered, Darcy thought as she pushed autodial for her boss. They were both going to be filthy in no time at all.

Struggling against his bindings got Jack nowhere at all except sorer. The skin on his wrists felt raw. The rope on his ankles didn't stretch in the least. And the man who held him captive hadn't returned.

Maybe the guy had gone somewhere. Maybe he wasn't coming back. Maybe he planned to leave Jack here to starve to death.

Maybe he'd driven back to the semiconductor plant to get an idea how much damage he'd done. That might give him away. Hope filled him as he remembered how quickly Darcy had noticed his interest at the high school. Yeah, she'd pick this guy out of a crowd.

Maybe.

And what if all Jack had managed to do was push the bomber's timetable up? What if someone got hurt or killed because this creep hurried ahead with his plan?

God, if his head hadn't already hurt so badly, he'd beat it against the post behind him. His mouth felt dry as cotton. No more water had been forthcoming. Those nutrition bars had long since vanished from his stomach and it rumbled annoyingly.

Well, he could make it. He just wished he could find a way out of the mess he'd created before it was too late.

What he had to do was find a way to connect with this guy. Get him to talk. Maybe even get him to feel sorry enough for Jack that he'd let him go. Hadn't he read somewhere that's what a kidnapping victim was supposed to do? Make the captor care?

But this guy had said he was going to be dead soon and didn't care. If that was the case... Well, maybe there was no reaching him now.

Still, there was a chance he could at least find out what this guy wanted to get even for. Because if Jack survived this, somebody was going to want to know what the bomber had been trying to do. Especially if he planned to blow himself up with his own bomb.

And all of that assumed, of course, that Jack got out of here alive.

Vince, Darcy's boss, said he'd see about getting some FBI agents out there to help. Exactly how they were going to help, Darcy didn't know. Local law enforcement knew this county like the backs of their hands. The FBI's having found that axle with a serial number hadn't happened because they were FBI. ATF or one of the locals could have found it, as well.

"FBI," she muttered.

"What about them?" Alex asked as she pulled into the diner.

"My boss is going to try to get me some agents. I'm just wondering what they can add to the mix. Extra hands, I guess, but the last I knew they were every bit as tied up with counterterrorism as we are, and they've probably got their hands just as full. The locals here don't need to be brought up to speed. I bet they know damn near everyone."

"Damn near," Alex agreed. "What do you want? I'll just run in and grab takeout."

"A ton of breakfast frics, a heap of scrambled eggs and enough coffee to float the Titanic."

He laughed quietly. "Got it. Be right back." He paused as he was climbing out. "I get why you're dubious, Darcy, but there's something the FBI can work on in much more depth than local LEOs."

"What's that?"

"Deep background on every possible suspect."

She hadn't thought of that. It made her feel marginally better as she waited for him. Heaven knew there was little enough making her feel good right now. Then this morning, on top of everything, she'd been about to cast caution to the winds and give herself over to pure pleasure... And the damn phone had rung.

Her body was still aching with disappointment and hunger even after a shower, a phone call, dressing... She wasn't used to this. Usually desire flitted by and then left. Usually. This time it was sticking and didn't want to abate even for work.

Great. That was all she needed. A thing for a Viking who lived in the middle of nowhere. No way could that jibe with her job. With her career. With her no-involvement rule so that her male colleagues wouldn't start using "family preoccupation" as a way to criticize her. Admittedly most of them wouldn't do that, but she only needed one to take it as his personal mission to make her look bad. She'd seen it happen once, and it had been ugly.

Alex returned swiftly with the bags of food and two tall coffee cups. She reached for a cup and gladly took a long drink before she backed out and started them toward the scene of the second explosion.

Without a word, he reached over and rested his hand on her thigh again as she drove with one hand and sipped coffee with the other. It made her feel good, made her feel as if he regretted the interruption to their lovemaking as much as she did.

Then the roads grew rougher and she had to put her cup in the holder so she could keep both hands on the wheel.

"This road's going to hell since the plant closed down," he remarked. "Next thing you know, it'll be sprouting grass."

"So it's not used for anything else?"

"Well, not much anymore. They paved it for the employee traffic, but obviously it's now only being used by the people who used it before, ranchers mainly. Not much traffic most of the time. An occasional police car, trips to town for supplies."

The plant had been built beyond the reach of the town, but by only a few miles. It gave the impression of wanting privacy. "Semiconductors, huh?"

"Yeah. Hush-hush, apparently. At least some of the work was for the DOD, but that's about all I know. The business moved out before I got here."

Even though it was no longer in operation on defense contract, Darcy wondered if some old grudge might be the reason it had been targeted. But that didn't explain the high school.

Chewing her lip thoughtfully, seeing the remains of the building rising before her as they approached, she wondered if this had been just another trial run. A bigger one. Another empty target seemed pointless. Unless they had a bomber who got all the kicks he needed from blowing something up. It was rare one of those went after buildings, however. You could make things go boom in an empty lot and run into a whole lot less trouble than when you destroyed property or threatened life.

No, this guy had a point to make with all this. She desperately needed to figure it out. Maybe this scene would offer more clues.

When she reached the end of the road and the beginnings of the fence, she saw two deputies standing guard, their cars on either side of the opening, roof flashers operating. They waved her through, but she halted just inside the fenced perimeter.

She wanted the larger view in the morning daylight, more than she'd been able to see last night. A big building, but not overwhelmingly so. Three stories. She wondered how much expensive equipment had been left behind. Judging by her early chemical analysis last night, some dangerous metals had been left, but possibly only in minute quantities that simply couldn't be located or cleaned up. A good reason, other than property protection, to keep this place behind barbed wire.

But the security guards had been removed. Well, it wouldn't be the first time a business had moved on and left its pollution for the locals to deal with. While that wasn't within her job description, she had a couple of friends at the EPA who'd told her about it. Anyway, there probably wasn't enough left here to constitute a real environmental threat.

She guessed she'd find out, though, because she

wasn't entering the remains of the structure without taking her detector with her. And wearing a mask.

The blast had been big enough to take out one entire corner of the building. How much additional damage had occurred in response to the fire or structural weakness was something she'd have to figure out.

Big, but not as big as some bombs she'd seen. Maybe this guy didn't want massive. Maybe he was after something smaller. Given that he'd proved to himself he could successfully build a bomb with the explosion at the high school, this one might have been done as a matter of scaling. Scaling up.

Alex had passed her a container and she opened it, eating scrambled eggs, home fries and toast while hardly tasting any of it. Fuel for the day ahead.

Her eyes kept roving the scene, from the undamaged end of the building to the blown-out and burned part. "The bomb was outside again," she said after a bit. "See the debris pattern? Implosion near the wall. Stuff blew inside."

"Yeah."

"So our guy doesn't want to get inside someplace. He wants to work from the outside."

Suddenly she put her breakfast aside. "I'm taking a walk."

She wasn't surprised when Alex came with her. The morning air still held the night's chill, and she was glad to be wearing her ATF jacket. She walked back toward the entrance and spoke to the first deputy, Marcus. "Is there another way through this fence?"

He nodded. "You mean from before the fire trucks drove through it? Yeah. Want me to show you?"

"Please. I want to walk, though."

He nodded. "Want me to bring my K9?"

For the first time she noted the dog in his back seat. "What kind of sniffing does he do?"

"Whatever I ask. He's not a bomb dog, though. Until recently we didn't have the need."

"Yeah, I can imagine."

So the trio and the dog began to walk along the shoulder. Here the road became mostly dirt, but not entirely. Patches of old pavement remained. Clumps of grass, a testament to nature's determination, popped up here and there.

"It rained yesterday," Marcus remarked.

"I was thinking about that," Darcy answered. "Tire tracks?"

"Two recent sets. I don't know if we're looking for two guys or it's coincidence. But I'm sure you'll want to see what we found down here a ways."

"I like the sound of that."

Marcus smiled faintly. "Say, Alex, you got a profile going yet?"

"Truthfully? There's not a whole lot to go on right now, but I'm inclined to think we're dealing with someone who wants to send a message. And this building isn't it."

"I was afraid you might say that."

Darcy spoke. "What kind of message?"

"I can't be sure. My guess would be he's mad about something, but don't hold me to that, please. It's early days yet."

"But that's the sense you're getting?"

"At the moment."

Darcy nodded. It would fit. There had to be a reason for blowing up empty buildings. For trial runs. An ultimate target. Someone who was angry about something? Entirely possible. A vet... Well, a vet could have a lot of reasons to be furious. "What about someone who just wants action?"

Alex shook his head. "I don't think so. There are lots of other ways to get action, like volunteering for another tour."

"I hear that's not why guys keep going back."

"Not usually. No, the psychology is more like, things were simpler on the battlefield. Clearer. Kill or be killed. Which is an extreme exaggeration, but you'll hear that from a lot of vets who keep going back."

"Well, that wouldn't fit this."

"No, so I'm thinking anger."

Darcy listened to the crunch of their boots on the gravel mixed in with the grass lining the shoulder. No silence existed out here. Not that there'd be any even if the ground wasn't so dry. Weary firefighters still stood around the building, smoking illicit cigarettes while watching the ruins for signs of smoke or more fire. As they walked farther, she could see inside the building—the damaged floors and ceiling and wires hanging down like threats. Going in there wouldn't be wise until things were shored up.

Another delay. Damn, she wanted something she could really sink her teeth into. Thing was, when you worked with bombs, evidence tended to be in small bits and pieces. Unless, of course, you were lucky enough to find the axle of the bomber's vehicle, and how often did that happen?

She was still staring into the open maw of the hole when she realized Marcus had pointed. She followed his gesture and saw the wire fence had been cut and inexpertly put back together.

"Hell," she muttered. Nobody casually driving by would even notice that, which gave the bomber time to set everything up. Then, when he was ready, he could close the gap, covering his trail temporarily, while he took off.

As they got closer, she saw the tire ruts in the wet earth and grass. "Pickup," she guessed.

"Looks like it," Marcus said. "Dasher, look."

At once the dog began sniffing around and decided the fence fascinated him, as did one spot on the ground.

"Reasonably fresh sign on the fence," Marcus said, watching his dog. "He could smell it even after rain, but after a few weeks he wouldn't be much interested. What's getting my attention is his focus on that spot right there. Guess? The guy relieved himself. Times like this I wish Dasher could talk. He'd be able to tell me a whole lot."

"Any way to tell if it was just one person?" Darcy asked.

"One set of blurry boot prints on the grass here. Maybe we should follow the tire tracks through the fence."

"That won't cause a security problem, will it?"

Alex answered, crooking one corner of his mouth, "No more than we already seem to have."

Almost in spite of herself, she laughed. "True that," she replied. "Well, let's walk back and follow the fence line around from inside. Maybe Dasher will notice something else. This bomber must have scouted and maybe he didn't always use the same hole in the fence."

The trip proved fruitless, however. The truck tracks rutted through the wet ground approaching the building but not too closely.

Darcy stared at where they ended, evaluating. "Bigger bomb, but not so big he couldn't carry it to the building. Maybe in pieces." She pointed. "Then he backed out, right?"

"I'd agree," said Marcus. "The tracks mostly run over each other. One set in, one set out—one vehicle and, from the trampled ground, my guess is one perp. From this point on, however, Dasher might have a problem tracking him because of the burn and explosion. Chances are he could, but unless it would serve a purpose, I'd rather not have him huffing whatever's in the debris zone."

Darcy nodded. "You've been a lot of help, but I agree. I registered some heavy metals last night while the fire was being put out. Nobody should go into the area without a mask."

"We need to know," Alex remarked, "what chemicals were being used in this plant. For safety reasons. Charity or Wade should have some idea in the firefighting plans."

Marcus took his dog back to the entry gate, leaving Darcy and Alex to walk around the perimeter, eyes glued to the ground for stray pieces of evidence.

Overall, however, the situation was looking overwhelming to Darcy. Working a scene like this with a team was one thing. Doing it solo? Even with all the help the fire department and police were providing, the technical aspects of an explosion this size were probably too great for one person to handle.

And maybe the bomber was counting on that.

Chapter 10

Damn kid, the bomber thought. He couldn't even go back now and see how much damage he'd managed to accomplish. If that kid had tracked him, someone else might have. Plus, he'd seen the kid talking to that female ATF agent. First he needed to pry every bit of knowledge out of that kid's head. He wasn't convinced the boy didn't know a whole lot about what ATF was doing. He'd learned long ago in a land far away that kids weren't exempt. No reason to think that just because someone looked young that they weren't an active agent. Or that they didn't know something important.

Then he had to get out of here. Quickly. Had to accelerate his plans as much as possible. He had one bomb almost ready to go, as soon as he was sure it was big enough and for that he needed to see the damage he'd done last night. But he also needed another one, and while he might be able to hurry the process, he wasn't sure that would be wise unless he wanted to risk a failure.

How soon would that kid be missed? Maybe by the end of the day. Then they'd start looking for him and find his car a little past here.

So he should probably deal with the car. Cover it in tumbleweeds, so it wouldn't be easily visible from the air. He doubted a cop would drive this road any-time in the next few days. There wasn't much out here that demanded their attention. Minimal camouflage was all he needed.

But he was tired. So tired. He'd burned up a lot of energy in setting up that bomb last night, then even more taking the kid out of the equation, at least for now.

Now the kid sat in an outbuilding by himself. He'd have to be fed and given some water soon, but not just yet.

Warren Trimble needed some rest. He was an angry man, but he was also a very sick man. He had a war he needed to finish, and he was rapidly passing the point of giving a damn whether any innocent people got in his way.

And that included the kid, whether he liked it or not. He had to tie the youngster up in a way that would make it clear to him he couldn't get away. Then he had to get him to talk. But first, better binding. That kid wasn't going anywhere ever again. Which meant drugging his water so he could chain him. Ropes and flex-cuffs wouldn't last much longer.

Sipping some muddy coffee, he closed his eyes, waiting for his energy to return a bit. Politicians started wars, but bureaucrats finished their dirty work for them. How many guys wound up killing themselves or living under bridges because there was no help for them when they got home? No help with the nightmares and the horror.

And then there were those like him who got physically ill and stayed that way, getting worse year after year and being told they were malingering.

Malingering! Every time he thought of that word he felt white-hot rage. Two Purple Hearts and they accused him of malingering. He'd proved he wasn't that kind of man by going back when he could have legitimately used his wounds to stay out of it.

And all his dead buddies—had they malingered themselves into early graves or severe disabilities?

Finally, many, many years later, they admitted maybe that Agent Orange wasn't so safe for humans after all. Then came the fight to have your particular illness diagnosed as being a result of exposure. They had every excuse in the book for getting around that. At last, a disability allowance which didn't begin to ease the pain, the suffering and finally the cancer that was killing him.

Yeah, he hated bureaucrats. And he was damn well going to make sure they remembered him and understood what they had done to him and so many other vets who had served their country. They deserved better than that. All of them. Your country called; you went; you bled, and if you were lucky enough to come home, you deserved proper treatment for your enduring problems, whatever they were, that had been caused by that service.

There was a time when he'd wanted to get even for

himself. Then he'd watched the new waves of vets returning. Listened to the news and realized they were getting the shaft, as well. Medical care in the field was saving lives, but as soon as those lives got back here, they were tossed on the heap of "used up." Not needed anymore. And all the talk about improving the VA wasn't getting much done at all from what he heard. Suicide rates were through the roof. Maybe those guys would have been happier if field medicine hadn't improved.

He didn't know. What he did know was he wanted to send a message for all of them, from past wars to future wars. Soldiers, sailors, airmen and marines weren't collateral damage. They weren't detritus. And if you asked young people to go, then you damn well ought to take care of them when they got home.

Nearly growling under his breath, he set to work soldering his final detonator. The last thing he'd do would be to mix the ANFO and put it in the ammo cases. He'd have to be feeling more rested before he could do that. Measurements were critical.

He rose, every inch of his body shrieking, and went to the cupboard shelf to pull out the det cord. For some reason he'd lately got edgy about whether he had enough of it. He knew he did. How many times had he measured it, the supply from years ago when he'd still been able to work and had lifted some from his job on a road construction crew.

But he measured it again anyway. He was past the point where he could afford a mistake.

At first he'd only wanted the bureaucrats, but he wouldn't mind taking some agents out, too. Somebody needed to start paying attention. And Warren Trimble was going to make them sit up and listen.

It was growing dark. The floodlights had an odd effect on vision. Big pieces of debris were very visible, but shadows were washed away by the surrounding lights. They provided security, but were beginning to become useless to help with finer work.

Darcy had taken measurements with the help of Alex and a few firefighters, and had a good idea of the blast radius inside and outside. She had the fire department's detailed description of the structure and saw that it was basically more of the same: concrete block with floors made out of reinforced concrete slabs.

"They really weren't expecting a fire," Charity remarked as the evening died. "Certainly not a bomb. Some of that collapse is just weak construction. To a point it was fireproof, but when temperatures get high enough…" She shrugged.

Darcy agreed.

"But I want you two to see something because it has a bearing on how you measure this."

They followed her, avoiding the blackened bomb radius as much as possible, and then, slipping inside, the gaping maw the bomb had made in the building.

Charity pointed. "This was part of the reason we had so much trouble putting this out. Something in here burned hot enough to make aluminum liquefy. That's about twelve hundred degrees, so add that to your calculations. It wasn't the bomb, though."

Darcy stared at the silver river running across the blackened concrete flooring. "Can you tell what else burned?"

"We're looking, but I don't think your bomber was planning on this. A side effect, maybe, but that's what was giving us fits last night. Most of the fires we deal with reach temperatures only half that high. Unless it's a forest fire anyway. So some of the damage you're going to be measuring here needs to take that into account."

"It certainly does." Again Darcy found herself wishing for a team. So many loose ends and she was trying to grab them all into her own two hands. "Thanks, Charity."

"I'll let you know if we find anything else. Meantime, I'm leaving it to the sheriff to guard this place. I need some sleep."

"That's a good idea," Alex said as he and Darcy circled away. She never stopped scanning the ground, as if some clue would leap out at her. But it had been a long day of sorting through detritus and she seriously wondered if she'd recognize a detonator if it leaped out at her.

Just as they were back on the grass and striding slowly to the gate, she paused and pointed.

"What?" he asked.

"Det cord." Squatting, she used her tablet to take a photo of it. Then she pulled a laser range finder out of one of her pockets and measured the distance to what she believed to be the point of the explosion. After taking a few steps to the right, she took another reading, triangulating.

"Okay," she said finally. "Tomorrow's another day. And this guy is going to need at least a little time to get another one of these ready."

She hoped. Because she sure as hell wasn't going to

find him standing here with bleary eyes. Meanwhile, the information she'd already uploaded was grinding along and would soon come back to her with a suggested plot of where everything had been placed.

Twelve hundred degrees? God.

Once again they picked up dinner at the diner and took it back to Alex's house with them.

Darcy joined him at his kitchen table and had a sudden thought. "Alex?"

"Yeah?" He was busy moving food from foam containers to real plates.

"How enlightened is this place?"

"Meaning?"

"Is my staying here going to get you in trouble with the school board or anything?"

He laughed. "I think we've moved out of the twentieth century."

"Are you sure?" But she liked the way his eyes twinkled as he smiled at her. He must be every bit as tired as she was feeling after this day, but he wasn't showing it.

"Absolutely." He pushed a plate her way with utensils and passed her one of the coffees. "I'm trying to remember the last time anyone around here gave a damn about a teacher's living arrangement. Oh, yeah, one time."

"Really? Why was that different?"

His tone turned dry. "Because the teacher was dating an underage student."

Darcy felt her jaw drop, then closed it. She wasn't *that* sheltered. "Is that growing more common or something?"

"I think we're just hearing about it more often. So no, I'm not worried that folks are going to get bent because the shop teacher has an ATF agent staying for a few days. *Everyone* knows the condition of the local motel."

"Might be a good project for someone, although I have to say the place is awfully clean. No complaints in that department."

Their meal was mostly quiet. Alex spoke briefly about some of the projects his students had been working on that the bomb had destroyed, but even that trailed away.

Darcy was sure they were both thinking about the second bomb.

But not just the bomb. The sexual miasma that had gripped them this morning before their phones rang seemed to be seeping into the room with them once again. She felt it begin to sparkle through her body until an ache built once again deep within her.

She tried to argue herself out of giving in to it. This wasn't professional. She had a job to do. She should be spending every single minute trying to find some link to the bomber that the local authorities would use. She wasn't even sure they'd have as much time before the next bomb, time for the FBI to send some agents to help.

Although she wasn't sure exactly how they'd help. From what she'd seen of the local police, they had a huge leg up on outsiders: they knew nearly everyone. If someone was out of kilter in this county, he was probably already under the microscope even if he didn't know it.

What could the FBI come up with?

Mainly, she wished she had superpowers and could just put an end to this now. This last bomb had seriously worried her. Someone could get hurt by the next one. They were getting bigger, so firefighters were at even more risk. And what if the next target was occupied?

So why was she sitting here feeling as if her body were turning into warm honey and the only thing that mattered right now was whether Alex was feeling the same?

When he rose to clear the table and put the dishes in the dishwasher, she didn't offer to help. Instead she sat there like a teenager, watching his every move, feeling that each stirring of his body stirred her passion even more, like hot coals on a fire.

A gorgeous man. Perfect in every way. There wasn't a thing about his appearance that she would change—except maybe to talk him into letting his hair grow longer.

When he turned from the counter, drying his hands on a towel, their eyes locked and she lost her ability to breathe.

Then a slow smile began to crease his face. "You look hungry," he drawled.

"For you," she admitted, astonishing herself with her own boldness. But not enough to change her mood. It was true, and lying didn't come naturally to her.

"I'm feeling the same way. And as near as I can tell, the rest of the world can wait until morning."

She decided it could. It was as if the day that had passed since they began to make love that morning had never happened. Her entire body ramped up to that exquisite place instantly, and all she wanted was to get every impediment out of the way immediately.

But Alex had other ideas. He led her down the hallway to his bedroom, where he turned on a single, dim lamp on his dresser. It created warm shadows in the room without casting too much light.

It was as if they had entered another world. Everything else dropped away like shedding an uncomfortable skin. Alex held out his hands to her, and when she clasped them he drew her close until she brushed against his chest.

"I've been trying to remain professional," he said. He released one of her hands and reached up to remove the clip from her hair. She felt it spill to her shoulders, a sensation of freedom, unexpectedly sensuous. "I'm sure you have, too," he continued. "We were raised that way, in our jobs."

She felt the corners of her mouth lift slightly. "All professional."

"Yeah. It made sense back then. But I'm not your coworker. So how about we leave all that crap behind and just be a man and a woman?"

A long, surprisingly happy sigh escaped her as he then ran his fingers through her hair like a gentle comb.

"So silky," he murmured. "Beautiful hair." Then he surprised a small laugh out of her. "I hear mine is too short."

"I certainly can't run my fingers through it," she murmured.

"But you can run your fingers everywhere else."

With fingers that were becoming surprisingly awkward as all her energy seemed to be sinking to a point between her legs, she unbuttoned his shirt. He let go of her just long enough to shrug it off, revealing a well-muscled chest.

"Sorry I don't have a shield or sword," he murmured.

"My Viking." It sounded so possessive, but not out of place in that moment. Then she shook her head a little at her own silliness, but before it could take over, he pulled the zipper on the front of her overalls and drove her thoughts and sensations in an entirely different direction.

Cool air slipped across her skin, feeling so very different from her overalls. The air's touch was immediately followed by the lightest brush of his fingertips as they traced her shoulders and collarbones before shoving the material down and out of the way.

Her eyes had closed, leaving room for nothing in her world except physical sensations that were weakening her and inflaming her all at the same time. When she felt the pop as her bra clasp released, her knees practically turned to water.

But then his hands roamed her even more, dragging material down her arms, then sweeping upward until they ran across sensitive skin above her breasts.

Anticipation and anxiety filled her, an eager fear that he might just stop. Fear that he wouldn't touch her breasts and longing that he would do so soon.

She felt herself puckering, reaching for his touches. When at last her arms fell free of the overalls, she reached out and found his waist, urging him closer, wishing he would answer all the promises his hands kept teasing her with.

Her insides clenched with longing, then began to squeeze in a steady rhythm, letting her know what she wanted as if she wouldn't have known otherwise. She became a throbbing mass of need and he'd barely begun.

"Alex," she whispered.

Alex heard his name escape her and it warmed him. She wanted him at least as much as he wanted her, but he kept banking the fires that threatened to consume him. He might never again get a chance to make love to this woman, and he wanted to stamp a memory of pure pleasure and joy in her heart forever. Though nothing could come of this, he still wanted to be sure that anytime in the future she thought of him, the memory would bring a smile to her face. It seemed like a small enough wish.

Lowering his head, holding her around her small waist, he found her breast with his mouth. A hardened nipple teased him, and he sucked it deeply into his mouth, enjoying her groan and the way her hands flew up to grasp his head. Wonderfully responsive, and her responses fired him even more.

His groin throbbed, hammering at him that he was ready, but he wanted to be sure that Darcy was, too. As ready as she could get. He wanted to take her all the way to bliss, out of this world and into a different realm.

He moved his mouth to her other breast and felt her fingertips digging into his scalp as if she wanted to pull him inside her. His hands around her waist felt her hips begin to rock toward him, reaching for him just as her hands did.

Raising his head, he found her lips with his and his tongue dived deeply into her mouth. She welcomed him generously, her tongue dueling with his in imitation of the final consummation.

At last he could restrain himself no more. Gripping her around her hips, he lifted her and placed her on the bed, forgetting all finesse in his need to have her.

Her boots at least didn't fight him. Then he stripped the last of her overalls and underclothes away and stood over her, drinking in her beauty by the dim, golden light.

"Perfect," he rasped.

"Hurry." She interrupted, lifting her hand toward him.

He was happy to oblige. He stripped off the rest of his own clothing, then tumbled down beside her, pulling her close, savoring the incredible sensation of warm skin against warm skin. She felt as smooth as satin everywhere their bodies met, and he felt her eagerness in the gentle rolling of her hips.

He was stiff and hard for her already, but pressing against her, flattening himself against her belly, felt exquisite. He could have stayed like that forever.

But then her hands began to roam, touching wherever she could reach. His back, his shoulders, his chest, squeezing the small points of his nipples until she dragged a helpless groan from him.

Later, said a devil in his mind, urging him to hurry. There'd be a later to take things slowly and draw out every perfect moment.

"Alex…" This time his name sounded almost like a keening cry. Rolling over her, he pulled the drawer of his night table open and brought out a foil packet. Even in the hazy, flaming hinterland of desire, he wouldn't put her at risk.

* * *

Darcy's eyes opened a bit and she saw what she was doing. Without hesitation, she reached out to help him roll the condom on. His hardness felt so good to her, the skin the softest thing she had ever touched, but then it was covered, concealed, but ready.

"I love the way you did that," he said gruffly, then bent his head again to seek her breasts with his mouth. As soon as he did, she felt herself rising, as if the bed beneath her was falling away and she was levitating into space.

Before she could completely drift away, however, he thrust into her, bringing her to him, spearing her in the most delicious way. A shudder of sheer pleasure ran through her as he stretched her, reminding her it had been so long…

Then she forgot everything else as he pumped into her and she began to levitate anew. Stars exploded behind her eyelids. Every nerve in her body drew tight as an archer's bow.

Up, like a lighter-than-air balloon, held to reality only by his plunging shaft. When the ache of need became almost too much to bear, it exploded, leaving a gentler ache in its wake that wouldn't let her stop moving, not until she felt Alex stiffen and find his own completion.

The fireworks inside her head kept on exploding, making her oblivious to everything except bliss.

Miles away, night had fallen and Jack was about to go nuts from his confinement. Something had happened earlier. Drugs? He didn't know for sure, because he'd had a bad blow to his head, but when he woke up, he found his bindings had changed.

Now he had a chain around his neck and another around his ankle. No matter how hard he pulled and yanked, it was soon clear the best he could hope for was to strangle himself. The chain wouldn't break; it just tightened when he pulled on it. Like a noose. *Trapped!*

He'd worked his legs as much as possible, pulling them up to his chest again and yet again. The chain on his ankle allowed that much, but the one around his neck wouldn't let him stand. When he rose more than a few inches, it tightened enough to make him choke. It was a wonder he hadn't strangled while he'd been unconscious.

At least his arms were free and no longer felt like they were being pulled out of their sockets. Not that it helped when he couldn't do anything with them.

And his butt! Damn, he'd never imagined the agony of sitting on a hard surface for so long. Hell, he'd never held still this long in his entire life.

Just within reach were a pile of protein bars and a plastic bottle of water.

So he ate because the consequence of growing weak might be a lost chance to escape. As for drinking, he stared suspiciously at the water bottle, wondering if it contained drugs. He held off as long as he could, but water was a much-stronger imperative than food. Eventually he wet his mouth and waited to see if he reacted in any way.

The guy kept his face covered on the rare occasions when he appeared, which Jack thought was probably a good sign. No reason to hide his face if he intended to kill Jack.

But this entire incarceration was beginning to be the worst experience of Jack's life ever. He was learning the true meaning of discomfort, and the guy who held him didn't give a damn.

"So you were in Vietnam?" he asked the next time the guy appeared with a bottle of water, since he didn't seem in a hurry to leave. Instead, he sat on that chair in the shadows and just watched Jack.

"Didn't I say so?"

"Yeah." *Great, Jack.* That would really get this man talking. "So does that have anything to do with this?"

"With what?"

Jack suddenly realized he was missing some important information and running on guesswork. He hadn't seen this man set the bomb. Hadn't seen any indication that he was building them. All he'd seen was a pickup drive away from the explosion at the semiconductor plant.

Admittedly, given that he was now a prisoner, it was likely that this man had something to do with that bomb. But he couldn't know that for sure, and maybe it would be best to play dumb about it.

"Keeping me prisoner like this."

The man didn't answer for a while. The chair he sat on creaked, but no other sound disturbed the night except for the hoot of a very distant owl.

"You think I get my jollies out of tying boys up?"

Jack stiffened. Not much he could do to protect himself from this man's ire. "I didn't say that."

"No? Then what are you saying, boy?"

Which led directly to the place Jack had been trying

to avoid. Although maybe that knock to his head had been worse than he thought. Man, he'd followed this guy out here, had come creeping back on foot... Yeah, that looked like idle curiosity. Some ATF agent he'd make.

"Just curious," Jack said. "I don't know much about Vietnam."

"Nobody does anymore. Those old enough to remember are happy to pretend it never happened."

Jack thought about it. "Does that make you feel bad?"

"Not as bad as knowing my own government poisoned me and my buddies."

"What!" The word was startled out of Jack.

"Agent Orange. You ever hear of it? No, of course not. They'd like that story dead and buried."

"What is it?"

"An herbicide. At first it was used against agricultural land, to destroy crops and drive people away. Some was used near the mountains to clear jungle as much as possible. Whatever the reasoning, it contained some really dangerous chemicals and a lot of people got sick. Even their unborn children were affected. A lot of court cases and finally we got a pittance out of the manufacturer. And I got a disability because I've been sick from the exposure for decades. Now it's killing me."

Jack didn't know what to say as horror crept through him, filling him with both disbelief and fear that this could be true. His government had done this?

"Lots of folks still don't believe it was that poisonous. But over the years... Well, over the years the diseases showed up, both among the troops and in Vietnam. People over there are still getting sick and

being born deformed because of it. But I watched my
buddies die, kid, and all the while the people who did
it to them denied all responsibility."

Jack swallowed hard. "That must make you mad."

"I'm past mad. They need to learn a lesson. They
need to learn that if you're going to send people out
to fight, then you need to take care of them when
they get home."

Now Jack was on certain ground. "I absolutely
agree!"

His captor fell silent for a long time. Jack considered asking for more water, but he was already uncomfortable enough. "I need a bathroom."

"Ain't gonna get one. Sit in it, the way I had to."

Then the man rose, little more than a dark shadow.
He moved slowly, whether by choice or necessity Jack
couldn't tell.

"But…what you're doing…"

"Call it a teaching moment. Next time I come back,
you're going to tell me everything you know."

"I know? I don't know anything!" Which had never
felt truer to Jack than it did right then.

"Think I'm fooled? I saw you with the ATF. You're
one of them. And you're going to tell me everything
you know or you won't see another sunrise." The
man's broken laugh followed him out as he left the
shed and locked the door.

Jack sat staring into the near dark, trying to ab-
sorb it all. Agent Orange. A long-ago war. A man who
clearly was not well using bombs to send a message.

But what kind of message could he send by blowing
up empty buildings? It wasn't making sense.

Maybe he had other targets in mind. Jack felt an unnatural chill trickle down his spine.

He needed to warn someone, but nothing he did freed him. This guy knew what he was doing, and he knew how to keep a prisoner from escaping.

What was worse, he seemed to think Jack knew something, that he was an agent. Jack wondered if he were facing the last night of his life.

Darcy, wrapped snugly in Alex's arms beneath a layer of blankets, never wanted to move again. She felt as if he had claimed every cell in her body, as if he was a deep-rooted part of her now.

Moving might ruin this marvelous feeling, might drive it away for good. She was quite sure she'd never felt so much magic running through her in her entire life. Maybe he wasn't just a Viking, maybe he was a Viking god. He'd transformed her so quickly.

The silly thought amused her even through her haze of happiness. She wanted to stay here forever, live in this moment until the end of time.

Alex pulled her a little closer, his lips seeking hers, his hands running down her back to her bottom, sending freshened sparks of hunger through her. She had a vague idea that it was around midnight, which meant there were a lot of hours left to them.

But Alex spoke quietly. "Sleep," he said. "I know I don't want to, but tomorrow's another day and you have to have your wits about you."

"You keep pushing me to rest," she mumbled, hating the way that reality persisted in returning. Wasn't she entitled to just a little escape? A few hours?

"Darcy, I've seldom seen anyone work as hard as

you do. But it's dangerous. You don't want to slip up. So as much as I'd love to ravish you again, I think that needs to wait. At least until morning."

She smiled against his cheek at the implied promise. "Have I told you I like you?"

"I kinda got that feeling a little while ago." Amusement trembled in his voice.

"You're bossy, though. But for some reason I don't mind. Anyway, I like you. And I don't want to go to sleep."

She doubted she would anyway, because his reminder of reality had caused guilt to start gnawing at her again. Important, dangerous matters needed to be dealt with, and she was ignoring them right now.

"You're getting stirred up again," he remarked. Then, without a word, he rolled over her until he lay on top of her. "I know how to wear you out."

He certainly did, she thought as he began to explore her entire body with his mouth and hands, teaching her things she'd never known about herself before, placing his mouth where no man ever had. Not that she'd had that much experience.

But when his tongue found her velvety folds and focused in on the exquisitely sensitive nub there, she felt pleasure and pain in equal measures, causing her to cry out and rise to meet him. Reality vanished to some dark hole as her world exploded in brilliant lights and intense sensations that blocked everything else.

Touch by touch, he teased her, lifting her until she floated somewhere in space, untethered from everything except him, his hands, his mouth, his heat.

This time there was no gentleness to him, just a demand for her response, and she gladly gave it. She felt a prisoner to his touch, allowing herself to be used however he chose and exulting in it.

Then, at last, he slid up over her and claimed her, following her to the dizzying heights he'd shown her before, then carrying her even higher.

Every brush of his body against hers, every thrust of his hips, taught her that ecstasy had many sides and many sources. When at last she could endure no more, she cried out, then heard his groan as he followed her into a new level of joy.

And he was right. Before he even withdrew, she slid into the netherworld of sleep.

Alex had the worst urge to beat the pillow when his cell phone buzzed on the bedside table. A couple of hours of sleep and now this?

He reached for it, hoping it wouldn't disturb Darcy. That woman worked way too hard. Not that he hadn't been guilty of the same thing in his time, but he knew where that kind of obsession led. It wasn't pretty. A human being had physical needs that couldn't be ignored for long. A need to take at least a brief time off to rest and recuperate. Failing to do that could lead to the kind of breakdown he'd had, a breakdown that had cost him the things he cared most about in the world: his wife and daughter. Some fences, once broken, could never be mended.

He hoped he'd learned his lesson. He hoped even more that Darcy never needed to.

Holding the phone to his ear, he said quietly, "Yeah." He recognized the sheriff's voice instantly.

"Just letting you know," Gage said. "Jack Castor's family reported him missing. He said he'd gone to stay with some friends last night and was supposed to be back hours ago. Anyway, no one's seen him since late yesterday, and he didn't stay with a friend."

"You need me?"

"We've got everyone we can spare out looking for him. We're assuming he might have had an auto accident. But if he vanished for some other reason, given his interest in the ATF, we're thinking he might seek you or Darcy out. I wanted you to know in case he doesn't call his family. I don't know what the hell has got into that kid."

Alex had some idea, and it worried the hell out of him. And, of course, Gage suspected. Tell him to keep his ear to the ground and what had he done? Even Gage hadn't thought that would be especially dangerous, but now Alex would have bet he'd gone haring off after some clue and got himself into trouble.

He just hoped the young man was still alive.

"Alex?" Darcy's groggy voice reached him.

He wished he could tell her to roll over and go back to sleep, but he was pretty certain she'd never forgive the lie.

"Jack. He's missing."

Stomachs full of cereal, two thermoses of hot coffee between them, they set out in Darcy's vehicle. Three o'clock in the morning. The birds weren't even up yet.

"It's my fault," Darcy said. "I should have told him to stay the hell away or I'd have him arrested for interfering with an investigation. But no, what did I do? Asked him to listen. To *listen*. I should have read him better than that."

"It's not your job."

"You were worried. You even told me I'd made a mistake. Then when he wanted me to clear his name... What if someone went after him because they think *he's* the bomber?"

"Look," Alex argued, "he could have had a car accident. Some of the roads in this county are bad enough that they ought to be marked with a skull and crossbones. Or a sign saying Drive at Your Own Risk."

She was not amused. Nor did Alex expect it. Although he had the fleeting thought that if he found out that boy was okay and sleeping at some friend's house where no one even suspected he was, he might give him a good verbal shaking.

His family was probably out of their minds. Local law was at full mobilization. Hell, there was even a helicopter overhead, probably using the new night-vision equipment they'd got a couple of years ago.

But it wouldn't see a cold dead body.

"Damn." He slammed his hand on the steering wheel, which wasn't exactly calculated to make Darcy feel any better. Not that words would do that. Only finding Jack safe and alive was going to help.

"You've got a bomb site to investigate today," he reminded her. "You need to let the rest of us hunt for Jack."

"To hell with it. The site isn't going anywhere. We've got to find that boy."

"Two of us looking isn't going to make a difference. I should have brought my own car so I could leave you and your equipment. Goddamn it, Darcy, we've got a bomber. You know that. And you know as well as I do that if we don't stop *him* he could kill a lot of people."

"Opposing priorities," she answered tautly. "Right now all I know is that it's my fault there's a seventeen-year-old boy out there trying to play ATF agent without any training, without any knowledge, without any backup. I can't blame anyone else for that. I should have realized I needed to stuff him in a cell."

"On what grounds? The stupidity of youth? Anyway, we don't know he tangled with the bomber. He probably just went off the road out in the middle of nowhere and it's a helluva long hike back to town or his ranch."

"We should be so lucky."

He agreed, but he wasn't about to say so. He thought Jack had more brains than to get himself into an untenable situation. But maybe he was wrong, too. Kids his age—their brains weren't wired to anticipate consequences. He *knew* that. So if anyone was to blame here, it was him.

And they still didn't know if there was any blame.

"We've got to find him, Alex. I'm going to call for more help from my boss this morning. We need bomb experts, more than me. No one can put this off as an experiment anymore. This bomber has a goal, and I've got the sickening feeling it isn't right around here."

Miles away in the middle of almost nowhere, in the rolling hills at the foot of the mountains, Warren Trimble had begun to load his van with what he needed. The kid finding him had unnerved him. He still had some work to do before these bombs were ready, but he was confident enough of his skills now to figure he could find some place isolated enough to finish.

The ANFO was packed into the ammo cans. Det cord hung in a coil from the side of the interior wall. The detonators, simple to the extreme, were almost done. He could finish them now without much trouble. The small holes in the ammo cans had been plugged by caulk, waiting for the det cord.

And if he couldn't get the detonators wired up properly, then he'd set the cord off by hand.

The nice thing, the only nice thing, about being a dead man walking was that he didn't care if his own bombs blew him up. It was the message that counted, a message that he was going to upload to the internet as soon as he filmed it. He'd say everything he had to say then.

Imagine that kid not knowing about Agent Orange or the ravages it created. He'd gone back to the Nam twenty years ago with a group of vets, and they'd seen how those people were still suffering from the effects of that defoliant. Little kids, two generations later, being born sick and deformed. The soil and water still poisoned after all this time. Farmers from that era living in small villages created to take care of them. Weren't many left.

He'd seen. He'd donated to their care.

But nobody took care of his fellows. Nobody wanted to admit the atrocity they'd created. They just wanted it all to die and be forgotten.

Well, he was going to make sure they got a loud reminder before the cancer took him.

So as soon as they were ready, he'd set the bombs at the state and federal veterans affairs offices in Casper.

Then, before he blew them up, he'd launch the message to the internet. As for the kid, he was going to give him one more chance to tell him how much the ATF had figured out. One more. The boy could deny he knew anything, but Trimble's own eyes had seen otherwise.

Probably didn't matter now, though. He was ready to move. All he had to do was wire the outbuilding in case they found it before he acted. Shut down anything that boy could tell about him, like the reasons for these bombs. He didn't want anyone putting it together too soon.

These next two bombs were designed to kill, unlike the first two. He wasn't worried about taking a few bureaucrats along with him. Not at all. They'd been making his life hell for an awfully long time. Sometimes he thought their only instructions were to obstruct.

But they'd turned Warren Trimble into a killer. A boy not much older than that kid he'd caught. They'd made sure he'd be their weapon. But what did you do with a weapon when you didn't need it any longer? Well, if it was a rifle or a nuclear missile, they'd find a use for it. A man—not so much. Especially if it appeared that you'd injured him in some way and maybe owed him something.

Warren had had a long time to grow bitter. He knew he was bitter and he didn't give a damn anymore. He'd spent most of his life since that damn war sick with one thing or another, living with a lot of pain, and he'd grown weary of being dismissed when he said it was the chemical exposure. Then, finally they'd started to admit it, and it was still a headache.

The company that made the stuff managed to get most of the money awarded by the court and the vets had been pretty much stiffed. He supposed he should be grateful that the volunteers at the VA had worked long and hard to get him on disability or he'd have been starving by the roadside.

Too sick to work the ranch he'd inherited, too sick to get a job, too sick except to feed his anger and plot his revenge. Pain was his constant companion most of the time. Now here he was, close to death with leukemia, and nobody tried to tell him this time it didn't have anything to do with the defoliants. Too late. Of course, it had been too late since the original exposure.

He thought of that kid sitting in the outbuilding. More hair than brains. Like they'd all been at his age. He didn't want the boy to come to harm, but he couldn't risk him getting out and telling everyone that Warren Trimble was the bomber. They'd know that as soon as they found this place. As soon as they triggered the bomb he was leaving behind. The kid wouldn't be able to talk, which was all that mattered, and right now he didn't give a damn about anything except finishing his mission.

Of course, Warren knew it wasn't easy to find a solo man unless he did something stupid. Which is why Warren had spare plates for his truck, so they couldn't find him that way. As long as he didn't get stopped on the road, he'd be fine. Anyone looking for him wouldn't recognize the plates.

Then there were other ways to avoid detection. He had magnetic signs for the sides of his battered van identifying him as a plumber. Treatment for his leukemia had left him bald, so he didn't resemble any photograph ever taken of him. He had a cell phone in another name that he'd never activated, so they wouldn't be able to track him that way, either.

He'd be safe from detection until he wanted to be found.

But that kid in the outbuilding.

What conscience hadn't been burned out of him bothered him. All that boy had done was follow him, probably hoping to find out who he was. A stupid but understandable reaction from a kid that age. Become a hero. Oh, yeah.

Except he hadn't been smart enough to creep up on an old soldier. For that he was going to have to die.

Warren finished loading the last of his materials into his big van. He'd put the magnetic signs on the side once he was out of here.

But first the kid. He knew perfectly well the kid had been suffering the tortures of the damned being confined like that for so long. Just so long you could sit in one position. Just so long your arms could take being unable to move. By now he must be about as miserable as it was possible to be short of torture. Now maybe he'd be ready to talk.

So he locked up the van and headed back inside his house for a beer. He needed to think of something, then get the hell out before someone found the kid's car.

Yeah, it was covered in sagebrush. Yeah, this road was in the middle of nowhere. But he'd heard a chopper in the distance, so he figured they were looking, probably with thermal technology.

Time was getting short, thanks to that boy.

Half a beer later, when he was sure no rotors were overhead, he made his way back to the outbuilding.

The kid looked gaunt now, his eyes hollowing out from the pain and discomfort of his position. Maybe even from the humiliation of not being allowed to use the facilities.

Warren didn't feel terribly proud of himself, but he was past caring.

"Kid, you better start talking or…" He made no secret of the ammo can he carried. He put it on the floor near the youth but out of reach. Then he plugged a length of det cord into it.

"You know what this is? It's a bomb. Ever seen det cord before?" He held it up. "If I wrapped this around you and set it off, you'd be a crispy critter in no time. But maybe I'll be kinder. A bomb is faster. And don't think anyone's going to rescue you. I'm putting a trip wire on this. Anyone gets close, they'll die along with you."

The boy gave him a hollow-eyed look. "What do you think you're doing? Getting even for what?"

"For all the lies. For them poisoning me and a whole lot of other people. You put on that uniform, son, and you aren't a human being anymore. Not in the eyes of the bureaucrats. You're like a pawn on the chessboard, and if you're lucky enough to get home, they kick you to the curb. They're still doing it. You reading about our boys coming home now?"

"I've heard some stuff."

"Bet it barely touches on the size of the problem. You see, nobody's got any use for a soldier when they can't fight anymore. Or when the war's over. No use at all. So the soldier pays. He got a family? They pay, too. They wish we'd all just died so we'd stop being a problem."

"I don't know anyone who thinks that."

"You ain't been around enough. They want us to be invisible. Don't want to be disturbed by reminders of what they made us do."

"Not everyone feels that way."

"Not everyone, maybe. But enough."

"So what are you going to do?"

"Finish my mission. And no, I won't tell you a damn thing more."

Jack tried to speak, but the guy silenced him.

"You see, boy, I'm a dead man walking. And I don't give a damn anymore about anything except being heard one last time. So now you're going to tell me what your friends at ATF know about what I'm doing, and maybe I won't wrap this cord around you and light it."

Jack closed his eyes. His entire body was quivering with terror. His voice cracked as he spoke. "I don't know anything. I'm not an agent. I'm a high school senior and I barged into the investigation because I want to be ATF someday, and they told me twice to get lost. That's all I know. So you might as well wrap that cord around me right now."

Just as dawn was breaking, when he was sure no chopper was flying over, Warren Trimble drove away from his run-down ranch one final time.

Tomorrow, he thought. *Or the next day.* But no longer. People were going to pay.

Chapter 11

As daylight began to illuminate the scene of the most recent bombing, Darcy spoke.

"Jack."

"What about him?"

"What if he was here? What if he saw the bomber and chased after him? Let's go look at those tire tracks again. They might give us a direction to look."

"They might," he agreed. "And neither of us might like what we find. You stay here, I'll go look."

She faced him squarely. "I feel responsible for him. The fire department is doing a good enough job at the moment. To get much more done, I'm going to need a team, or this is going to drag on forever regardless. This second bombing makes it imperative we move swiftly. And damn whoever was so sure the first one was an accident."

When they reached the place where muddy tire tracks had alerted them yesterday, they climbed out of Darcy's truck and began to walk the road.

"Away from town," Darcy suggested.

"Agreed."

Unlikely the bomber would have fled back to Conard City, although it was possible. Anyway, they had to find a second set of tracks in the mud in order to follow them.

"No guarantee it was Jack, though," he remarked.

"No, but Jack's the only person reported missing. Isn't your radar pinging?"

He nodded. Indeed it was. One of the deputies had mentioned that Jack had been seen driving around the college campus on the cart path late the night before last. So he was out and doing something, clearly not staying with a friend.

The college wasn't that far from this building. Jack could have arrived here very quickly, and if the bomber had hung around briefly to watch the results of his work... Well, Jack might have been foolish and brave enough to follow him.

No guarantees, but it was obvious to Alex that Darcy had put Jack ahead of everything else. And while he didn't disagree with her priorities, he also was worried that they needed something to lead them to the bomber before someone got killed.

As they climbed out to survey the tracks left in the muddy soil during the rain, he reached a decision.

"Finding Jack alive might be our best lead to this bomber."

Darcy nodded, her lips compressed into a tight line. "He might be. But I can't rest until we find him. Jack is out there because I put him up to it."

"Like you ever suspected he might go chasing after a bad guy."

"It doesn't matter what I suspected," she said tautly. "It remains I didn't shoo him off. I didn't threaten him with interfering with an investigation... I didn't do anything to make him stay away from this mess. That's on my head and no one else's."

"Look, the sheriff said they'd all be keeping an eye on him."

"You ought to know how hard it is to keep an eye on one person. If anyone saw him the other night, they probably thought he was just tooling around the campus before going home to bed. Nobody would be uptight about it."

"Exactly."

He hoped she heard him. He hoped she understood. But nobody would have predicted anything like what they suspected right now. That Jack had risked his neck to try to find out who the bomber was.

No, he thought. *Not alone*. Jack was bright, unusually bright for someone his age. But apparently this time he hadn't paused to consider what might happen. Partly due to his age, but Jack had never really fallen into that group before. As well as he knew Jack, Alex wouldn't have anticipated this possibility. Not that he'd chase someone. Call the cops? Yes, he would have expected that from Jack.

Apparently he hadn't known the young man as well as he'd thought.

Darcy didn't think she was abandoning her post. The likelihood that she'd find the clue to the bomber's identity and his intentions in that heap of rubble was small. Even all the helping hands of the firefighters and cops had turned up little that was useful except a potential ammo can. How many people in this county had probably served in the military and understood the use of that container for an improvised bomb?

Too many. The sheriff was talking to some vets he trusted to see if anyone suspected that someone they knew could be capable of this. So far, no one.

FBI was arriving tomorrow. Well, they could dig deeper into military backgrounds, but they'd probably be left with a stack of names to go through, of people who might have improvised bombs during their careers.

Then there was that deputy—Micah Parish. He'd run those metal fragments to the state lab. Maybe the results would come in soon, although that would lead them to another place too full of suspects.

Online purchases of ammo cans? The sheriff had been looking but it was amazing how many places sold that kind of surplus, mainly as watertight storage containers for food. Another blank.

One blank after another, and now maybe Jack had got himself into trouble, maybe even killed, because he might have followed someone away from the explosion.

At this point, she didn't much care about anything except finding Jack. She needed a whole damn team now that there'd been a second explosion. She needed background checks, maybe VA medical records, enough people to sift through the debris to find some more useful clue than a possible metal can.

And if, by the grace of God, Jack was still alive, he might turn out to be the most useful clue of all. Once she got through dressing him down, she was going to ask the ATF to find a scholarship for that young man. Best to send him to college, then train him, for his own sake.

Jack knew the bomber was gone. He felt it as if the air had changed. Before, he'd felt a weight surrounding him, as if darkness were trying to close in, but now the world felt normal again. The darkness had moved on.

Maybe he was just being fanciful, but he was past caring. He was tethered by that chain locked around his throat. No way to wriggle out of it or break it without strangling himself. He knew because he'd tried repeatedly.

But there was food and water within reach, and somewhat-softer hay to sit on, and feeling was beginning to return to his butt.

There was also an ammo can sitting ten feet away with that cord running out of it toward the door. Apparently that cord was some kind of fuse, because the guy had said if he wrapped it around Jack, it would fry him.

All he'd done, all he'd risked, and he still didn't know who the guy was. Right then he felt like one great big failure. His parents were probably worried to death. The sheriff had to be searching for him. Work on the bomb scenes had probably halted because one teenage boy, a stupid one evidently, had disappeared.

No one had asked him to follow anyone. All Darcy had asked was that he keep his ears open in case he heard something. If he'd followed his orders, he wouldn't be stuck right here, unable to do anything to help.

After this, assuming he survived that bomb that

was keeping him company, even if he managed to go to college and apply to the ATF, they'd probably tell him to get lost. He'd screwed everything up.

For all he knew, after this they might even charge him with something, like getting in the way of an investigation or whatever it was called. Maybe he'd be better off dead.

Especially since the guy had taken off. He might still be here, within reach if they found the right clue, so he could be stopped.

But no, Jack had scared him into leaving. Now the bomber was out there, probably making sure no one could find him even if Jack was found and they learned who owned this place.

Jack half wished the bomb would just go off so that someone would come quickly enough to hunt the guy down.

Alex found the tire tracks. Here and there they ran over the first set that had pulled away from the building the night of the explosion, but that indicated they were fresher. They called for the opinion of one of the deputies. Sarah Ironheart and Sergeant Beauregard came quickly.

"We think Jack might have seen the bomber," Alex explained.

"And possibly followed him," Darcy added. "We've got two sets of tracks here. One belongs to the truck that went through the fence but is the other set newer or older?"

"Hard to tell given the rain the other day," Sarah remarked, squatting. "Beau?"

"Yeah." He, too, squatted, then looked farther down the road. "Maybe we should follow a bit."

Sarah nodded. "Just what I was thinking. And we need to know how many people might have driven along here since the rain."

Together the four of them walked up the road a way, then Darcy suddenly stopped. "Are those fresh tracks overlaying? Breaking up the dried mud?"

Sarah squatted again, poking a finger into the crumbled earth. "Yup. Someone drove through here since the road started to dry out. During the night maybe. We have to find out if anyone saw a vehicle from the scene."

Beau walked a little farther down, then spoke. "Different tire treads, longer wheel base, slightly bent frame. It wasn't the truck that pulled away from the building. Not a car at all, I'm thinking."

Darcy felt her heart sink. "I'm going to get my vehicle and keep heading out this way, unless there's a reason I shouldn't."

"I'll go with you," said Alex.

Sarah stood and looked at them. "Remember, you two, you might be chasing a bomber. You find anything, Darcy, anything at all, you radio immediately."

Of course, she'd radio immediately. She wasn't foolish enough to think she could stand up to a crazed man who might be armed, even with Alex's help. But she had to find Jack. First and foremost, find that young man alive.

Guilt rode her like a heavy weight and gnawed at the edges of her mind. No way could she convince herself she wasn't in some way responsible for Jack's disappearance. Nothing Alex said could relieve her of that burden. Even the bit about what was she supposed to have done—lock him in a cell?

But if he'd actually seen and followed the bomber...
God, she couldn't stand to think of it.

When she and Alex were in her truck, ready to follow the road to wherever it led, Sarah flagged them.

Darcy rolled her window down. "Yes?"

"I'm going to check with the sheriff. You may find that you've got some deputies on your tail. He might pull some of us from elsewhere in the search, okay?"

"Thanks. If we find anything, we're going to need you guys."

Sarah's smile was faint. "I know. Now, get going."

For the first time in his life, Jack understood true loneliness. Sitting in an outbuilding probably somewhere near the guy's property, in the company of a bomb, kind of made cold winds blow inside him, like he was in a desert in the middle of the night all by himself.

No one to call. No friendly face to look for. No one to find him who probably wouldn't be blown up the instant they opened that door.

He hoped that if someone found him, they'd make enough noise that he'd hear and could call out a warning. He didn't want anybody else to die or get hurt because of his idiocy.

And he had been an idiot. What did he think he was going to accomplish following that guy? He should have kept driving, but no, he'd thought he could creep up on the house and maybe get some information to take back to Darcy. Be a hero. Solve the case.

When he thought of the painstaking work he'd seen

Darcy and everyone else doing as they sifted through the evidence... He should have known he wasn't going to fly in like a comic-book hero and save the day. He should have had more brains than that.

He'd disappointed himself, and now maybe he'd die for it. *Probably die*, he amended. The guy had left him some power bars and a few bottles of water, but that would only delay the inevitable if no one found him. And that bomb sitting there made him think it might be better if he just died of thirst.

Yeah, noble thoughts, he told himself scornfully. That was a *bomb*! Even if he were dead, someone else might be killed trying to get to his bones.

No, he had to ration that water, make it last, in the hopes he could shout a warning to anyone who came out here. That mattered more than everything else now. It was the only good thing he had left to do with his life.

He leaned back against the post, feeling the pressure of the chain around his neck, his fingers already bloody from having tried to break it. It let him move a little, let him lie down, but it wouldn't break, and every time he pulled on it he felt its strength. If he pulled too hard, he'd strangle.

He'd even struggled to grip the length that was tied around the post, hoping he could break that or pull it loose. No go.

But once he'd stopped trying to find a way out of this mess—as if he could with a bomb wired to the door—and stopped dousing himself with self-pity for being a fool, he started thinking about the man who had done this to him. What he had said.

It was like a puzzle. That man was a Vietnam vet.

He wasn't the only one around here. Lots of them—
from the last sheriff to the guy who currently headed
up the Emergency Response Team; even Micah Parish, his favorite of all the deputies, because Micah
was like dark, still waters, saying little but seeming
to know so much.

Lots of Vietnam vets, but he hadn't met any who
seemed as crazy angry as this guy. From more recent
wars there were even more vets around here. Some
occasionally went off the deep end a bit, but everybody understood and tried to help.

This guy was different. Dying, he'd said. Agent
Orange. What the hell was Agent Orange? A defoliant, Jack had gathered. Probably something like the
weed killers people used in their gardens, only worse.
Apparently, it had made the guy sick. Maybe a lot of
guys, from the little he'd said.

The things he'd said about soldiers being disposable
when they could no longer fight? When Jack thought
about it, he squirmed inwardly because he suspected it
was true. He didn't have a whole lot of experience with
the larger outside world, but he'd heard things. High
rate of suicide. Not enough medical care from the VA.

But to build bombs to get even? This guy had a
major grudge, and maybe he wasn't exactly sane.

He was going to get even with bureaucrats? What
the heck did that mean? It seemed to Jack that anyone who'd given this guy a hard time in the past was
probably long gone. Retired.

Send a message? By blowing something up? That
didn't make much sense to Jack, either. It didn't seem
like a good way to get the kind of attention anyone
would want.

But maybe the bomber couldn't see any other way. In his rough voice, Jack had heard frustration, even when he seemed weary. Terrible, ugly, endless frustration.

He tried to focus his mind on the pieces the man had given him. A defoliant that had apparently killed his friends. That was still having an impact all these years later. Maybe it was the reason the man said he was dying.

Even so, after all this time, wasn't it too late to send any kind of message about that? Unless his captor thought similar things were still happening.

But no, he'd just said he wanted to get even. Over forty years seemed like a long time to want to get even. Something must have pushed this guy over the edge. Or maybe he'd just been simmering for an awfully long time, and finally he blew a gasket.

Maybe the fact that he was now dying had been the last straw.

Jack sighed and leaned back against the post. What did it matter? he asked himself. He was chained in here with the bomb. His own time was probably limited, and if he didn't live he couldn't pass along even the small bits of information he'd gathered.

Useless, Jack. Just useless.

He looked again at the bomb and decided to just be grateful it didn't have a timer ticking down. That would have made the tension even more unbearable.

Because right now he felt wound tighter than a drum. As if he could explode himself.

Much as she would have liked to race, Darcy drove slowly. The grasses on either side of the road had deepened with spring and fresh water, and Alex had mentioned they needed to keep an eye out for disturbance.

"If he went off the road into the grasses, it might be hard to see his car because that grass is growing in drainage ditches in a lot of places."

Good advice, she thought. Plus, she didn't want to roar by a house that might hold information.

After what seemed like forever, she caught sight of a group of ramshackle buildings that hadn't been painted in so long the wood had slivered. There was a mailbox out front, dented and rusted and tipped on its rotting post.

"Looks like nobody lives there," she said, slowing down even more.

"I'm not sure. Stop for a minute, okay?"

She obliged. Alex climbed out and walked slowly across the road, then to the end of what was probably once a driveway, overgrown by grasses now, but still showing two ruts through the grass. If anybody came here, they didn't use it often.

He stood staring up the drive, then turned around and spoke as she leaned out the window. "Somebody came down the drive recently. Some of the grass is still crushed." Then he pointed toward the road ahead. "Only one set of tracks continuing. Let's drive a little farther. If we don't find something, we'll come back and check this place out."

"Okay." As they started moving again, she spied a rusted pickup way down there near the house, but it looked as if it could have been abandoned a long time ago. The whole place looked as if it had been deserted for decades.

Kinda creepy, actually. But they needed to find some sign of Jack, if he'd come out this way, and stopping might delay them.

A half mile farther down the road, her heart suddenly lodged in her throat. "Alex?" His name could barely escape, but she managed to point. "Under the sagebrush," she whispered, trying to regain control of her breathing.

"His car." Alex didn't even wait for her to fully brake. She was still rolling a bit as he leaped out and ran forward. She pulled up closer, then climbed out to join him.

"Be careful," he said as she ran over. "When the brush is dry like this it can scratch you."

"Is it useful for anything?" she asked, feeling oddly frustrated as she tried to pull the tangle away from the car. What if Jack was in there and needed help?

"Provides most of the food for antelope and elk," he responded.

At last, between them, they broke the tangle enough to see inside the car. "No one."

Her heart sank, then lifted rapidly. Okay, he wasn't dead beside the road. But where had he gone?

At almost the same moment, the two of them turned and looked back toward the seemingly deserted ranch.

"He might have been hurt," she said.

"Seeking shelter," he agreed.

Both moved swiftly, climbing into the car. Darcy turned it without going into the ditch herself. As they headed back toward the ranch, Alex used her radio and called the sheriff's office.

She barely heard him explaining the situation and

where they were. All she could think was, *Dear God, let that kid be okay.*

She knew so little about this area that she had no idea if turning into the rutty, overgrown driveway might get them shot, but she never hesitated. The truck jolted and bumped, and only the seat belt kept her head from hitting the roof.

At last they reached the house. No one had appeared. No faces in the windows, the few curtains that remained never twitched. But she was right behind that pickup truck and could tell it hadn't been abandoned. As she climbed out and approached it, she could see fresh metal exposed in the bed. The tires were full of air.

"This place is occupied," she said.

"Well, someone lives here," he corrected. "Stay back while I knock on the door."

The porch looked as if it might fall through at any moment, but it supported his weight. He more than knocked—he banged. When there was no answer, he banged again.

Darcy dared to climb up beside him and when he got no answer to his second knock, she framed her face with her hands and peered through the window.

"Somebody lives here," she said.

"Hell." He banged again. "I guess we should walk around outside and look."

Her radio crackled and she heard Sarah's familiar voice. "Darcy? The guy who lives in that ranch that Alex asked about? Vietnam vet named Warren Trimble. Apparently he's been ill for years and is dying of some kind of leukemia. That's from a vet who's talked to him a few times. Anyway, be warned. Trimble is an angry man. He was the victim of Agent Orange."

Darcy and Alex exchanged looks as she hooked the radio back onto her belt.

"Sounds like a good prospect," he said. Then without another word, he stepped back, raised his foot and prepared to kick the door in. "You aren't going to see this."

"Emergency doctrine," she retorted. "We think Jack is being held prisoner in here." But just as quickly, she reached out a hand and said sharply, "Don't. We're dealing with a bomber, remember?"

Alex seldom swore, but he raised a cloud of blue language that stained the air. "What the hell…"

Darcy pulled her radio again, raising Sarah. "We're going to need help. No one's home, and if this is the bomber…"

"I read you. We're on our way."

"So what do we do?" Alex asked, frustration lacing his voice. "What if he's in there?"

"Let's walk around, calling for him. If he's in any of these buildings and still alive, he'll answer. Maybe he can even give us some intel, like whether there's a bomb."

She could easily understand Alex's frustration. She shared it. But it wasn't going to do a single soul a bit of good if they blew themselves up. That was one thing her line of work had taught her: if you got anywhere near a bomber, you had to look out for traps.

It was awful, though, trudging around slowly, scouring the ground and windows for trip wires, for anything that looked out of place.

It was when they reached the outbuilding way to the back that their calls were finally answered.

"I'm here," they heard Jack shout. "But don't come in. He's wired some kind of bomb to the door."

The two of them froze, then Darcy looked for a crack in the wall. "Jack? You okay?"

"I'm chained up, but I'm okay."

"Did he wire the bomb just to the door?"

"I think so. But I don't know what kind of switch he used."

Alex frowned at the door, then looked at her. "Back window maybe?"

"Not dressed like this," she answered. "Bring my truck over here?"

"Sure." He took the keys from her and ran fast back to her truck.

She put her mouth to the crack. "We're going to try to come in from the back. You look around carefully and if you see anything that doesn't look right, you have to let me know."

"I don't think he went near the back."

"Can you be sure?"

"I can't be sure of anything. He knocked me out when I first saw him."

Great. Darcy's heart was pounding with awareness. One wrong move and she could kill Jack. She wasn't nearly as worried about herself. But it was her fault Jack was in there with a bomb. And no, she wasn't going to excuse herself. She should have stomped on him with both feet instead of trying to be nice.

"Darcy?"

She leaned closer to the wall. "Yes, Jack?"

"I shouldn't have been so stupid. I'm sorry. And

I don't see any other possible triggers for the bomb. He was in a hurry. Maybe he thought the door would be enough."

"We'll talk about you later. Right now I just want to get you out of there in one piece."

Then her truck rolled up. She called, "I'm coming in, Jack. Just hang on."

"You'll need some bolt cutters."

"First I have to get in."

Jack realized he was feeling weak. He'd been trying to preserve his supplies. The best thing he could do, he'd decided, was eat and drink so he wouldn't be useless if Darcy could get to him.

God, he hoped he was right. He hoped he hadn't made another inexperienced mistake. But honestly, he hadn't seen the bomber attach that bomb to anything but the door. Just the door. Kinda like he was hoping it might not be triggered.

"Jack, hang on. I'm coming."

Alex hated this. He hated it with a passion beyond words. Helping Darcy suit up in protective bomb gear made him sick. He should be doing this. Someone else should be doing this. He hated it when he saw that the suit left her forearms and hands unprotected. He understood why, but he hated it. She'd need her dexterity for dealing with the bomb.

But this was Darcy's job; she had the equipment and she knew how to use it. God willing, if that bomb exploded she'd be okay. But then there was Jack. That made him even sicker. That young man didn't deserve to die just because he'd got too big for his britches.

When she finally looked like an olive green Pillsbury Doughboy, she gazed at him through a faceplate. "In the back there's a blanket that looks like this suit. When I manage to get inside, pass it to me. It's a blast blanket I want to throw over Jack."

He nodded, feeling the grim set of his mouth and jaw.

"Stand back while I pull these boards away."

That was too much for Alex. If that bomb was going off, he wasn't going to be hiding behind her truck. He wouldn't be able to live with himself.

"Did you tell the sheriff to bring a bomb squad?"

"Such as they have," he answered. "Darcy..."

She paused. "I know," she said quietly. "Now, get behind the truck."

But when she reached for the first board, he reached for the one beside it. He was determined not to let her do this alone.

Four boards were all she needed. No explosion, thank God. In the distance she heard the wail of sirens. She pushed herself through, then turned to grab the blanket from Alex.

"Now," she asked, "will you get behind the truck?"

He scowled, but this time followed directions. There was certainly nothing else he could do right now.

Inside, the light was dim and dusty and she paused a moment to let her eyes adjust from the bright morning sunlight. Then she switched on the flashlight over her faceplate so she could see better.

"Here," said Jack.

Stepping carefully, searching for any possible trip wires or triggers, she approached him.

She could scarcely believe the way he was chained, like some kind of animal. "I'm going to throw this blanket over you," she said. "It'll be hot, but it'll protect you. It's a blast blanket, okay?"

"Okay," he said.

"Where's the bomb?"

He pointed. Her heart stuttered when she saw the ammo can. Micah had been right. For all she knew, the state lab was about to call with the results of their examination of the twisted metal they'd recovered. It didn't matter now.

"Here's the blanket," she said.

It was hard to move inside the suit. Her usual agility was beyond reach. But she was capable of drawing the thick blanket over Jack's head. "I need to go back for the bolt cutters. Don't move."

She turned and went back to the opening she'd made in the wall. The bomb suit didn't release her body heat and she was warming up considerably. Only the coating on the face shield was keeping it from fogging over on her.

The bolt cutters lay on the ground where she'd left them. Wrapped in tape, with only the metal jaws exposed, they shouldn't be much of a spark hazard, but she'd seen the dust in that place. Dust could be extremely explosive all by itself. She might hurt Jack without ever triggering the bomb.

When she got back to his side, she knelt with difficulty. "When I cut the chain off you, I want you to get up and move slowly to the opening I made in the wall. Keep the blanket around you. Make sure the bulk of it is toward the bomb for maximum protection. You can do that?"

"I ought to be able to get at least that much right."

Another time she'd worry about his load of self-blame. Right now, however, she was more worried about getting him out of here in one piece.

The sirens outside were getting closer. "Alex?"

"Yo."

"You told them this building is wired?"

"I told them every building could be wired. No chances."

"Thanks."

Then she tugged the blanket to one side and looked at the chains. Tight around his neck and ankle. Impossible to cut with the tool in her hand. But that didn't matter. A length of it was hooked to the post behind him, and she could cut there.

Grabbing the cutters in both hands, she surrounded the chains with the strong blades and snapped them together. The chains fell away at once.

"Anywhere else?"

"No. I'm just stiff from not being able to move much."

"Okay, I'll help you up, then we'll get you out of here. Walk in front of me. I'm extra protection for you."

She hardly noticed how hard her heart was galloping. All her focus, every cell of her being, was intent on getting this right, getting Jack out of here and then dealing with the waiting bomb.

There was no room in her for anything else. Not one thing. The cold that crept through her, freezing her in the moment for Jack's safety and her own, was contradictorily as hot as hell. She could feel the sweat running down her back, over her body, wetting her hair. It prickled and she didn't care. The damn suit was hot.

She finally eased Jack to the opening and urged him through. "Take him away from here," she told Alex.

"What about you?"

"Someone has to deal with that bomb. You got a bomb squad around here?"

His silence answered her. Small towns rarely did. Small towns almost never needed them. The best they had was probably Charity, the arson investigator.

"Make sure Jack calls his parents. They must be sick with worry. Oh, and bring me the black case from the back of the vehicle before you drive him away. Tell everyone else to back off. We know we have this bomb, but I'm not sure there aren't others."

"I know" was all Alex said as he urged Jack into her truck, then brought her the black bag. "Are you sure about this?" he asked as he passed it to her.

"I'm the tech" was all she said.

And she was. The only trained tech they had. While she wasn't called on to defuse bombs as a rule, she knew the principles. Now she'd need to apply them.

She waited until she heard the truck drive away. Then she turned to look at the bomb. A shaft of sunlight had found its way through a crack, illuminating the dusty air and falling right on the ammo can.

With her case, she walked slowly over to study it.

Alex was now living out his own version of hell. He'd got Jack safely away from the building and was pouring bottles of water into the boy while cops gathered, but Darcy was still inside, about to try to deal with a bomb.

At a safe distance from all the structures, tense deputies waited. Then three guys from the FBI appeared, looking travel worn in their jeans and FBI windbreakers.

"Seems we're late," Josh Hargreaves said to Alex after introducing himself around.

"Far from it," Alex said. "Jack here says the bomber is trying to get even and he talked at some length about Agent Orange. You might want to background the guy who owns this place."

Josh nodded and took his crew to one side where they plugged a laptop into a satellite connection in their car and began to check things out. The sheriff, Gage Dalton, joined them to share all he could about Warren Trimble.

A fireman came over to remove the chain from around Alex's neck. All that remained was a raw line where it had rubbed.

Warren Trimble. The name seared itself into Alex's mind. He'd never heard of the guy. At this point, he didn't especially care. He wanted Darcy to walk out of that ramshackle building in one piece, the sooner the better.

Darcy doubted the guy's other bombs had been built like this one. A four-inch piece of det cord was plugged into a hole in the side of the can, surrounded by caulk. Once lit, that cord would burn hotter than hell.

But running away from it were slender wires coated in plastic. They undoubtedly led to the trigger mecha-

nism that would have sent a spark through the wires
to ignite the det cord.

Wishing she could wipe the perspiration from her
forehead, she knelt and studied the setup. She couldn't
see any possible way that det cord could ignite without a charge coming through the wires. He hadn't put
a double detonator on it, from what she could see.

Without the det cord, the ANFO would be a dangerous but unexplosive lump of fertilizer and fuel oil.
Being cautious, she looked around the entire bomb,
seeking another trigger while taking care not to disturb the black wires running back to the door.

No, that was it. He'd either been in a hurry, or only
cared that he slowed everyone down. Did he really believe they'd just come busting into this building without looking for a bomb?

Maybe. Maybe the guy had gone so far around the
bend he wasn't thinking clearly. Remembering that
Alex had been ready to kick the door of the house in,
maybe the bomber wasn't that far around the bend
after all. Regardless, he must have known that if Jack
were still coherent when they found him, they'd be
warned about the bomb.

Screw it, she thought suddenly. It was getting so
hot inside this suit that she might well start to suffer
from heat stress and do something stupid.

She opened her bag and grabbed a fully insulated
pair of wire cutters. *These shouldn't even send a spark
along the electrical line. Maybe.*

Then she paused, took one more look and made
up her mind. Without hesitation, she grabbed the det
cord and pulled it out of the box.

Just in time. A spark shot down those wires and the

next thing she knew that det cord was burning with white heat. Moments later it melted into a twisted piece of plastic on a blackened floorboard.

Well, she'd made the wrong choice. Maybe. Evidently pulling the cord had caused the original detonator to register movement and it had sent the necessary spark.

It didn't matter now, though. She had disarmed the bomb. The next thing she needed to do was follow the wires back to the detonator and make sure it wasn't a threat, either.

Damn, she was hot!

For Alex, a lifetime seemed to pass before the door on the distant outbuilding opened and Darcy emerged. She was practically staggering, and she pulled her headgear off immediately.

He ran to her, forgetting everything else. When he reached her, she was struggling to open fasteners with fingers that didn't work. Her hair was plastered to her head.

"God, get me out of this," she said.

He was glad to oblige, even though he didn't really know his way around it. Tugging at tapes, he helped her until finally the suit fell to the ground. She looked as if she'd been through a shower or heavy rain.

"Let's get you some water."

"Let's find out who this bastard is."

"We can do both," he said mildly. He could tell the heat had made her irritable, but it didn't bother him. "Want me to bring the suit?"

"Leave it. We can get the car to pick it up and use it again if we need to. But everyone's okay?"

"Everyone except you," he answered. "Jack is reeking of embarrassment."

She just shook her head as they started walking toward the car and the crowded cops. Then her step hitched. "FBI?"

"Three of 'em. They're looking into this guy's background right now."

"Hallelujah. Why do I think it's more important to find him than to check out the rest of these buildings?"

"From what Jack said, he's on a mission of vengeance. On the other hand, there might be clues inside."

"So how much time are we going to waste checking these buildings out for bombs? He's already been found once. You don't think he's in a hurry now?"

Alex couldn't argue with that. But the FBI agents were busy checking out Warren Trimble, and that might provide the only information they needed without taking additional risks by breaking into his house.

Finally Darcy propped herself against the side of her truck and guzzled the water he passed to her. The morning air felt positively frigid after the blast furnace of that suit. She saw Jack standing over by the agents and walked that way.

"Are you okay?" she asked immediately.

He gave her a shamefaced look. "I'm fine. I was so worried about you, though, and it was all my fault."

She shook her head a little. "All's well that ends well," she said, then sighed. "Jack...just hang on. In the future let the pros do the work, okay? On the other hand..."

"If you hadn't found me, or someone had come busting through that door, somebody would be dead," he said seriously. "I was stupid and I know it. I won't do that again, I swear."

As she shed the excess heat, and tendrils of her wet hair began to dry, she felt a faint smile dawn on her lips. "I sincerely hope you won't have to. Anyway... because of you, we know who we're looking for now."

"I guess. The FBI agents got the name from the sheriff."

Alex joined them, passing them each another bottle of water. For a few minutes, they watched the crime scene techs enter the outbuilding with cameras and other equipment to log everything in there.

Darcy spoke again after draining half the bottle. "So I guess we wait to see what we can learn about him. I honestly don't want to break into the house unless we can't find out enough. It might be wired, too."

"Jack says he wants to get even and it has to do with Agent Orange. The sheriff said the guy has been suffering from illness for a long time. Cancer now, he thinks."

Darcy looked at Alex, felt again that amazing ripple of desire and awareness. Maybe the adrenaline she'd been feeling as she dealt with Jack and the bomb had left her with some other needs. From the beginning, he'd made her aware of her womanhood. That didn't seem to be about to wear off. She had to drag her thoughts back to business, and she didn't believe that was a good thing.

"Agent Orange," she said after a moment of gathering herself. "That might explain a lot."

Jack spoke. "He said they'd killed his buddies and wouldn't believe it was the Agent Orange."

"That's for sure true," muttered Alex. "Sadly true."

"He said that soldiers mattered only as long as they could fight, and then they just got thrown away."

"Ouch." Darcy winced. She hadn't expected to experience any sympathy at all for the bomber, but that reached her. It also gave her an understanding of what might be going on with him. "What a terrible way to feel."

"And at least partly true," Alex said. "That Agent Orange thing… Wasn't there a long fight about it? Didn't it take decades for the VA to recognize it as a source of a lot of problems?"

"I think so," Darcy answered. "I'm not sure. My history is weak on some things. It doesn't matter anyway. What matters is that this man believes it has blighted his life and the lives of people he knew. What more does he need? Graphs and charts and mortality statistics? But who the hell could he go after? It's been more than four decades since that war ended."

"But the effects of Agent Orange didn't stop there. That battle is still being fought, if I remember. Just fewer people to fight it."

Darcy felt her energy returning as she cooled off. Now she was hungry. Fat chance of eating something just then.

"Bureaucrats," Jack said. "He was blaming bureaucrats."

"Did you hear when he left?"

"Before dawn, not long before. And he took a different truck. It didn't sound like the one over there."

"Where do you go to find bureaucrats to bomb?" Darcy asked rhetorically. "They're almost everywhere."

Alex's head suddenly snapped up. "But not VA bureaucrats." He looked around. "Anybody know if this guy had any trouble with the VA offices in this state? Or anywhere else for that matter?"

Josh Hargreaves, who'd been peering at a laptop with the other agents, stepped back and spoke. "He was removed for disturbing the peace and making threatening statements at the VA office in Casper. But that was eight years ago."

"Long enough to learn how to make an ANFO bomb," Darcy said.

"I wish we could be sure that's where he was headed," the sheriff remarked. "He could have his eye on the state capitol. It'd be a bigger target."

"We need more information," someone else said.

Then Hargreaves spoke to Darcy. "Alex will never tell you this, but he's a legend around the Bureau. Listen to his psychological assessments."

But Darcy's gaze was already fixed on the front door of the house. "Alex? I want my gear. And a power bar if anyone has one." Adrenaline had drained her. She needed her energy once again. An EMT shoved one into her hand and she ripped it open without finesse. "Thanks."

Alex shut up. He wanted to protest but no matter how much he might want to suggest someone else, he knew full well she was the only one with the training to deal with a bomb. There might be important information inside that house, information that would indicate where he was heading. Lives were at stake, obviously, and he knew Darcy well enough by now to know that she wasn't going to stand by and let it all fall out, not when someone might get hurt.

He drove over to get her equipment from the out-building while she drank more water and got ready for another tour with another power bar. When he brought the truck back with her bomb suit and case of equipment, she was standing a little to one side by herself, staring at the old house.

He pulled up beside her and climbed out. "You do know if a bomb goes off, nothing in there is likely to be of much use to us anyway."

"He's after someone. Probably a number of people. I don't want them on my conscience."

He could understand that easily enough. His job had left him with deaths that still haunted him and questions about why he hadn't been quicker. "You need to separate your actions from his. You're not responsible for what he does." He'd tried to learn that with BSU. Evidently he'd failed with the bicycle killer, so he knew what was coming next.

"I'm responsible if there's some way I could have stopped him and I failed."

He couldn't rightly argue with that.

"The thing is," she said, "I'm wondering if he would have left enough inside there to tell us where he was headed. It doesn't seem likely unless he has the place ready to blow up…which is a problem we're going to have to deal with sooner or later. But the other thing…"

She fell silent, and he waited, wishing he could just wrap his arms around her and offer whatever comfort a hug could. Except in this situation, with so many cops milling around, it would have been damn stupid and she'd have every right to be furious with him. He'd gathered that she hadn't found it easy to be a woman in her job. Why announce they were more than colleagues and start tongues wagging? She'd leave in a few days anyway. Better for her if her reputation was intact.

But he'd have given an awful lot to be able to comfort her.

At least she was beginning to dry off from her time in the bomb suit. He imagined no one could wear one of those for very long without suffering from heat stress.

"What are you thinking?" he asked.

"That I'd very much like to know who he went after. And something else, Alex. He didn't mean for Jack to die."

"But he put a bomb there!" But as soon as the words escaped him, his training and experience kicked in, making room for themselves amid his worry about Darcy. "You're right."

She turned her head and looked at him. "Exactly. He had to have known Jack would warn us, assuming we found him before he died of thirst. And he only wired one door, when we could have come from any direction. It was a simple disarm, too."

He nodded. "I agree, at least as far as his motivation. Can't comment on the bomb. So what are you thinking about the house?"

"I'm thinking it's probably not wired. I'm thinking he probably didn't leave much behind to give himself away. We're not going to walk in there and find maps with X-marks-the-spot. But from what Jack said, he doesn't care about being caught because he's dying anyway. All he cares about is buying the time to complete his mission."

Alex nodded, in full agreement with her assessment. "I think you're right. But he'll guess that we'll be stymied outside for at least a while because of the potential for bombs in there. So maybe he didn't clear everything. Regardless, he's bought time for himself, and I'd judge that at this point he doesn't want much time. He's going to act soon."

"Yeah." She rubbed her forehead. "I need to go in."

God, he wanted to stop her. To prevent her from taking the risk. But she was the only experienced bomb tech they had. Did they dare wait until new ATF guys arrived to help her? How many others might die? They had to find out where he was going.

He looked over at the FBI guys. They appeared to be learning everything they could about Warren Trimble. The sheriff's men looked ready to charge the house, but they also knew better.

Which left Darcy.

Everything inside him squeezed into a tight knot as he gave her permission he knew damn well she didn't need. She'd do what she judged to be the right thing no matter what he might say about it. "Okay, go for it. But is there anything we can do first to make it less likely you'll trip a trigger?" He needed and wanted a sliver of hope.

"He hasn't used a motion trigger yet." But she paused. "While I suit up, ask the cops to shoot a few rounds into the building, enough to create a pressure wave. Just in case our Mr. Trimble got fancy."

"They could use a flash-bang outside."

"As long as they don't set the building on fire. That place looks like tinder."

"I guess," he said mirthlessly, "that you've been

too preoccupied to notice the fire truck parked out at the road. Everyone was worrying about you after you went into the outbuilding. Now we can keep this heap of boards from igniting."

Darcy waited, every nerve in her body aching with impatience. That bomber was out there pursuing his deadly mission. Who knew how long it would be before he reached his target and killed someone? "Alex? Talk to me. Do you think Jack might have sped this guy up?"

Alex's gaze grew distant as he flexed mental muscle he hadn't needed in years. "Yeah. Probably. He thought he was perfectly hidden out here, unknown to most people, just another old man who was dying. Then Jack followed him. He had to have known we'd find the kid's car eventually. So yes, Jack sped him up. I don't know much about this guy except he's short on time, as far as his life goes. Maybe he expects to die at almost any moment. Add that to Jack following him... Yeah, he's in a race against the clock now."

The pump truck pulled up close to the house, and doused it with water. When everything was dripping wet, two deputies moved forward, called a warning and threw their flash-bangs.

Darcy had her ears covered and eyes closed, but it was still deafening even in the open space. Nothing ignited, though.

She pulled on her bomb suit as fast as she could and headed for the front of the house. If it was a trip trigger, she could spot it. At this point she'd bet there wasn't a pressure-sensitive bomb or a motion-sensitive one. That left the same kind he'd placed in the out-building with Jack.

She could handle that. No sweat. Well, except for what was inside the suit.

Alex stopped her. "Be careful," he said, but his eyes offered something much hotter and more concerned.

She managed a nod and plowed forward in the awkward, hot suit. Twice in one day. Some kind of record.

But this time was different. Before she'd been concerned about Jack, worried enough about him that she hadn't been able to run through any emotions of her own. This time she was scared for herself. This time she was aware that her forearms and hands weren't protected. This time the adrenaline pumping through her in huge quantities wanted her to run as far and as fast as she could.

No dice. They had to get inside to find out if the bomber had left any clues. She simply wouldn't be able to live with herself if she walked away and left others to die.

Alex stood back with Jack and the others, a safe distance between them and the house, vehicles ready to act as shields in an instant if they had to duck.

"Is she crazy?" Jack asked as he watched.

Alex looked at him, at his pale worried face. "No," he answered. "We need information, if it's in there, to save other lives. So she's going in. You still want to be with ATF?"

Jack gnawed his lower lip. "Yeah. I do."

"Why?"

"Because she saves lives."

Good a reason as any, Alex thought, returning his attention to Darcy's approach to the building. Another few steps and she was going to push in that door. Or break a window. He had no idea which way she'd try to enter. Those windows were big enough to step through if she broke out the panes.

His heart had climbed to a place it hadn't visited in a long time: his throat. His chest had tightened as if steel bands bound it. If anything happened to that woman…

That was when he noticed the hush. Not a person around them was talking. Not one, not even the FBI. Every eye was pinned to her, every tongue silenced with concern for her.

Alongside his building anxiety that something might go wrong, Alex felt a huge admiration for that woman and her determination. He was sure she was afraid. How could she not be? She had to be acutely aware that even if her bomb suit protected her from death, she could lose her arms and be crippled for life.

Yet in she went, because she didn't want to risk other people, people she didn't even know. Because inside she might find the key to a madman's plan. No one would have blamed her for letting it ride, letting others do the detective work, hopeful they'd figure it out in time.

But one scene Trimble had made at the VA office in Casper wasn't enough to commit their resources there. He might have a wholly different target in mind.

He'd understood fully when she'd walked into the jaws of potential hell to save Jack. The victim was right before her. This time—an empty house.

But he also understood something else from his own experience: the nightmares that would haunt her if she didn't go in there hunting evidence and people died. She didn't want to live with that. He wouldn't either, which was why he'd become so obsessed with the bicycle killer, unable to turn it off, day or night. Unable to sleep unless exhaustion caught him unwillingly. To save another little girl, some faceless child that some parent loved the way he loved his own daughter...

Darcy was feeling the same. But she wasn't seeing her own daughter as a victim. Not even kids like Jack. No, she was concerned for the nameless, faceless bureaucrats that Warren Trimble evidently loathed.

Alex would have liked to punch the man. He'd known a lot of those so-called bureaucrats in his life. Good people who went to work early, stayed late and were devoted to their jobs. What Trimble didn't get was that all too often their hands were tied. No authority, no rule, no law to do what they probably wished they could for a sick vet.

That came from higher up. It would have made more sense for Trimble to take his bombs to Washington, to the secretary of defense or to the Congress. Anyone who held the real power. The little guys in their offices could only do so much.

But Trimble was going for the immediate cause, from his perspective. They just needed to know who he was blaming right now.

Evidently there had been a piece of two-by-four on the porch. He hadn't noticed it earlier, but he watched

Darcy struggle in the confines of her suit and lift a four-foot length from the porch floor.

Then he tensed from head to toe and waited as she swung it against the window beside the door. He was braced for an explosion, but none came. Darcy swung again, taking out the rest of the window. Then she leaned inside and looked around.

There was no measure for the relief he felt when she at last pulled her upper body out and turned to face the gathered cops.

"Bring a ram up. I don't see any trip wires or ammo cans, not in the front room. But we've still got to clear the premises."

The front door caved in quickly before a cop wielding the heavy battering ram. Then Darcy, after a deep drink of water, moved in, scanning carefully, using not only her headlamp but also a flashlight she'd taken from one of the cops.

An eternity passed before she emerged at last and sagged against the porch railing.

"Clear," she called as she pulled her helmet and face mask off. "Anybody ever heard of Triple T Plumbing?"

This time the EMTs moved in to look after her. She was determined not to go anywhere, but she sat on the back of the ambulance and let them check her out after she doffed the suit. Water and more water was passed to her while the dry morning air began to suck the sweat from her body.

"God," she said, "I hope I don't have to put that suit on again."

Alex was just relieved that she was okay and for once was willing to let the cops and FBI agents take over checking the house for evidence.

A call had gone out about a vehicle bearing the logo of Triple T Plumbing. That had been a find. A template that had been used to spray paint the name in blue. About the size of a magnetic sign you'd want to put on a big truck or van. A vehicle big enough to carry his bombs.

"I must stink," Darcy remarked, then waved Jack over. When he reached her, his head down, she didn't say a word. She just threw her arm around his shoulders and held him beside her, reassuring the kid.

"You know," she said finally, "this is a huge state. Lots of roads. He could be anywhere."

"Yeah," Alex agreed.

"I feel like I should be out there."

"Where exactly?"

He felt so happy when she smiled faintly. "Are you always so logical?"

"Not usually. I'm a psychologist, not a logician." He also reckoned that she wanted to keep moving, chasing the guy, so she didn't have time to reflect on the risks she had just taken.

"There might be more in the barn," she remarked.

"Probably. But unless we need something straightaway, may I suggest you've put on that suit enough for one day? Let someone else do the barn."

"If we can wait."

He had to be content with that. "You're amazing," he said finally.

"Why?" Her green eyes met his, reflecting little except lingering tension and fatigue.

"Not everybody could put on that suit and certainly not twice in one day."

"Somebody has to. Besides, the meltdown will probably come." She shrugged one shoulder and drank more water.

Jack spoke. "There's no way to protect your hands?"

Darcy looked at him. "No. You need the dexterity to work with the bomb. Imagine trying to handle delicate wiring with fingers the size of doughnuts."

He nodded. "What's going to happen to the bomb now?"

"Someone is going to have to detonate it safely. I don't think that will be me."

"Why not?"

"Some more ATF agents should be arriving today. I'll let them deal with it."

"Good idea," Jack said judiciously. "What you did already was radical. Amazing."

She turned to face him directly. "I did my job. Keep that in mind, Jack. I just did my job. If you get into ATF, that could be your job sometimes, too. Nothing radical about it."

He nodded. "But I'll never get there. My dad wants me to ranch."

"You never know," Darcy said. "You never know."

Then the agents came out of the house. Hargreaves was evidently the spokesman for the three. "He's heading for Casper. There are two VA offices there, one state and one federal. He had a map of the area in his drawer. Our guess is he plans to set the bombs tonight." He looked at Alex. "Your evaluation?"

Alex's mouth tightened. "I agree. You want my assessment?"

"Whatever you can with as little as we got."

"I think he wants to plant those bombs late tonight when nobody's likely to see. He plans to detonate them in the morning after the employees come to work. Maximum carnage, maximum message. You've got one thing going for you, Hargreaves."

"Which is?"

"This guy doesn't want to kill anyone he doesn't have a grudge against. Maybe he won't consider you and the cops to be bureaucrats. On the downside, Trimble doesn't care if he dies as long as he can trigger his bombs."

"Thanks." Hargreaves paused. "You ought to come back, Jansen. We're still talking about you. We could use your talent."

Then Darcy pulled on her ATF windbreaker and climbed into her truck to make the trip with them. Alex could hear Casper law enforcement already being radioed.

Before she pulled away, Alex put his hand on her arm through the open window. "You coming back?"

She bit her lip and looked at him. He felt the sizzle pass between them and wondered if she did, too. It would be a perfect time for her to make a clean break with him. So perfect that he doubted he should have even asked the question. Places inside him, long put on ice, had thawed. This was going to hurt.

"Yes," she said after the briefest pause. "As soon as we get this tied up."

Then she drove off, leaving him and Jack in a cloud of dust. He wondered if he'd ever see her again.

Alex looked at Jack. "Think I can hitch a ride home?"

Chapter 12

Even though the investigation was ongoing and Alex, lacking any official capacity, had no right to any information, Gage Dalton shared the important items with him. Warren Trimble had been caught around midnight outside the federal VA office in Casper. Since he possessed a string of ANFO bombs, they didn't need anything more to take him into custody. He'd probably spend the rest of his short life in a jail hospital.

Alex spent his free time setting up a shop room at the junior college where the high school had been lent the use of facilities until their own building could be repaired. He also helped Jack deal with his parents, who were pretty horrified by what he'd done.

At least all his training in psychology proved useful there. He was also bugged by Hargreaves's suggestion that he return to the FBI. After what had happened with the bicycle killer, he didn't want a rerun and wasn't sure he'd pass the psychological testing anyway. He'd gone around the bend once. Not in any way that harmed the case, but it had ripped his marriage apart. Maybe they'd overlook that, maybe they wouldn't. But he still had his nightmares.

But mostly when he was busy with his hands, his mind free to roam, he thought about Darcy. She'd shown incredible courage in rescuing Jack. In checking the house for more bombs. Not everyone could do that. Most people would probably head the other way as fast as their legs could carry them.

She was admirable, but she was also beautiful, and when she allowed her guard to drop, she was warm and sexy. He wouldn't mind having her around a lot.

But each time that thought danced through his mind, he shoved it away. She had a career she apparently loved, and she showed no signs of missing him at all. Not even a phone call.

He figured he'd never see her again. No reason he should. No promises had been made, and she'd get swept up into the Trimble investigation and then into another investigation somewhere. From the sound of it, ATF was so shorthanded she probably couldn't expect even a vacation anytime soon.

He wondered where she'd be off to next. The Georgia bombings? Or some new case? Then he wondered if she only worked bomb cases or if she was involved in other operations. Alcohol, Tobacco and Firearms covered a lot of territory.

There was so much he hadn't had a chance to learn about her, and now he wondered if he ever would. A kind of heavy acceptance filled him as he admitted he'd allowed another woman to take up residence in his mind and heart, and that she could inflict the very kind of pain he'd wanted to avoid forever after his marriage broke up.

He'd taken a risk with Darcy, maybe foolishly believing that he could prevent himself from caring deeply. After all, he claimed to have learned his lessons. He should have built some nice psychological protections against involvement. He was a psychologist, damn it. He knew how easily walls could be erected, creating an emotional fortress. He'd tried to knock down a few for patients during his clinical days. It wasn't easy. Yet here he was, knowing better, and already in it up to his neck. As if it had happened behind his back. Maybe it had.

Ten days later, shortly after dark with a surprisingly crisp spring wind blowing, he was standing on his porch, watching the spring leaves on the trees toss and rustle. Summer was around the corner, but lately the weather hadn't felt like it. Astonishing when he thought about how warm the last few years had been.

He heard a vehicle approaching and thought he recognized the engine. No, he was deluding himself. Lots of people drove trucks and Darcy hadn't even phoned.

A neighbor's car passed by, the driver waved, and he experienced a sense of deflation. At times over the last ten days, he'd been either amused at himself or angry. Apparently he'd given more than he should have to a woman who was passing through. Or any woman for that matter, he thought when he remembered his ex. How many times did he need a mule to kick him in the head before he learned his lesson? For a lot of people once was enough.

But he hadn't intended to invest so much in Darcy. Hell, he hadn't even realized he was doing it until she drove away. Now it was time to pick up and carry on.

But the engine was growing closer, right down the street now, and he couldn't make himself turn and go inside.

He waited, his heart accelerating, until the big black truck pulled up right in front of his house. For an instant he closed his eyes, hardly daring to believe, but then he heard the engine switch off and a door slam.

When he looked, the only thing he could see was Darcy.

She walked briskly toward his porch, a smile on her face. "Sheesh, it's chilly," she said. "Am I still welcome? I don't have long—a case I need to get to but... Alex?"

He threw caution to the winds. When she reached the bottom step, he bent, caught her in his arms and lifted her until she was pressed tightly to his chest.

"Why the hell didn't you phone?" he demanded roughly, then, without waiting for an answer, he kissed her as if he wanted to devour her.

At some level he knew he was opening himself up again, giving someone all they needed to gut him once more, but he didn't care. Not at all. He was past caring about anything except the woman he held so snugly in his arms.

"Alex..."

He had to let her go. He had to. He had no right to

trap her in a hug. But even as he started to loosen his hold, he felt her arms snake around him.

"Let's go inside," she murmured huskily.

Yeah. Inside. It was cold out there. More privacy in there. If she was about to tell him she'd never see him again, a visit was certainly kinder than a phone call or a text message. Internally his heart warred, fearing crushing disappointment, hoping for a fairy-tale happy ending.

Inside he tried to offer her coffee, something to eat, but she wasn't having it. She drew him into the living room and down on the couch beside her.

"I'm sorry I was gone so long," she said before he could speak again. "I know I could have called but there was nothing I could really say because of the investigation, and then they were briefing me on my next job, and I feel lucky to have got a couple of days to come back."

"I'm glad you did," he managed, bracing himself to hear that she was leaving for good but just wanted to say good bye.

"You told me to," she said, her smile crooked. "Did you mean it, Alex? Did you really want me back?"

"I meant it." What was she driving at? "I've learned not to say things that I don't mean."

She nodded, her expression growing serious. "When I was away I spent my nights thinking about how... If you want me, Alex, could we make it work? I'd be in and out but could we still have...something?"

He drew a long breath, getting ready to take a plunge he'd sworn never to take again, yet as eager to do it as a kid standing on a diving board for the first time. "We could have something. We could have more

than something if you want to try. In my marriage…
my job dictated everything. Do you think I'd be un-
willing to give your career the same respect?"

He watched her eyes brighten, and as they did so
he felt his heart begin to lift. Maybe this wasn't going
to be so bad after all.

"So you could live with me coming and going?"

"I could live with my *wife* coming and going."

Her entire face transformed, beaming with joy.
That smile brought an amazing warmth and peace to
his heart. "Seriously?" she asked.

"Seriously. I don't know how it happened, Darcy. It
must have happened when I wasn't looking, but I fell
in love with you. So… All or nothing. I don't want to
be a layover. I want to be your husband. I'll tend the
home fires. You save the world."

She laughed then, such a happy sound that he
couldn't help joining in as his heart leavened in a
way it hadn't for so many years.

"Marry me, Alex?"

"Hell, yeah, but I'm not going to grow my hair
long."

They were both laughing when he swept her up
and carried her back to the bedroom. Joy had come
home with her.

It might prove to be a balancing act, but the happiness would more than make up for it.

* * * * *

Don't forget previous titles in Rachel Lee's
CONARD COUNTY: THE NEXT GENERATION
series:

UNDERCOVER IN CONARD COUNTY
CONARD COUNTY MARINE
CONARD COUNTY SPY
CONARD COUNTY WITNESS

Available now from Harlequin Romantic Suspense!

Get 2 Free Books,

Plus 2 Free Gifts—

just for trying the Reader Service!

HARLEQUIN®
ROMANTIC suspense

"I fled to Syria to escape war," she continued. "I returned to Iraq for the same reason. I do not wish to settle in another unstable place. Armenia has known many years of peace, and our people are welcome there."

"Do you speak Armenian?"

"A little."

"How many other languages?"

"Four or five."

"Which is it? Four or five?"

"I am fluent in English, Arabic, Assyrian and Kurdish. I also know a bit of Farsi and Armenian."

He counted on his fingers. "That's six."

"But I only speak four well."

"I only speak one well. If that."

"You can learn another."

He turned toward her and studied her face. A week ago, he'd had no interest in learning Arabic. Now he wanted to learn her ways. He wanted to know every inch of her. When he cupped her chin with one hand, she didn't pull away. He rubbed his thumb over her parted lips. "What is the word for this?"

"Mouth or kiss?"

"Both."

"*Bosa* is kiss."

"*Bosa,*" he said, then touched his lips to hers.

"Mouth is *fum*."

"Fum." He kissed her again.

"*Tongue* is *lisan*."

"*Lisan,*" he said, and gave it to her, plundering the depths of her mouth. She returned his kiss with a low moan. Her tongue touched his shyly and her fingers laced through his hair. She tasted like Yazidi liquor and female spice, a delicious combination. He settled against her, learning all her sensitive places. His lips traced the silky column of her throat while his hands roamed. Her hijab fell away, and he pulled his shirt over his head. Her fingertips danced across the surface of his chest.

Don't miss
NAVY SEAL RESCUE by Susan Cliff,
available April 2018 wherever
Harlequin® Romantic Suspense books and ebooks are sold.

www.Harlequin.com

HRSEXP0318

SPECIAL EXCERPT FROM

Love Inspired.
SUSPENSE

*A serial killer is on the loose on a military base—
can the Military K-9 Unit track him down?*

*Read on for a sneak preview of
MISSION TO PROTECT by Terri Reed,
the first book in the brand-new
MILITARY K-9 UNIT miniseries,
available April 2018 from Love Inspired Suspense!*

Staff Sergeant Felicity Monroe jerked awake to the fading sound of her own scream echoing through her head. Sweat drenched her nightshirt. The pounding of her heart hurt in her chest, making bile rise to burn her throat. Darkness surrounded her.

Where was she? Fear locked on and wouldn't let go. Panic fluttered at the edge of her mind.

Her breathing slowed. She wiped at the wet tears on her cheeks and shook away the fear and panic.

She filled her lungs with several deep breaths and sought the clock across the room on the dresser.

The clock's red glow was blocked by the silhouette of a person looming at the end of her bed.

Someone was in her room!

Full-fledged panic jackknifed through her, jolting her system into action. She rolled to the side of the bed and landed soundlessly on the floor. With one hand, she reached for the switch on the bedside table lamp while her other hand reached for the baseball bat she kept under the bed.

Holding the bat up with her right hand, she flicked on the light. A warm glow dispelled the shadows and revealed she was alone. Or was she?

She searched the house, turning on every light. No one was there.

She frowned and worked to calm her racing pulse.

Back in her bedroom, her gaze landed on the clock. Wait a minute. It was turned to face the wall. A shiver of unease racked her body. The red numbers had been facing the bed when she'd retired last night. She was convinced of it.

And her dresser drawers were slightly open. She peeked inside. Her clothes were mussed as if someone had rummaged through them.

What was going on?

Noises outside the bedroom window startled her. It was too early for most people to be up on a Sunday morning. She pushed aside the room-darkening curtain. The first faint rays of sunlight marched over the Texas horizon with hues of gold, orange and pink.

And provided enough light for Felicity to see a parade of dogs running loose along Base Boulevard. It could only be the dogs from the K-9 training center.

Stunned, her stomach clenched. Someone had literally let the dogs out. All of them, by the looks of it.

Don't miss
MISSION TO PROTECT by Terri Reed,
available April 2018 wherever
Love Inspired® Suspense books and ebooks are sold.

www.LoveInspired.com

LISEXP0318